Shabnam Minwalla writes for newspapers, plays mother to three teenagers, shops for saris and gobbles murder mysteries by the bookshelf. But her absolutely, totally, completely favourite activity is writing books for children.

Her popular books for children and young adults include *The Six Spellmakers of Dorabji Street*, *What Maya Saw*, the laugh-a-minute Nimmi series and the shiver-inducing *Saira Zariwala Is Afraid*.

Shabnam has been a speaker at the Jaipur Lit Fest and has conducted workshops and book readings at Bookaroo, the Kala Ghoda Festival, the Tata Lit Live festival and lit fests around the country.

Also by Shabnam Minwalla in Talking Cub

On Your Marks (2018)
Nimmi's Bizuper Birthday (2020)
Nimmi's Dreadtastic Detective Days (2019)
Nimmi's Spectabulous Schooldays (2018)

Also by Shabnam Minwalla in Speaking Tiger

Colaba (2020)

MURDER AT DAISY APARTMENTS

SHABNAM MINWALLA

Speaking Tiger
YOUNG ADULT

SPEAKING TIGER BOOKS LLP
4381/ 4, Ansari Road, Daryaganj
New Delhi 110002

First published in paperback by Speaking Tiger Books in 2021

ISBN: 978-93-5447-014-1
eISBN: 978-93-5447-015-8

10 9 8 7 6 5 4 3 2 1

Typeset in Adobe Jenson Pro by Jojy Philip
Printed at Chaman Enterprises, New Delhi

MURDER AT DAISY APARTMENTS

1

Mr Sevnani was taken away in an ambulance on the forty-third day of the lockdown.

This was not exactly headline news. Mr Sevnani was seventy-eight years old. He had a bad heart and an even worse temper. He had often been ferried across the city in a white ambulance with a flashing red light and a weee-oww weee-oww wail.

This time, though, it was different.

This time, Mr Sevnani was taken away by a swarm of men wearing masks and flapping blue safety suits. The neighbours didn't pop out to say, 'Get well soon, uncle.' Instead, they stood at their windows and shuddered as the white vehicle drove off with its trembling invalid and its sinister blue crew. After which they tried to remember if they'd shared the elevator with Mr Sevnani over the last few days.

This was the most OMG moment in the history of Lily Apartments, so it seemed totally unfair that we'd missed the action.

Ved and I had woken up late. While events were unfolding one floor down, we were slumped at the dining table with uncombed hair and unscrubbed faces. Our mum, in turn, was drinking her tea, phoning the vegetable shop for the seventeenth time, and delivering her standard 9.57 a.m. lecture. The one about waking up on time, brushing our teeth and keeping our bedrooms tidy.

It bugged my mother that Ved and I had turned into spineless, blobby creatures who looked and behaved like twin jellyfish. She refused to accept that, at the moment, we had no reason to use our toothbrushes, our hairbrushes, our brains or our backbones.

What was the point?

This nasty virus with the nastier name—Covid-19—was zipping around the globe. The whole world was in lockdown. Everyone was staying home, staying away from others, staying safe. Every day that passed was the exact shade of brown-grey as the day that had gone before.

Our trip to Croatia had been cancelled. Our birthday dinner had been cancelled. Ved's band's concert at the Royal Opera House had been cancelled. And the school summer holidays might as well have been cancelled—they were about as much fun as munching on cardboard.

Forget about a Caramel Frappuccino at Starbucks or a swim at CCI, we weren't even getting butter in the shops. Our mum was googling recipes for cakes made from Aashirwad aata and vegetable oil. Seriously, that's how grim things were.

Amazon was not delivering. Waffle Wonderland was not delivering. Zara Online was not delivering. And on days when Colaba Market shut down suddenly, even the bhajiwala was not delivering.

I didn't mind about the brinjals and cabbage, I preferred Maggi 2-minute noodles anyway. What I did mind was that we were all at home, pained and bored. Which was a lot of pain and boredom squished into a 1027-square-foot Mumbai apartment.

We could really have done with some drama. Which is why it was cruel that when the drama came along, we missed it. Why? Because Ved and I were spreading Nutella on cold toast, my mother was chasing an elusive bhajiwala, and my father was WFHing. (WFH is the new way of saying Working from Home. My father's version of WFH is to sit in the bedroom and nod at a laptop screen which is crowded with other people nodding at their laptop screens. He usually wears an ironed shirt, a striped tie and a pair of shapeless trackpants that he's rescued from the 'cut into kitchen rags' pile.)

Even Alfonsa—who usually spends hours standing on stools and contorting herself to see if Neville Khambata is smoking or Amrita Aunty is wearing a too-short skirt—was chopping onions on that fateful morning and had forgotten to peep out of the window. (An oversight that caused her untold anguish in the days to come.)

This is why the big news trickled into the Venkat household a full forty-five minutes late. It arrived in the form of a cryptic message on the Lily-Daisy Apartments WhatsApp chat and, at first glance, sounded like pure gobbledygook.

Ved and I had finished breakfast and relocated to the sofa, where we were checking our phones and continuing to do the jellyfish thing. My mother was dusting the Ganpatis and pausing to check if Salman of Citypoint Vegetables had responded. He hadn't. This made her jittery. 'Do you think the police have shut the market down again?' she asked. 'How will I make pasta in red sauce with half a squishy tomato? Should I change the menu?'

The freshly dusted Ganpatis didn't care to reply. Nor did the jellyfish impersonators. So my mother clucked in irritation and returned to her phone, where she found a new target for her irritation. 'That man really needs his head examined,' she exploded. 'I'm starting to think he's actively dangerous.'

This time, the jellyfish impersonators did look up.

'What?' Ved asked. 'Who needs his head examined?'

'What?' I said at exactly the same time. 'Who's actively dangerous?'

'Baman Marker,' my mother barked. 'He's written some nonsense on the building chat. As usual.'

'What has he written?' Ved and I asked in perfect sync, sounding revoltingly like those xerox-copy twins in storybooks.

'Listen,' my mother said, and started reading from the phone screen. 'Residents will refrain from rumour-mongering and needless panic. As of now, the individual has only been taken for testing. There should be NO discussions or dissemination of Fake News. You are expected to adhere to these instructions and stay indoors.'

Ved and I blinked.

'Which individual?' I asked. 'What instructions?'

Ved and my mother didn't have answers, but I had more questions. 'How will Baman Marker know if we're adhering to these instructions anyway?' I demanded. 'Do you think he's padding around Lily and Daisy Apartments on his fat feet, eavesdropping outside each house?'

The idea thrilled Ved who capered around our rust and moss green living room, rapping in a low voice:

Beware, beware, he's out and about,
So be careful 'bout the rumours you monger, the panic you spread.
The Big Bum's at the door, revenge cooking in his head.

'Seriously,' I said, half joking, half unnerved. 'What do you think the Big Bum will do if he catches us discussing that which is not to be discussed?'

'Maybe he'll stop us from getting milk in the morning,' Ved suggested. 'Or maybe he'll sack Raghunath and the two Mishrajis and put us on water-filling or staircase-mopping duty.'

Raghunath was the cleaner and errand boy of Lily and Daisy Apartments. The two Mishrajis were the security guards. Day Mishraji guarded the buildings during the day. And Night Mishraji guarded the buildings during the night.

'Actually, Raghunath hasn't been around for a couple of days,' my mother muttered as she tiptoed to our main door, opened it a crack and then swivelled around to glare at us. 'Now stop this, you two, you're making me nervous! There's nobody outside.'

True, there was nobody outside. But that didn't change the fact that it was startlingly easy to imagine Baman Marker—aka The Big Bum and The Hon Chairperson—standing outside with his ear pressed to the door.

By now you're probably imagining Baman Marker as an arch criminal—a sort of Macavity the Cat without the tail and whiskers. Please erase that image from your mind.

Baman Marker was a highly respectable chartered accountant. He lived on the fifth floor of Daisy Apartments with the equally highly respectable Mrs Binaifer Marker. Mrs Marker was stick-thin and stick-straight. She had a beaky nose, a cawing voice and called her husband 'daaaaarling'. Their two daughters were married to men who were also highly respectable. I am pretty sure that they also called their husbands 'daaaaarling'.

Baman Marker was around sixty-five years old and looked as if he'd been assembled from pinkish foam cushions. Like a cuddly Teletubby Grandpa with a silver bob. His soft, sing-song voice added to the snuggly vibe. And it was only when you spotted his eyes—pale and wily behind round spectacles—that you had reason to wonder.

We had long stopped wondering. We knew exactly what lay behind that bland, doughy face and bleach-white reputation. Baman Marker was the chairperson of the Lily-Daisy Cooperative Housing Society. This was unfortunate, because he was the human equivalent of pesticide-laced apples or carbon monoxide-infused air.

Most buildings in Mumbai are run by housing societies that are basically made up of the people who live in them. These societies choose a chairperson, a secretary and a treasurer to do stuff like sign cheques and scold the security guards for sleeping on the job.

Being the chairperson of a building society is not a big deal. You don't get paid for it. You don't get famous for it. And you're never going to meet a little kid who asks for your autograph and announces, 'When I grow up, I want to be the chairperson of my building society.' Actually, if that kid ever existed, he'd grown up to become Baman Marker.

Baman Marker loved being the chairperson of the Lily-Daisy Cooperative Housing Society. He loved lording it over the twenty families that lived in Lily Apartments and the ten that lived in Daisy Apartments. He imagined himself as a mash up of CEO and chief torturer. He sent bossy messages over WhatsApp and rude messages via the security guards.

Building societies are supposed to be democratic affairs. Ours was not.

Of course, the Hon Chairperson solicited our opinions. (His words.)

Then he considered these opinions. (His words again.)

After which he went ahead and did exactly what he wanted. (Our words.)

Till about four years ago, Lily and Daisy Apartments had been modest, middle-aged buildings that perched at the edge of Colaba, next to the smelly fish market of Sassoon Dock. The twin buildings were painted a wistful sky blue and stood in a cement compound amidst a happy muddle of badam trees, two ramshackle garages and children with rattly bicycles and skipping ropes.

Then Baman Marker struck. He decided to give our buildings a makeover, just in time for his older daughter's wedding. Of course, he didn't put it quite like that. Instead, he talked about beams and leakages. He delivered half-truths and quarter lies.

Everybody forked out money to make the buildings strong and leakproof. The workmen arrived with their yellow hats. But instead of making the buildings strong and leakproof, they did exactly what Baman Marker had intended all along.

They slapped granite slabs on the building entrances and passageways. These were the brown-red of congealed blood, so that you felt you were penetrating an infected wound whenever you stepped inside. After that, the workmen uprooted the lovely but unruly badam trees and replaced them with six joyless Ashokas that cast miserly needles of shade. They scraped away at the dreamy blue paint and replaced it with a septic shade of mustard.

Right at the very end, a team of men arrived with wires and poles. They wore T-shirts inscribed with the words, 'Wide Eye'. They installed four grey CCTV cameras, also inscribed with the words 'Wide Eye'. One camera watched over the entrance of Lily Apartments, another over the entrance of Daisy Apartments, and a third gazed upon the patch of street outside the gate. The last camera kept guard over a corner of the compound where Baman Marker parked his black BMW. (Or so everybody said. We could never be sure. The feed from the cameras could only be viewed in the offices of Wide Eye Security Systems and on the phone of the Hon Chairperson. Nowhere else.)

The weird part was that after all that money and inconvenience, the buildings continued to leak and the balconies continued to sag. If anybody complained, the Hon Chairperson bristled. He said he had spent a year of his life walking over rubble and standing in the sun. He had destroyed two pairs of leather shoes (bought from Joy Shoes at the Taj for thousands of rupees). Then he demanded a public apology.

The amazing part was that Baman Marker got his public apology. But then, Baman Marker always got what he wanted.

For many years now, Baman Marker had been an unpopular figure in our fishy, salty patch of Colaba. But by Day 43 of the lockdown, his ratings were at an all-time low—somewhere between Jack the Ripper and the coronavirus-carrying bats of China.

By the time you read this, the lockdown and the virus that caused it may be a fading memory. What you need to keep in mind, though, is that during the May of 2020, Mumbai was a jumpy city. People were terrified of falling sick. They gazed with suspicion at their neighbours. All it took was a single case of Covid-19 for a building to be sealed and for hysteria to erupt.

Baman Marker made the most of this fearful atmosphere.

Lily and Daisy Apartments had always been relaxed about security. If a particularly piratical individual sauntered in, wearing an eye patch and flashing a cutlass, Day Mishraji might ask him his business. Otherwise, the unofficial motto was 'All are welcome'.

Then the virus came along and suddenly all were unwelcome. The Hon Chairperson placed a table in the middle of the compound. On the table he placed a notebook and on the notebook he stuck a label stating 'Compulsory Register'.

As its name suggested, the Compulsory Register was compulsory. It was used to monitor not just the delivery boys and Swiggy agents who arrived at the gate, but the residents of Lily and Daisy Apartments who were irresponsible enough to venture out for a strip of Crocin or a breath of fresh air.

The Hon Chairperson decreed that every family must maintain a temperature chart that had to be emailed to him between 5 p.m. and 5.30 p.m. on Wednesday evenings.

He accused families of harbouring coughers and sniffters. He reminded the chat that he and his wife were vulnerable senior citizens. He sent menacing messages that stated, 'Do not shop at Modern Stores. My sources have confirmed that 3 people on the same street have tested positive for coronavirus.'

He sent threatening messages: 'Mr Shetty, I do hope everything is As It Should Be. You were seen leaving the compound at 9 a.m. and returning at 11.45 a.m. May I ask where you have been? We need this information to ensure the Safety of the Building.'

Or: 'Mrs Doshi, you failed to enter your time of departure and destination when you left the building yesterday. Everyone is Expected to Obey the Rules of our society.'

The latest message on my mum's phone—the one prohibiting rumour-mongering and panic-spreading—fit right in. Even if it was more dumbfounding than most.

We were still discussing Baman Marker's descent into insanity when my mother's phone rang. She took the call with a beam on her face and a smile in her voice. 'Hi Amrita. All okay? I've been trying to phone the bhajiwala all morning. What will we do if they shut down the market for a week or something? Things are getting crazy.'

Amrita Kapadia lived in Daisy Apartments. She was my mum's great friend and gossip-mate. Her daughter Shanaya was my BFF. And if that was not reason enough to adore her, Amrita Aunty was the only person this side of Regal Cinema who dared to challenge Baman Marker and his diktats. (She also made the most addictive pankis, dhoklas, pani puri and undhiyu ever. And I'm pretty much a world expert on these dishes.)

I was hoping that Amrita Aunty had called to invite me over for lunch, when my mother switched from smiling voice to gunshot voice. 'What?' I heard her snap. 'No, no. Are you serious? No, we didn't hear a thing.'

Ved and I stirred and tuned into the conversation. Compared to the rest of the lockdown, this Wednesday morning was positively action-packed. We waited while my mum spent six long minutes saying pointless stuff like, 'Then what will happen? Oh gosh. We are totally unprepared.' And, 'This is terrible. I better stock up.' And, 'I don't have a single tomato. But at least my mixer hasn't conked out like poor Rashida Habibullah's. I have no idea how that poor woman is managing.'

Finally, my mother finished chatting about random neighbours and their random kitchen appliances. The moment she wrapped up her conversation, we pounced. 'What?' we demanded. 'What happened? Tell us.'

My mother didn't tell us, which was most mean-spirited of her. Instead, she glowered at us and asked a question of her own. 'Have you had anything to do with Mr Sevnani in the last few days?' she snarled, sounding like a police officer with mouth ulcers. 'Have you spent time with him or shaken his hand or anything? Have you taken sweets or mangoes or something from him?'

This was so unexpected that Ved and I could only gawp. I mean, this was our mother. Surely she must know that we were as likely to hang out with cranky, red-faced Mr Sevnani as with the Abominable Snowman.

'No,' Ved said after a befuddled pause. 'I think the last time I spoke to Mr Sevnani was when I wished him Happy Diwali. Maybe last year, maybe two years ago. I can't remember if he coughed. But he definitely didn't give me a sweet or a mango. I don't think it was mango season.'

'Me too,' I lied. I actually doubted I'd ever wished Mr Sevnani for Diwali. Or for New Year or for Pongal or for anything at all. Ved was the sunny, social, festival-wishing twin. I was the secretive, sullen, sarcastic one.

Our words reassured my mother. 'That's a relief,' she said. 'I was so, so worried.'

It was at this moment that my father wandered into the living room, seeking banana chips and a break from the computer screen and tinny voices. 'What's going on?' he asked. 'Why are you worried, Priti?'

'Something terrible has happened,' my mother blurted out. 'Mr Sevnani has been taken to hospital.'

'Poor man,' my father said, trying to sound all love-thy-neighbourly. 'Listen, have those pepper banana chips gotten over? I can't find them.'

My mother glared at my father and repeated, in a high, strained voice, 'Mr Sevnani has been taken to hospital.'

'Yes, yes,' my father said. 'Very sad.'

'He has been taken,' my mother squawked, 'To. Be. Tested.'

Ved and I gasped, as we were meant to. My father looked dubious. 'Tested for coronavirus?' he asked. 'That seems unlikely. We've all been stuck in the house for weeks. How would he get it?'

'How do I know?' my mother retorted. 'All I know is that those men in blue plastic suits came for him. Amrita saw them from her balcony. The whole building saw them except for us. This is so unfair. We've been so careful, not gone anywhere or met anyone. And all the time the danger has been in our own building.'

'Mr Sevnani is only being tested,' my father pooh-poohed. 'Nothing has happened yet.'

'But Amrita says he definitely has the virus,' my mother wailed.

My father's face tightened. Unlike the rest of the family, he was not a fan of Amrita Aunty. He didn't even like her panki and samosas. 'And Amrita knows this how?' he scoffed. 'Is she a human coronavirus-testing kit or something?'

My mother did some face tightening of her own. Then she stalked into the kitchen and returned with a bowl of peppery banana chips and plonked them in front of my father. 'The results will come soon enough,' she said. 'But I know exactly what they will say. Amrita is always right about these things.'

2

I'm really glad that this is not a graded assignment. I would probably have gotten a C+. (The plus because our school believes in encouraging students.)

Sir Paulash has spent so much time and energy teaching us how to write stories. All that stuff about settings and plots. All those tips about introducing the main characters and theme at the very beginning. But somehow, I've managed to crash through all the rules.

I've managed to tell you all about Baman Marker and the maroon granite stone that clads the building entrance. I've managed to tell you about Amrita Aunty's pankis and my mother's lectures. But I haven't told you about the main characters in this story.

About Ved, who is my twin.

Or Shanaya, who is my absolute, total, forever best friend.

Or Daniel, who is my someone special, even if he doesn't know it yet.

I haven't even told you about myself. Not even that my name is Nandini Venkat. Which is pretty pathetic and doesn't say much about my abilities as a narrator.

It's seriously time to rectify matters and conduct a round of introductions.

We are the Venkats of Lily Apartments. When people meet us, they immediately think 'Oh, south Indians' and they tell us that they love idlis and sambar. No matter what our last name indicates, Ved and I are standard issue South Bombay brats.

Two months ago, I was a fourteen-year-old schoolgirl at Bright Minds School who loved mathematics and physics and was rotten at making friends and winning hearts. Ved was a fourteen-year-old schoolboy in the same school, who was fabulous at playing the drums and even better at being cool and popular.

Although Ved and I are twins, we're very different.

People know me because of my marks. They think that I am broody and dour (if they know the words, that is). They look at my oval face and regular features and think, 'She could be pretty enough if she took the trouble.'

Every year, the paragraph at the bottom of my school report card reads: 'Nandini is an excellent student with an analytical mind and an impressive power of observation. She does, however, need to curb her competitive spirit and learn to work with others.'

People know Ved because of his wisecracks and because he's the drummer for the school band. They think he's charming and they all want to be his friend. They look at his oval face and regular features and think, 'That boy will grow up to be a heartbreaker.'

Every year, the paragraph at the bottom of his school report card reads: 'Ved is a pleasure to have in class. He brings positive energy and works well in teams. He is bright but needs to focus more on academic goals.'

Clearly, the Venkat twins are as unidentical as they come.

My father used to be a banker, who spent more time at airports than in our living room with its Ganpatis, Pattachitra paintings and furniture fashioned out of antique trunks. My mother was a furniture designer and partner in a trendy store called Reincarnations—one of those shops with exposed brick walls, industrial pipes along the ceiling and tables made out of old truck parts.

Then somebody in China decided to eat a bat. Or some evil genius cooked up a virus in a laboratory. Or the universe decided that human beings were a menace and said, 'Chalo. Let's exterminate them.'

Whatever. All of a sudden, the newspapers were full of this new illness. A lockdown was declared. Bombay turned into Bandit City and Earth turned into a depressing planet.

Sometime during the last six weeks, Ved and I moved from Grade 8 to Grade 9 without clearing our desks or giving Thank You cards to our teachers. Sometime in that period we celebrated a birthday and turned fifteen, without new jeans or Red Velvet Cake. And along the way we regressed from human beings to jellyfish which—as anybody who has done an hour of biology will know—is a gazillion stages down the evolutionary ladder.

My father is still a banker, but now spends a lot of time at the dining table, after which he worries about his weight and his job. My mother is still a furniture designer, but she doesn't have staff either at home or at the workshop because of the lockdown. So instead of turning ancient sewing machines into cute little tables, she spends the day stressing about tomatoes, sanitizing the doorbell and reading articles about 'Positive Parenting during the Pandemic'.

(Inspired by these articles, she and Amrita Aunty have launched a 'Let's teach the kids life skills' drive. Invaluable Life Skill No. 1 is cooking. We haven't made much progress, which is why we haven't reached Invaluable Life Skill No. 2. If I have my way, we never will.)

Only one person in our house remains what she has always been, and that person is Alfonsa. Alfonsa is our help. She is a lugubrious woman with a concave face who has been with us since Ved and I were born. Alfonsa fills her days with a little ironing, a little dusting, some plant watering and vessel washing—and lots of information gathering. She keeps careful tabs on the neighbours and their misfortunes. There is just one thing that thrills her more than sudden death—and that is sudden death with violence and black magic thrown in.

For Alfonsa, the lockdown is an upgraded version of Christmas.

Alfonsa is besties with two housekeepers from Daisy Apartments. In normal times, the three friends went to church every Sunday evening, followed by a meal and gossip at Madras Cafe. At the moment they make do with long chats on the phone, after which Alfonsa gives us the news from the other side of the compound.

Over the last six weeks I've spent way too much time listening to these news updates, squabbling with my twin and refusing to tidy my room. But I really shouldn't grumble. I still have Shanaya. And in a way I also have Daniel. Both Shanaya and Daniel live right across from me in Daisy Apartments.

Shanaya is Amrita Aunty's daughter and my soulmate. She's eight months older than me, has crazy curly hair, alert eyes and a deceptively delicate air. She's just 4 feet 11 inches tall, but they are 4 feet and 11 inches crammed with energy, ideas and determination.

Shanaya's parents are divorced, but she's okay about it. In fact, she's generally okay about most things—with one exception. Her father.

I tell Shanaya every itty-bitty little thing. Almost.

Shanaya doesn't tell me everything. But she tells me more than she tells anybody else.

Shanaya and I have lived in each other's pockets and messy bedrooms through the lockdown. Of course, Baman Marker has discouraged interaction between the Lily and Daisy Apartments. But Shanaya and I have managed to out-sneak the sneak. We've done sleepovers and wake-overs, fight-overs and dress-overs at each other's houses. And when we're not together, we're chatting over WhatsApp. At the moment, most of our chats centre around Daniel Carvalho.

Daniel Carvalho has always lived in Daisy Apartments. I have a vague memory of him as a neat, pale schoolboy in a white shirt, white shorts and blue and yellow tie. I think he was one of the boys who used to cycle around the compound on dented bicycles till, one day, Baman Marker banned cycling in the compound.

I'm not sure when I started to notice Daniel. Like really notice him.

Perhaps it was when his mother died about a year ago. Everyone was shocked because it happened so suddenly. My mum went to Wodehouse Cathedral for the funeral and came back sad and shaken. 'That poor, poor boy,' she'd sighed. 'He gave such a loving, dignified speech. And he must be only two or three years older than you.'

Or perhaps it was after an ugly incident that erupted some months later on a rainy, blowy day. Baman Marker's large daughter had come to visit her parents. Ignoring the 'No Parking for Visitors' sign, she left her SUV in the middle of the compound.

The gleaming, muscular car blocked Mr Carvalho's small Hyundai. Mr Carvalho came down a few minutes later and realized that he was trapped. He started honking and demanding that the offending SUV be moved. Day Mishraji looked helpless. After about five minutes, Mr Carvalho stormed out of his car into the pelting rain. He screamed at Day Mishraji. Then he tried to phone Baman Marker. Then he shouted through the rain and wind at the Marker balcony.

Mr Carvalho was wearing one of those long, translucent raincoats that came down to his calves. Even so, he was soaked to the skin within minutes. It was another five minutes before Baman Marker strolled into his fifth-floor balcony. He didn't apologize or rush down to move the SUV. Instead, he acted as if Mr Carvalho was the problem. 'I really don't think that you are in any position to throw your weight around,' he called down. 'Be careful how you talk about my daughter. We could say many worse things about you.'

By this point, half of Lily Apartments and half of Daisy Apartments was watching the spectacle. I was in the middle of my exams and studying at my desk. I peered out and spotted Daniel at his bedroom window. The stricken look on his face hurt my heart.

Perhaps I began to notice Daniel when he shed his school uniform and started attending college in jeans, grey T-shirts and sneakers. Or when he started practicing the guitar in his bedroom, where I could see him and sometimes even hear him. Or when one day, at the end of the monsoons, he and

I were stuck outside Patel General Stores during a sudden downpour. Neither of us had our umbrellas. I remember that we smiled at each other a bit awkwardly. I remember the dimple in his left cheek and the lock of damp hair that kept falling into his left eye.

Or perhaps it was during the dreadful Lily-Daisy Diwali dinner last year (the one in which Amrita Aunty got tipsy and described Baman Marker as a fungal infection). I was behind Mini and Kysha in the queue for the palak paneer and veg au gratin and heard them agree that Daniel was cute. Mini and Kysha are three years older than me. They have purple streaks in their hair and glittery polish on their nails. Mini has 17,000 followers on TikTok. Kysha wears tops that look like shrunken bras. She has a navel piercing and a snake tattooed on her shoulder. Naturally, I deferred to their judgement.

I really don't know when my thing for Daniel began, but by the Christmas holidays I was properly besotted. I spent a large part of the vacations at my bedroom window. By New Year, I knew his schedule better than I knew my quadratic equations. And please remember, I'm the Maths topper in my class.

On holidays, Daniel woke up around 10 a.m. and ate his breakfast alone, because his father had already left the house. He played football on Mondays and Thursdays, and he liked slow, syrupy music of the kind that Ved described as 'jalebi pop'. I knew that Daniel had formed a band with two boys and one dauntingly glamourous girl who wore skimpy miniskirts, fluorescent tank tops and had blond streaks in her hair.

Still, there were many things I didn't know.

Was Daniel dating the girl with the too-tight tops and the clutching, touching hands? You could tell from a mile away that she was interested in him. But was he interested in her?

Was he still aching for his mother, who had died about a year ago? Had he even noticed that a fifteen-year-old schoolgirl named Nandini Venkat lived right across from him in Lily Apartments?

I was determined to find out. After all, I had a surveillance set up that was worthy of James Bond.

First, I had Shanaya. Shanaya lived on the second floor of Daisy Apartments, just beneath the Carvalhos. She could hear Daniel shifting the furniture when his bandmates came over to practice. She could hear his apartment door slam and his sneakered feet thuck-thuthuck on the stairs when he was going out. She could even hear the occasional sentence when he was standing at the window and chatting on his phone. And although she said he was wimpy and called him Drippy Daniel, she was not above a bit of spying for her best friend.

Second, Daniel and I were both on the Lily-Daisy Kids chat. It was a sleepy chat that spluttered into life every few months when Jeh Khambata posted photographs of dogs that were up for adoption. Or Mini Kurien forwarded memes. Or Aashu sent unsolvable riddles.

Other than the standard Happy Birthday posts, I'd sent just one message on the chat. It was after I lost my biology jotter and wanted to know if anybody had spotted it in the compound. Daniel had never posted a single message. Still, there was something cosy about being on a chat together.

Third was the fact that Daisy and Lily Apartments were built facing each other. Between the two buildings was a patch of cement, broad enough to allow a game of rubber-ball cricket. This served as the venue for the annual Diwali dinner, the Dandiya Nite and the big society meetings. During the rest of the year, it was used as a car park and a place for residents to form huddles and mutter about Baman Marker and his stooges.

My family lived on the fourth floor of Lily Apartments. I had always resented the fact that Ved's bedroom opened onto a triangle of fishy sea and a wide banyan tree, while mine overlooked a patch of asphalt, the roofs of two garages, six prim Ashokas, a bunch of parked cars and the bald head of Day Mishraji.

Now, though, I was grateful. For beyond the patch of cement stood Daisy Apartments. And in Daisy Apartments lived Daniel in a third-floor bedroom that was right across from my fourth-floor bedroom. This made it convenient for me to keep an eye on him. To see if he was wearing his yellow T-shirt. To try and figure out if he was talking on the phone with a lover-like expression.

When Daniel ate his dinner in the living room, I could see the white bowls and plates on the table. And when he left the house, if I peered at the five small windows that ran along the stairwell of Daisy Apartments, I could catch flashes of his legs climbing down the staircase. (Daisy Apartments and Lily Apartments had old and temperamental elevators that routinely got stuck between floors. As far as possible, we used the staircase.)

Shanaya found all this wildly funny. She had given me various names of the Nosy Nandini variety, so now I was more discreet. I didn't want to be stuck, either with a reputation or a title like The Lily Lurker.

I know. I know. All of this makes me sound like one of those lock-picking, pet-murdering stalkers. But honestly, I'm not a nutjob with a glinting knife. I'm just a girl with a big, fat crush and loads of time on her hands.

3

Mr Sevnani's test results arrived on the forty-fourth day of the lockdown.

They confirmed that he had coronavirus.

They proved yet again that Amrita Aunty was always right.

They provided Baman Marker with an excuse to behave as though Lily Apartments was more dangerous than Dracula's crypt.

They induced the BMC and the police to arrive soon after lunchtime, with cans of chemicals and a banner that announced to the world:

> MUNICIPAL CORPORATION OF GREATER MUMBAI A WARD
> THIS AREA HAS BEEN DECLARED AS 'CONTAINMENT AREA'
> AS A RESIDENT IS FOUND POSITIVE IN CORONA VIRUS TEST
> THE ENTRY TO THIS AREA IS RESTRICTED AND VIOLATION OF RULES IS PUNISHABLE.
> MAINTAIN SOCIAL DISTANCING. STAY SAFE.
> BY ORDER.

The message was delivered in shouty black and red letters that you couldn't miss even if you were as blind as one of those infamous, virus-carrying bats. As a resident of the building that had been declared a 'Containment Area', I found the banner rude and offensive.

But not as offensive as our Hon Chairperson.

Baman Marker stood in the middle of the compound, glaring at Lily Apartments and all who lived in it. He was careful to keep a safe distance from the BMC workers in their white safety suits and floppy yellow gloves. He was wearing a mask of course. Over that he was wearing one of those plastic face shields that make you look like a minor character from *Star Wars*. The mask and the face shield, we could understand. What we couldn't understand was why Baman Marker was holding a long, thin wooden stick.

'A curtain rod,' my mother whispered, in full furniture-designer mode. 'What's he doing with a curtain rod? In the middle of the lockdown?'

'Maybe he's planning a home makeover,' I quipped.

'Maybe he'll use it to beat anyone who emerges from infection-filled Lily Apartments?' Ved suggested.

'Maybe he's twisted his ankle and he's using it as a walking stick,' my father offered. 'It's decent of the guy to be overseeing stuff in the middle of the afternoon.'

This statement was met with a series of pchahs and poohs. None of us was in the mood to be reasonable about Baman Marker. We'd just realized that we wouldn't be allowed to leave the building for fourteen days. Not even to buy Oreos and Laughing Cow cheese. Not even to take a walk in the compound around the same time that Daniel was out and about.

My father had popped on his blue mask and gone to have a word with the BMC officials who were spraying chemicals, hanging their banner and sweating in their white safety suits.

'They were pretty decent,' he said when he got back ten minutes later. 'They said that it was okay to leave the building in a real emergency. They also said that we could order food and soap and things. They said the things could be dropped off with the security guard and then we could go down and pick them up.'

My mother sagged with relief till my father added that most insidious word. 'But…'

'But what?'

'But then Baman Marker quoted from some notification. I think he's going to make his own rules. May not be a bad thing, but we should be prepared for an inconvenient couple of weeks.'

Naturally then, we were feeling uncharitable towards Baman Marker. Naturally, we were unwilling to accept an innocuous explanation for the curtain rod. My mother—who'd realized that we were low on butter and coconut milk—accused my father of signing up with the forces of darkness. My father criticized her for not making shopping lists, and then wandered away to his computer.

The rest of us sat mesmerized, watching the theatre of the absurd.

We were not alone. All our neighbours had abandoned their online meetings, their sibling spats and their onion-chopping to gather in their balconies. Ved and I were with our mum in the living-room balcony which, along with my bedroom window, offered the best view.

Shanaya and Amrita Aunty were right across from us, and we raised our eyebrows at each other. Amrita Aunty was wearing trackpants, a T-shirt and a ponytail. She looked girlish, trim and totally sneery of the Hon Chairperson and his curtain rod.

Kysha was at her window in Daisy Apartments. She gave Ved a lazy wave and pulled exaggeratedly grumpy faces at someone else in Lily Apartments—probably Mini. Daniel was also at his window. He kept glancing towards the gate and I felt a stab of jealousy. Could he be waiting for Miss Miniskirt?

Downstairs, Baman Marker was speaking through his yellow mask and plastic face shield. From our perch on the fourth floor we could only hear faint bleats, but his body language was loud and clear. What he really, really wanted was to stuff Lily Apartments into a vacuum-sealed plastic bag for the next six months. As this was impossible, he was looking for alternate strategies.

It was during this lull that two new actors arrived on the cement stage. Both wore masks. Neither wore plastic face shields. Neither carried a stick. But then they were merely stooges.

Stooge No. 1 emerged from Daisy Apartments in a chickoo-brown churidar kurta. Kavita Lamba was the secretary of the Lily-Daisy Cooperative Housing Society. She was Shanaya's neighbour and had a daughter named Thea who was a bit younger than us. Kavita Lamba was a strapping, masterful woman who had taken numerous employers and cousins to court. She was the sort who could stare down a Bengal tiger or a ganglord with three gold teeth. But when it came to Baman Marker, she turned hunched and submissive.

Stooge No. 2 emerged from Lily Apartments in pink track pants, a black T-shirt, and rainbow-coloured curls. Ruby Vaz was a well-known hairstylist. She had 167,000 followers on Instagram and had done the styling for a Hinglish movie, many advertisements and innumerable celebrity weddings. She was also the treasurer of the Lily-Daisy Cooperative Housing Society.

Why would someone with 167,000 Instagram followers, monthly junkets to the Maldives, and designer shoes spend her free time writing out cheques for the lift company and the gardener? The reason was simple: Ruby Vaz's husband was a chartered accountant who worked under Baman Marker. Ruby was forced to play the part of amenable treasurer, whether she liked it or not.

That Ruby was an unwilling stooge was apparent from the way she tossed her pink-green-lavender head and stomped towards Baman Marker in her sparkly flip-flops. That she was an unwanted stooge became apparent a minute later.

Baman Marker had hailed Kavita Lamba with a gracious nod. He greeted Ruby Vaz with a sharp, shooing gesture. Then he jabbed the curtain rod in the direction of Lily Apartments. 'Scat,' he was clearly saying. 'Keep yourself and your infection inside your sealed building.'

Ruby halted. She stared at the wagging, banging stick. Then she shrugged, turned on her heels and flounced back into the building. After which she probably spent the rest of the day convincing her husband to switch from chartered accountancy to pet-food testing or termite-harvesting or any other profession that did not involve Baman Marker.

Up in our balcony, Ved was jubilant. 'WhadidItellyou, whadidItellyou?' he crowed. 'The Hon Chairperson needs the stick to protect himself from the dangerous dwellers of

Lily Apartments. Us, in short. He's scared that the virus will sneak across the compound into his precious Daisy Apartments.'

Ved was right. Our Hon Chairperson stood in the bright afternoon sunlight, tapping on his phone. Seconds later, a series of messages flashed on the Lily-Daisy Apartments chat. Each was designed to make this Thursday more miserable than it already was:

'Residents of Lily Apartments will NOT leave the building for 15 days. After 15 days the situation will be Reviewed.'

'Outsiders will NOT enter the building for 15 days.'

'Gate of the building will be LOCKED AT ALL TIMES and ONLY be opened upon instruction by Hon Chairperson or Hon Secretary.'

'The elevator of Lily Apartments is to be switched off to discourage movement in the building.'

'We have two security guards. Ajay Mishra is our Day Guard. Chandu Mishra is our Night Guard. From today, both will do Day Duty. Ajay Mishra will sit at the gate of Daisy Apartments and Chandu Mishra will sit at the gate of Lily Apartments.'

'Two New Guards have been appointed for night duty. They will report for duty at 7 p.m. They will answer ONLY to the Hon Chairperson and the Hon Secretary. Please do not think that because they are new, you can Disregard them.'

'Residents of Lily Apartments will order only Basic Essentials. Orders can be placed only through the Hon Chairperson.'

'There are many High-Risk Individuals in our buildings. Binaifer and I are Extremely Vulnerable and have been advised to stay indoors. It is Only to fulfill my Duty that I am Risking my Health.'

'We expect full Cooperation and Support.'

'Thank You.'

If Baman Marker had expected applause, he was in for a disappointment. The silence that greeted his messages was so cold that you could hear icicles crackle and snap. Our Hon Chairperson, though, was not a let-sleeping-dogs-lie kind of person. He waited for five minutes before sending a final message that reeked of petulance.

'Please Acknowledge.'

This time, the Hon Chairperson got the response he wanted. 'We are blessed to have such an efficient and caring Chairperson,' Lina Almeida wrote on the chat. 'Thank you Baman for everything. You can count on our support.'

Lina Almeida lived on the first floor of Dairy Apartments. She was an imperious, white-haired woman who, for thirty-four years, had been principal of one of the most exclusive schools in the city. Although she was too old to be principal any longer, she still wielded immense power at All Saints School.

Lina Almeida was a useful person to cultivate and Baman Marker was a cultivator of useful people. Especially principals of posh schools. After all, he had two (plus one on the way) grandchildren who would soon be needing admission into a posh school.

It was only natural then, that Baman Marker and Lina Almeida should form a mutual admiration society and coo at each other on the building chat. 'The arrangement of the Christmas lights this year is delightful,' Lina Almeida would write. 'Thank you dear Baman, for your personal attention to detail.'

Two days later, dear Baman would return the compliment. 'Mrs Almeida makes the Most Fabulous immunity boosting juices,' he would gush. 'Thank you for your Papaya Smoothie today. You must conduct a class for us. The Green Glow Detox and Carrot Energy Shake are Superior to anything I have sampled in the best European spas.'

We had made puky faces then, and we made puky faces now.

'Speak for yourself,' my mother snarled at her phone. 'Baman Marker cannot count on my support. How dare he make everything worse than it already is? Shweta's building is also sealed. But they order Mediterranean platters whenever they want. Shweta even sneaked out to buy hair colour. And what if there's a fire? I'm sure it's unsafe and illegal to lock us in like this.'

Ved and I nodded in doleful agreement. No football in the compound of Bhagwan Nivas. No afternoons with Shanaya. No cheese pillows and wafers from Camy. How could we possibly survive the next fortnight?

The afternoon sun was getting to me. I was about to get up from my white cane chair when, quite suddenly, a figure hurtled out of Lily Apartments, uttering a string of words. We leaned forward to make sense of them.

The newcomer was frighteningly dishevelled, with a lopsided mask, sticky-out hair and a long, lavender garb that looked like a nightgown (though it could hardly be a nightgown at this hour of the day). Ignoring Baman Marker's stick and gestures, the lavender figure rushed straight towards the BMC officials, who were loading their van. 'Please!' The cry pierced the locked-down city and rose all the way to the fourth floor.

The voice was unmistakable. Sheela Jagtiani. Of course.

'I hadn't thought about Sheela,' my mother exclaimed. 'This will be terrible for her. How will she manage?'

Sheela Jagtiani lived two floors below us. Her husband had gone to Chennai for a training programme before the lockdown and got stuck there. Sheela was managing her two small sons, her own house and her father's house across the compound in Daisy Apartments. Her father was old, feeble and dependent on his nurses. But the nurses had stopped coming since the lockdown was enforced.

'Sheela goes to give Mr Alimchandani his medicine, check his oxygen and deliver his food,' my mother said. 'He's alone in the apartment with just one new, untrained man to help. Poor Sheela is really worried.'

This was apparent at a glance. Sheela Jagtiani wrung her hands as she spoke to the officials. They listened with sympathy and seemed to be comforting her. Sheela Jagtiani was mopping her eyes and thanking the officials when Baman Marker sidled into the conversation.

Baman Marker never shouted. That was not his style. Instead, he sing-songed on and on: a steady stream of tweaked facts, half-lies and faulty arguments that lulled his listeners into a stupor. (I don't know if you've seen that Disney movie, *Jungle Book*. But the Hon Chairperson was a padded, SoBo version of Kaa the python.) This time too, Baman Marker hypnotized his audience. The BMC officials looked dazed and said something stern to Sheela Jagtiani. Then they sat in their van and juddered off to seal yet another building.

In the suddenly vacated compound, Baman Marker stood talking, talking, talking and brandishing the curtain rod to keep the purple figure at bay. Sheela Jagtiani slumped dispiritedly for two minutes before she whirled around and charged towards Daisy Apartments. Day Mishraji blocked her path and she wailed, 'Just once a day. Only so I can give my father his medicines and one meal. I will wear a mask and gloves. Anything.'

Standing next to me, my mother looked ready to cry. My father came running to the balcony. But Baman Marker merely shrugged and turned away.

Sheela Jagtiani had already stepped into Lily Apartments, so we could no longer see her. But we heard each word that she hurled at the Hon Chairperson. 'Do what you want,' she screeched. 'Tell whom you want. I am not afraid of you. Tell the whole world everything. After that you won't have power over my family any longer, will you?'

Baman Marker raised an offended hand. But Sheela Jagtiani was not done. 'You will be punished,' she declared in the ringing voice of a prophet. 'Not after years and years, but soon. Very soon.'

If this had been a movie, lightning would have flashed and thunder crashed through the sky. Instead, a nervous silence fell over the compound, dispelled only when another figure strode onto the scene.

Mr Burman, the banker.

All I knew about Mr Burman the banker was that he lived on the fourth floor of Daisy Apartments behind a screen of glossy banana plants. Mr Burman was dressed in a grey mask, trendy trackpants and chunky orange sneakers. He didn't seem to notice that the Hon Chairperson and Hon Secretary were standing in his path. He continued on his way and would have barrelled into the two Hons if they hadn't jumped backwards.

It's not often that you see a Teletubby quake with fury. Baman Marker did just that. Then he pointed to the

Compulsory Register with an accusatory finger. Mr Burman froze. Then he turned very slowly, like one of those tai chi types, and raised his fist. Then he extended two fingers to form the barrel of a gun which he aimed at the Hon Chairperson.

'Did you see that?' my mother yelped. 'Is Mr Burman mad? Not that I'm complaining, but—'

'It's been a bad year for Ranjit Burman,' my father remarked.

'And it's been a bad day for Baman Marker,' Ved guffawed. 'Two threats in one day. Go Jagtiani. Go Burman.'

'It definitely looks like Ranjit and Baman have fallen out with each other,' my father mused. 'I was wondering.'

'What do you mean?' my mother asked, twisting around in her blue cane chair.

'Baman Marker is Ranjit Burman's chartered accountant. Isn't that how Ranjit bought the flat in Daisy Apartments?'

'Oh yes, I remember now,' my mum said. 'But then they had that nasty fight some months ago. Water from the Markers' bathroom was leaking into the Burman's house. Baman Marker ignored the complaints and Mr Burman turned aggressive and copied everyone on the mail.'

My father looked blank. 'Must have been when I was travelling,' he said. 'But that explains why things soured between them.'

'But why is it a bad time for Ranjit Burman?' my mother asked. 'How do you suddenly know so much about him? How come you haven't mentioned any of this before?'

'Ranjit Burman's pretty well-known in the financial world,' my father replied. 'And there are suddenly lots of whispers about him. He's made some questionable decisions. But please don't say anything to Amrita. I don't want this announced on All India Radio.'

My mum was saved from having to lie by a flurry of activity in the compound. Kavita Lamba hurried into Daisy Apartments. Then the Hon Chairperson took a deep breath, looked around the empty compound and waved his plump, white hands as if he was conducting an orchestra. Instead of violins and cellos, it was Night Mishraji who responded.

Night Mishraji was stationed at the entrance of Lily Apartments. We couldn't see the security guard, of course, but we could hear his struggle with the heavy gate. Both Lily and Daisy Apartments had black metal security gates. I couldn't remember the gates ever being shut in the seven years that we had lived here. That was about to change.

The clang of metal on metal was shocking in the afternoon hush. Then came the scraping of a key in a rusty, uncooperative lock. The faces at the windows and balconies of Daisy Apartments wore expressions of pity and relief. 'Thank God it's not us,' they seemed to be thinking.

Somewhere below us, Night Mishraji fiddled with the reluctant lock. A minute later, it clunked into place and Lily Apartments was sealed. My eyes swam and Daniel blurred into smudges of green and brown.

I shuffled away to my bedroom and stood at my desk. Then I picked up a red marker, leaned over my calendar and made a thick angry cross on Thursday, 7 May. After which I burst into tears.

We'd only been prisoners for thirty seconds and I was already freaking out. It was not a good sign.

4

The forty-fifth day of the lockdown was grimly satisfying. At least for the residents of Lily Apartments—aka Azkaban@Colaba.

It wasn't such a great day for the people living in Daisy Apartments, but I was low on empathy. To be honest—and I'm not sure that honesty is always such a great policy—I felt more and more gleeful as the day progressed.

In fact, it's a pity that my chapters don't have headings. For this particular chapter at least, I would have been spoilt for choice:

- 'The Tables Are Turned'
- 'She Who Laughs Last'
- 'Mr Marker Gets His Comeuppance'
- 'The Hon Chairperson Gets a Taste of His Own Medicine'

Any of these would have worked, as you will see soon enough.

My Friday began with a bowl of Choco Pops and a nasty message on the Lily-Daisy Apartments chat. The message was sent by Kavita Lamba, but we knew that every phrase and comma had been dictated by the Hon Chairperson. My mother read the message and was nauseated. She then proceeded to read it out and nauseate us. This is what Kavita Lamba wrote:

'This is in connection with Mr Ramesh Sevnani, a resident of Lily Apartments, who has tested positive for Covid 19. We would like to state on record that Mr Sevnani did not take precautions as advised by the Hon Chairperson. Despite objections he continued to visit his daughter in Puja Towers. It is unfortunate that he has exposed our two buildings to grave danger.'

Mr Sevnani was nobody's favourite. But we still felt bad. The message spread way quicker than the virus and, within an hour, had popped up on the Colaba Rocks chat and the Residents' Welfare Association chat. At this rate, Mr Sevnani would need to hide his face behind a mask for the next two years.

If he pulled through, that is. Amrita Aunty told us that he was critically ill. 'Somebody is going to do something to that Baman Marker one of these days,' my mother muttered, dusting the pots and vases with needless force. 'We should protest.'

'Don't get into a battle with Baman Marker,' my father warned. 'He's already hinted that he will complain to the BMC about the extra bathroom in our flat.'

'But we didn't build it,' my mother said as she pulled out the dead leaves from a fern. 'It was done by the earlier occupants.'

'Who knows what Baman Marker will tell the authorities,' my father sighed as he turned on his computer. 'Do you really want to be involved in a war that we're bound to lose?'

'No,' my mother admitted. 'But I'm sick of that man. He finds out nasty little secrets about everyone, and he uses them to manipulate people and get his way. It's downright disgusting. He's no better than a common blackmailer.'

Hearing my giggle, my mother turned her wrathful attention our way. 'Nandini, Ved, are you going to nibble at your breakfast till lunchtime or what?' she snarled. 'Take your bowls to the kitchen. Now. And Nandini, your room is in such a mess that Alfonsa and I are finding it impossible to sweep it even. I want it tidied up. Today.'

My mother's words were as forceful as a kick and Ved and I scurried to the kitchen. She was still frowning when we returned to the living room and Ved attempted to cheer her up. 'There has to be someone in our buildings who doesn't have a deep, dark secret or a third bathroom,' he said. 'Maybe they'll protest.'

My mother snapped that it was unlikely. So we were pretty amazed when someone did protest. We were even more amazed when that someone turned out to be Rashida Habibullah, the mild, smiling woman who lived on the ground floor of Daisy Apartments.

We didn't know Rashida Habibullah well. We didn't know if she had a deep, dark secret or a third bathroom. But we now knew that she had courage. 'The police and authorities have said repeatedly that it's illegal to name and shame people just because they have fallen sick,' she wrote on the chat. 'We should not lose sight of our humanity at a time when the world is in such trouble.'

'Good for Rashida,' my mother crowed. 'I've always liked her. She's really suffered at the hands of Baman Marker.'

'She has?' Ved and I gawked. We were learning new things about our neighbours every couple of hours.

'Yes. Her husband has some serious anxiety issues, so they were really depending on her catering business for an income. Once the lockdown happened, people didn't have help at home and Rashida began to supply meals to half of Colaba. Baman Marker didn't like it that she was doing well. He called the police and said that she was running an illegal business. But Rashida had all her permissions and was following all the lockdown rules.'

'Then?' I asked, wide-eyed.

'Then someone spread a rumour that one of Rashida's staff had tested positive for coronavirus. A complete lie, but the damage was done. And we all know who was behind the rumour.'

'Who told you all this?' my father asked, looking up from his phone. 'How can you assume Baman had anything to do with it? You hardly know the Habibullahs.'

'I know Rashida well,' my mother bristled. 'We've shared a compound for seven years. I even sent Ved to fix her mixer some days ago. And anyway, Amrita told me that Baman Marker has been harassing Rashida for years and years now—complaining about the sound of cooking, about her delivery van, writing to the police. He made a rule that only cars could be parked in our compound. So even though they have their own parking spot, the Habibullahs can't park their van here. Which is ridiculous.'

'There must be some reason,' my father protested. 'Baman is not a madman.'

My mother laughed sardonically. 'Oh really?' she asked. 'Well, he certainly drives others mad. Mr Habibullah has been so disturbed by the harassment that he's stopped leaving the house. Meanwhile, the catering business has taken a big hit.'

'Very convenient for the Big Bum,' I said.

'And sad for the Habibullahs,' my mother added. 'You remember their son Ibrahim? One of the boys who used to cycle around the compound when we first came to live here? He's in a university in Ohio and they're not sure they can pay for his final year. As Amrita says, only a monster would kick someone who's already down.'

Given this back story, it made perfect sense that Amrita Aunty should fire the next salvo. 'I agree with Rashida,' she wrote on the chat. 'We would hardly want our Chairman and Secretary to break the law. That might cause uncomfortable problems for them and for us.'

We were still chuckling when a most unlikely neighbour lolloped into the debate. Darius Khambata lived on the third floor of Daisy Apartments. He taught yoga and floated around Colaba with a long beard, batik shorts, knobbly knees and bead necklaces.

He never engaged in building controversies, which made his words even more peculiar. 'Only kindness works at times like this,' he had written. 'Remember that old saying from our childhood? When you point one finger at others, there are three fingers pointing back at you? Let us be mindful of this. Otherwise, one doesn't know how this will end.'

I had always viewed Darius Khambata as eccentric but harmless. Someone who was not to be taken too seriously. But one person was taking him extremely seriously. 'Baman Marker typing…' kept flashing at the top of my mother's phone, but it was a full half hour before a message arrived. It was pretty short for all that typing and thinking, thinking and typing.

'In most cases one knows how it will End,' Baman Marker had written. 'When Money is moved that should not be moved. When Papers are sold that should not be sold. When Plants are bought that should not be bought. Then we Know that it can only end Badly.'

My mother read out the message in a startled voice, after which we wrinkled our brows, shook our heads and decided that this was yet another indicator of Baman Marker's mental collapse. (We didn't spot the meaning hidden in those words until much later. How could we? But there were others who had understood exactly what our Hon Chairperson was implying. And they didn't like it one bit.)

After this, the Lily-Daisy Apartments chat turned to mundane matters. Aashu's mother complained that the new night chowkidars were causing mayhem with the morning milk and bread delivery. Lina Almeida agreed that they were 'disobliging and dull'.

Rashida Habibullah asked if anybody knew of an electrician who would fix her mixer. Baman Marker hit back with a brusque message saying that no handymen were permitted to enter Daisy Apartments. Five minutes later, the Hon Chairperson was back with another message: 'A Parcel meant for me was Inadvertently delivered to Someone Else in Daisy Apartments by the new Night Guard. Immediately inform me if you have it.'

Bored by these prosaic matters, I trailed away to my bedroom and winced when I stepped inside. Much as I hated to admit it, my mum was right. My room looked as if an army of marauding bandicoots had battled their way through it. Every available surface was heaped with crumpled clothes. Some of these should have gone into the washing machine weeks ago. Others, I had modelled and then tossed into a corner along with broken anklets, lonesome earrings and dusty scrunchies. Some of the clothes belonged to Shanaya. She must have forgotten to take them home after our sleepovers. A black bra sat on my desk and a ghagra covered half my dressing table.

I surveyed the chaos for a few minutes and wondered if a poltergeist had taken possession of my room. Then I wondered if I was reading too many horror books. Then I resolved to tidy the room.

To my credit, I even began the process and put two black T-shirts into the cupboard. But then I stumbled upon a pleated purple skirt with the price tag still dangling from the waist. Naturally, I got distracted and tried to call my personal fashion consultant. Shanaya's phone refused to connect and, when I looked across the sun-struck compound, I saw that her bedroom windows were shut and the yellow curtains drawn. She must still be asleep.

One floor up, Daniel wasn't visible either. I wondered if he had slipped out to go wherever he went and meet whoever he met. The thought filled me with acrid resentment. Life during the lockdown had been slow and unyielding—like swimming through condensed milk. But being stuck in a sealed building was way worse, more like wading through sticky toffee.

I was trying on the purple skirt with a white vest when Alfonsa stuck her head in at the door. 'Chemmen Saab is going somewhere,' she hissed, and waggled her head in the direction of my bedroom window.

'Okay,' I said, wondering where the Hon Chairperson could possibly be going. Baman and Binaifer Marker were petrified of the pandemic. They behaved as if the virus had sprung into being for one reason alone—to sneak into Daisy Apartments, climb five floors, and infect the pudgy chartered accountant and his bony wife.

Baman Marker was not the sort to ever venture into Colaba Market or Sahakari Bhandar for his own cauliflowers and jeera powder. In normal times he had a fleet of drivers and housekeepers. Not to forget a parade of delivery boys who trotted in and out of the compound bearing farm-fresh pineapples, gluten-free brownies and milk from cows raised on Mozart and organic grass.

What amazed me was that even during lockdown—when so many people had no food to eat, and others couldn't get basic stuff like Amul cheese and tomatoes—the Markers still managed to get their organic avocadoes and Rose Pista White Chocolate Cakes delivered to the door. Baman Marker really had no reason to go anywhere. Alfonsa must be imagining things.

I turned back to the mirror, but Alfonsa was not easily discouraged. She edged into the room and spoke in her most sibilant whisper. 'A car has come for Chemmen Saab. And they are putting bags into it. Big bags.'

'A car?' I asked dubiously. 'And bags?'

Puzzled, I headed to the window and looked down. Alfonsa was right. An unfamiliar car was standing in the compound. Two matching brown suitcases were being loaded into the boot by a driver in a white uniform, while Baman Marker stood at a safe distance and gave instructions. Then the thin, hockey-stick form of his wife hurried out of the building, dashed through the compound, leapt into the car and slammed the doors shut. The way she was behaving, you would have thought that blood-dripping, fang-baring werewolves were yapping at her heels.

There was some rapid waving and Daaaaarlinging, and then the car drove off. It was all very strange.

By this point, Alfonsa had summoned my mother. Who in turn had phoned Amrita Aunty, the usual solver of Lily-Daisy riddles. This time, though, she was as zapped as the rest of us. 'She must have gone to one of her daughters',' Amrita Aunty decided after some thought. 'Nothing else makes any sense.'

'But Baman Marker was horrible about Mr Sevnani, only because he visited his daughter,' my mum protested. 'It's hardly likely—'

'Priti, you are an innocent,' Amrita Aunty snorted. 'Surely you know the rules by now. If WE leave the house, we are mass murderers. But if THEY leave the house, it is because God has personally printed out a permit for them. Still, if that man can poke his nose into our business, I don't see any reason why we can't repay the favour.'

Ved and I chortled and agreed that Amrita Aunty was bomb. Our mother was less gleeful. 'Be careful, Amrita,' she warned, 'That man is capable of anything.'

'He's a bloody coward,' Amrita Aunty retorted. 'And anyway, I'm only going to do to him what he does to us. I'm even going to copy-paste his words from his messages. How can he possibly object to that?'

Amrita Aunty's message arrived on the Lily-Daisy Apartments chat a minute later: 'Mr Marker, I do hope everything is As It Should Be. Mrs Marker seen leaving the compound in a car this morning. May I ask where she has gone? We need this information to ensure the safety of the building.'

Amrita Aunty had followed this up with a hands-folded emoji.

We waited near the phone till Baman Marker wrote back five minutes later: 'Thank you for your concern. Everything is as it should be with us.'

Amrita Aunty must have been waiting as well, phone in hand. She swooped like a fierce bird of prey. 'Good to hear,' she replied. 'It was noticed that Mrs Marker didn't fill her time of departure and destination in the Compulsory Register.'

The message was greeted with silence, but Amrita Aunty was not in a mood to leave well alone. 'Do let us know where Mrs Marker has gone,' she prodded. 'We are all anxious.'

The reply came after a longish time and further confirmed our suspicions about Baman Marker's mental deterioration. 'No cause for worry,' he'd written. 'Her family knows where she is. She is not in Banyan Tree Resorts in Phuket. She is not in an apartment in Worli. Thank you.'

My mother read the message aloud, shaking her head and announcing that the Hon Chairperson had officially gone dotty, pagal, paithyam. I agreed, even though the Hon Chairperson's message had given me a pinprick of unease. It had poked something buried deep in my memory. Something that refused to rise to the surface.

My mum was so eager to discuss the unravelling of the Hon Chairperson that she decided to feed us Maggi noodles and use the time to gossip with Amrita Aunty. But Amrita Aunty didn't answer her phone. I guess she must have been making her fabulous aamras or falafels.

After this, all was quiet on the chat till Lina Almeida struck while we were eating an early lunch. As I've mentioned earlier, Lina Almeida lived on the first floor of Daisy Apartments. She was a silver-haired woman who wore a neat bun and spectacles on a golden chain. She was famous for being the strictest principal of the strictest school in the city. And there wasn't a student in All Saints School who didn't dance a jig when she finally, finally, finally gave her retirement speech.

The celebration was premature. Lina Almeida vacated the principal's office. But that was only so that she could shift three doors down, to an even bigger office with an even wider desk. The board outside the new room read, 'Mentor and Guide'. It was generally agreed that the signboard-painter had made a mistake. The sign should have read 'Tormentor and Guide'.

I didn't attend All Saints School, but Shanaya did. So did Thea and Kysha and three of the littler kids from Lily Apartments. Which meant we had a lot of tormented and guided children in our compound.

During the lockdown, Lina Almeida must have found herself woefully short of victims. Which probably explained her revolting message. 'Dear all,' she had written on the Lily-Daisy Apartments chat. 'We are witnessing a unique moment, when the universe has paused for breath. Let us fill this pause with meaningful activity.'

Ved and I gagged as my mum read on, 'We must teach our children to be of service to others. On my part, I am insisting that my granddaughter become handy in the kitchen. Yesterday she made a passable Spinach Frittata and Scalloped Potato Casserole. She also made an excellent jug of Green Glow, a detoxification smoothie that I have perfected over the last year.'

'Kysha made a whatever and a whatever?' I interrupted. 'Is she even the cooking kind?'

'She isn't,' Ved confirmed. 'She must be pissed about this. Hardly goes with her snake tattoo and her image. But why is Granny Gruesome telling us all this anyway?'

'Listen for a minute,' my mother said, before continuing to read out Lina Almeida's message. 'We should all encourage our youngsters to help in the kitchen. After their experiments, they can share their successes and failures, as well as their recipes. To get the ball rolling, I have shared my Green Glow recipe here.'

My mother started reading out the recipe. It began with a list of ingredients that included kale, spinach and celery. I quaked. Not all the cucumbers in the world could possibly balance out that evil threesome.

I was pretty sure that Lina Almeida's scheme would fade and die. I mean, who on earth would agree to play Masterchef in the middle of a lockdown? I got my answer soon enough. Mini's mum—an exhaustingly energetic type—wrote back within minutes, 'Lovely idea, Mrs A, We're on.'

This set off a chain reaction. Other mothers—especially those whose children attended All Saints School—felt compelled to raise their hands as well. After all, Lina Almeida was not a forgetting, forgiving sort of Tormentor and Guide.

One after another, they began to sign up for the teach-our-children-to-be-of-service-to-others scheme. 'Thea has been making chapatis since the beginning of the lockdown,' Kavita Lamba wrote. 'Today I will have her make rajma using my grandmother's recipe.'

Then Mrs Doshi from the ground floor of Lily Apartments went on about how Tariini had been making perfect brownies since the day she was born. After which Amrita Aunty, who had been uncharacteristically silent, responded with a brief, 'We are on.'

Which was when I knew that my goose was cooked. (We are a vegetarian household, but that doesn't stop my mother from cooking my goose pretty often. Or my dad from snacking on the occasional chicken tikka at office parties.)

Before we could stop her, my mother had jumped in with a thumbs up. She informed us that I would be making dinner that evening, and that Ved would be making dinner the next day. After which there was nothing to do but to wish various plagues upon Lina Almeida. 'May her kitchen be infested with termites,' I said. 'And her ladle be riddled with rust. May her bread turn moldy and her—'

'And her nose turn coldy,' Ved jumped in. 'May she fracture her pinky, and her frittatas flop…'

My mother frowned. 'I don't often agree with Lina Almeida. But this time she's right. High time you children learnt to help. You should know basic cooking. You should keep your rooms tidy. Nandini, I don't have words to describe your room. It's covered in clothes and crumbs and I-don't-even-want-to-think-whats. Go and clean it up. And you can look up some recipes if you like.'

I did not like. I made that pretty clear and stomped off to my bedroom to glower at heaps of clothes and earrings and single sandals. Then I made the bad mistake of looking out of the window.

The residents of Daisy Apartments were flaunting their freedom to the prisoners of Lily Apartments. Mr Burman was wheeling out a sleek, lemon-yellow bicycle from his garage. Jeh Khambata was giving his motorbike a wash and polish. Kysha was leaning on a car, posing supermodel style and chatting with him. 'Let's call the others down,' she was saying in her loud, confident Kysha-bray. And I immediately wondered who 'the others' were. Shanaya? Daniel?

The thought made me so anxious that I stayed at the window for a bit, watching Kysha preen and sparkle. Literally. Her many piercings glinted, her trademark silver Nikes glittered and her purple hair shimmered in the harsh sunshine. After some time, I saw sullen Thea and her even more sullen father walking Muffin, their yappy puppy. But it looked like 'the others' weren't coming after all. Comforted by the thought, I wandered away from the window and phoned Shanaya.

'I've called you about a hundred times,' I said when she finally answered. 'Don't tell me you were sleeping all this time?'

'Ummm…yeah,' Shanaya said. 'My mother was hassled about something and forgot to wake me up. What's been happening?'

I gave Shanaya a quick update about the morning. My forgotten-and-found purple skirt. Baman Marker's odd messages on the chat. Lina Almeida's abominable suggestion. As usual, Shanaya handled it all with aplomb. She decided that the purple skirt would go with my dull green stretchy T-shirt. She announced that Baman Marker was a horrid bore. And she said that she would make toast and butter for dinner. 'My dinner, my menu,' she said with bracing decisiveness. 'Lina Bloody Almeida can take it or leave it.'

We spent a few minutes giggling at the thought of the foods that would be posted on the Lily-Daisy chat. Perfect brownies, spicy rajmas, fancy frittatas—and a plate of cold toast with a scrape of butter. 'My mom will somersault with irritation,' Shanaya chortled. 'She's pissed off anyway.'

'I am too,' I sighed. 'It would have been such fun to cook together. I'm really feeling depressed about this sealed-building business.'

'Pity you're on the fourth floor,' Shanaya agreed. 'I bet we could have figured out a way to get you out if you'd been on the first floor.'

'I'm not sure I would risk broken bones just for the joy of making cold toast with you,' I laughed. 'Guess we'll have to wait for the fourteen days to get done.'

'You are such a wimp,' Shanaya snorted. 'A perfect match for Drippy Daniel.'

I ignored the first part of the remark and focused on the Daniel bit. 'What's Daniel doing?' I asked eagerly. 'Can you hear anything?'

'Being drippy I guess,' Shanaya retorted. 'All is silent for the moment.'

We argued about Daniel's drippiness for a bit. Then Shanaya hurried away for a shower, before Amrita Aunty got mad. I settled on my bed, cheered by my masterful best friend and her brisk attitude towards purple skirts, cooking competitions and life. I wondered if I could get away with making cheese toast for dinner. Somehow, I didn't think so.

The day stretched ahead endlessly. I had plans to watch Netflix, but the WiFi was down so I read Stephen King's *The Shining* instead.

The book is about a haunted hotel and not recommended reading for someone who's already gloomy and stuck inside a sealed building. I could only handle two chapters, after which I took myself and my grouch to Ved's room. I made him turn off the smashing-crashing sounds that he calls music. Then I paced around while we tried to solve the mystery of Mrs Marker. 'I'm not that interested in where she's gone,' Ved said again and again. 'What I really want to know is why.'

'We'll never find out,' I replied gloomily. But my pessimism was unwarranted. We did find out—just a few hours later.

At 5.05 in the evening, a BMC van drove through the compound gate. Once again, the men in white jumped out with their sprays and banners. Once again, the residents of Lily and Daisy Apartments gathered at their windows and balconies. Once again, Baman Marker arrived in his yellow mask and his face guard.

It was an eerie action replay of the events of yesterday. Except.

Except this time the focus was on Daisy Apartments.

'Has someone tested positive in Daisy Apartments?' I asked my mother. 'Has Amrita Aunty said anything?'

My mother shook her head. And, when I glanced across the balcony at Amrita Aunty and Shanaya, they seemed as dazed as the rest of us.

This sense of déjà vu intensified when a figure darted into the compound, masked and furious. For a bewildered moment I thought Sheela Jagtiani had burst through the metal gate of Lily Apartments. But no.

This figure had emerged from Daisy Apartments. And this figure was male.

It took us a couple of minutes to recognize the wiry little man who lived on the ground floor of Daisy Apartments. Old Mr Shetty, who was usually so chatty and cheerful and full of stories about stray dogs and mango trees.

At the moment, though, he was neither chatty nor cheerful. He was rattling with rage. 'How?' he shouted at Baman Marker. 'How could you do such a thing? Raghunath has been a part of this building for more years than you or I have. And you throw him onto the streets? You don't even call for an ambulance? You are a murderer. Nothing more, nothing less.'

Baman Marker tried to manage the situation as usual. He talked in his soothing singsong and served up his usual half-truths and quarter-lies. But Mr Shetty was having none of it. He raised his head and looked up, first at the packed balconies of Daisy Apartments and then at the packed balconies of Lily Apartments.

'Shame,' he shouted. 'Shame on all of us.'

Then he trudged back to his ground-floor flat in Daisy Apartments with a bowed head and bony, hunched shoulders.

The BMC men were unfazed, or maybe they were just in a hurry. There were many of them today and I counted five men in white, flapping suits wandering up and down Daisy Apartments. They were impressively meticulous. I spotted one of them in Daniel's living room, wraithlike in that gloomy space. A couple of them headed for the garages and, later, another even climbed beyond the fifth floor to the roof.

Most of the men were back in the compound and packing up when Amrita Aunty lobbed her question on the Lily-Daisy Apartments chat. 'Can we please know why Daisy Apartments is being sealed?'

Kavita Lamba responded: 'Raghunath told us two days ago that he was having trouble breathing. We asked him to leave the premises immediately and to go to a hospital.'

'Did he test positive for coronavirus?' Amrita Aunty demanded.

'We have just been informed that he did.' Kavita Lamba wrote.

Mr Shetty added to that terse reply. 'We have just been informed that Raghunath, who cleaned our buildings for

35 years, died of the illness. We did nothing to help him get medical help. We didn't even call for an ambulance. We didn't give him 500 rupees to make things easier. We didn't even phone his wife in the village. I am ashamed of myself. I am ashamed of all of us.'

The news shocked everyone. A series of messages popped up, first sorrowful and then angry.

'How terrible! May his soul rest in peace.'

'This is shocking.'

'We should have been informed earlier.'

'I agree.'

'Mr Marker, will the same rules that you imposed on Lily Apartments now apply to Daisy Apartments as well? Only ordering essentials? Turning off the elevator? Being locked behind a gate? We are all wondering.' (This last message was sent by Aashu's father, a shy scientist who rarely interfered in building matters. The fact that he broke his own rule was an indication of how high emotions were running.)

While these messages flashed on the chat, the BMC workers were wrapping up their job and gathering near the van and packing away their cans and bags. Then, one of the officials pointed a firm finger at Baman Marker.

The message was loud and clear. Baman Marker needed to return to Daisy Apartments. The Hon Chairperson ignored this and continued to talk, talk, talk.

The BMC official appeared dazed by the outpouring of honeyed words. He nodded and started to climb into the waiting van. Watching him, I felt a moment of confusion. There was something off with the picture. What?

The answer crept into my head—but was pushed out by a high-pitched voice. 'Now we know why Mrs Marker left so quietly this morning,' Sheela Jagtiani cried out from a window two floors below us. 'Now we know what people mean when they say that rats desert a sinking ship. Now let's see how Mr Marker deserts Daisy Apartments.'

My mother clapped. Actually. 'Well done, Sheela,' she said. 'Hit the nail on the head. The Markers must have suspected that Raghunath would test positive. They didn't want to be stuck in a sealed building where other people might be infected.'

'And where they couldn't get their organic mangoes from Ratnagiri,' I added.

'So Binaifer ran away. But why didn't Baman run away with her?'

'Bet he was planning to leave once the BMC guys left,' Ved said. 'Bet that white car is parked near Sassoon Dock. Bet he was planning to creep away.'

'I hardly think Baman Marker was planning to sneak away,' my father said, once again playing reasonable, empathetic neighbour and fully getting on our nerves. 'We would know if Baman Marker left. And if he sneaked away like this, he would lose his moral upper hand. Knowing him, he'd rather get the virus than have that happen.'

'But would we even know?' I asked. 'We'd all be sealed in our own flats. He could get his information from Kavita Lamba. And he could send his pompous messages from wherever they're holed up. How would we know for sure if he was in his apartment or not?'

'Maria would say something to Alfonsa,' my mum said. She spotted our blank expressions and explained. 'Maria is the housekeeper. She didn't go with Mrs Marker. I think she's still in Daisy Apartments…but maybe…'

'Her name is Maria?' I asked. 'The fattish woman who's Alfonsa's soulmate? The squinty one who claims that the fishermen caught a mermaid at Sassoon Dock? And who said that a ghost lived in the garage? She's the one who fights with the crows in the balcony and—'

'I haven't written a PhD thesis on Baman Marker's housekeeper,' my mother protested. 'She's one of the church gang. The plump one. But I don't know about crows and mermaids.'

'Looklooklook,' Ved interrupted, pointing down at the cement compound, with its parked cars, stingy Ashokas and ample Hon Chairperson.

We looked and realized that the BMC official had made up his mind. He was pointing towards the door of Daisy Apartments and his body language said it all. For the first time in the seven years that we had known him, the Hon Chairperson was not getting his way.

For a moment Baman Marker glanced at the compound gate and I actually wondered if he would make a dash for it. He didn't. With an air of acute injury, he turned around and stalked towards the entrance of Daisy Apartments. Seconds later he had been swallowed up by the blood-red gullet of the building.

The metal gate of Daisy Apartments shut with an emphatic bang. Which is how the tables were turned and the Hon Chairperson got a taste of his own medicine.

5

While Day Mishraji struggled with the lock and key, tense faces peered out from the windows and balconies of Daisy Apartments. Some I knew well. Others I would barely identify if I spotted them at Inox or H&M.

The strange thing is that I can see those faces still, as vivid as a photograph. It's that split second that's still lodged in my head. And it's that image that I turned to again and again over the next few days, whenever I needed to examine my gallery of suspects.

But all that comes later. In that frozen moment, this is what I saw when I stared across the compound at Daisy Apartments.

Fifth Floor:

The balconies on the fifth floor were empty, and all the windows were shuttered against the insistent sunlight. The Markers occupied both flats on the top floor. Their daughters were married and no longer lived with them. Mrs Marker had driven off in a white car that very morning. Somewhere inside the apartment was a trapped Baman

Marker—with or without his gap-toothed, gossip-loving, mermaid-spotting housekeeper whose name, I had just discovered, was Maria.

Fourth Floor:

In the apartment directly across the compound from us lived the Burmans. The Burmans had moved into Daisy Apartments a couple of years ago. They were youngish and worked in high-pressure jobs. They had a house in Alibaug and three expensive-looking cars, which seemed an overkill for two people.

The Burmans were always in motion, always doing three things at the same time, always going out or presiding over parties loud with clinking glasses and bursts of laughter. I remember watching Mr Burman as he set out for work one morning, some months ago. He had stalked out of the building into his waiting car, the phone jammed to one ear and some papers in his hand. Behind him came the two women who helped in the house. One of them was holding Mr Burman's briefcase and a pair of mirror-polished black shoes. The other one was holding a white plate which held toast, fried eggs and fruit arranged in a bowl. The two women fussed about, arranged the plate on Mr Burman's lap and made sure he was comfortable before the car drove off.

That day, though, the Burmans looked quite as rumpled and lockdown-weary as the rest of us, and I remembered my father saying that Ranjit Burman was going through a bad patch. The couple was watching the events in the compound with utter intensity. As if it really mattered to them that the lock of Daisy Apartments had clicked into place. (I'm not explaining myself too clearly. It mattered to everyone. But it seemed to matter to them that little bit extra.)

The other apartment on the fourth floor was home to Sheela Jagtiani's father. I hadn't seen Mr Alimchandani in ages. He no longer came for the building dandiyas and Diwali dinners. He'd stopped coming down in his wheelchair. His balcony was empty, except for a threadbare brown towel hanging on a metal clothes stand. There was a figure sitting a little away from the bedroom window, but it was impossible to make out if it was Mr Alimchandani. I hoped that he hadn't been at the window yesterday, while his daughter sobbed and screamed in the compound. I wondered how he felt about stonehearted Baman Marker. Then I wondered who was giving him his medicines and cooking his food.

Third Floor:

If Mr Alimchandani's balcony was silent and bare, the one beneath his was raucous with banter and laughter. Darius Khambata was a yoga teacher who said eccentric things and wore merry batik shorts. Most unlike Baman Marker, who was a chartered accountant who sent bossy messages and wore laundered blue shirts. Even so, both were cousins. It surprised no one that they worked hard to downplay this connection.

Darius and Silloo Khambata appeared on the cover of glossy magazines, standing on their heads or their elbows or whatever. Their sons were the most active members of the Lily-Daisy Kids chat. Neville and Jeh were dashing collegians with toned bodies, white smiles and vrooming motorcycles. They spent hours lavishing love on those bikes and invariably had beautiful girls riding pillion. But the stereotypical college dude façade didn't tell the full story. Both boys were animal lovers and had adopted a bunch of stray dogs, abandoned tortoises and injured monkeys. They had set up a big compost bin in their balcony and planted a thriving herb garden. They were also rumoured to be harbouring a killer snake in their apartment.

Baman Marker tried to block every single thing that the Khambatas did. He put in place rules that were yoga-class-unfriendly, animal-unfriendly, composting-unfriendly, killer-snake unfriendly. It was hardly surprising that the four Khambatas should stand in their plant-filled balcony and watch Baman Marker walk back into the building with jeering amusement.

In general, Darius and Silloo Khambata seemed calm about being stuck in a sealed building, probably thanks to those deep-breathing exercises, headstands and stuff. Jeh and Neville looked mildly irritated. I guessed they would miss their motorcycles and glossy girlfriends.

Next to the Khambatas were the Carvalhos. That, of course, was the apartment on which I most often set my sights and my binoculars. (They're not powerful binoculars, almost toys, but still…)

Daniel was at his bedroom window. There was no sign of Mr Carvalho and I wondered for the gazillionth time why Daniel and his father never did anything together. Not even look out of the same balcony. Once again it was clear that Daniel was in need of some tender, loving care. It was a good thing that he had a volunteer right across the compound. Now all that was left was for him to realize this.

Second Floor:

Just below the Carvalhos lived Amrita Aunty and Shanaya.

Amrita Aunty looked fed up. Shanaya looked tousled and hassled. Her hair was doing the wild, cartoon-character-after-an-electric-shock thing and her eyes were half-closed. It struck me that she looked really upset. And my always-on-top-of-things friend didn't often look really upset.

Next to Amrita Aunty and Shanaya lived the Chief Minion. All three people in the Lamba balcony were sitting on stiff red plastic chairs. The two adults were staring down at their phones. The Secretary, herself, was busy fielding messages on the building chat. Her quiet, bespectacled husband was looking at his phone with a rapt, lip-licky expression. I can't be sure, of course, but I think he was watching a movie on his phone. Something intensely violent, with dismembered bodies and exploding buildings.

Thea sat a little away from her parents. Every few minutes, she glanced towards Lily Apartments with anxious, searching eyes, but she never once glanced down at the compound. Watching Thea, I wondered. For the millionth time.

Thea was not bad looking. She did decently in school. So why was she always so switched off? Like Shanaya, Thea was in Grade 9 of All Saints School. They were in different divisions but rode on the same yellow school bus. Shanaya said that Thea was madly conscious about her weight, which had made her touchy and reclusive. I wasn't convinced. There were so many plumper, plainer girls who didn't feel the need to hide in smelly, paan-stained corners and make themselves invisible.

Every few months, my mother would insist that Shanaya and I include Thea in our plans. We even invited her to lunch once, a couple of months before lockdown. But Thea was hard work. She barely spoke, she rarely smiled, she never, ever laughed. She looked like a hunted creature and flinched when I asked her ordinary questions like, 'What is your favourite subject in school?' She cringed when Shanaya looked at her and she shivered—literally—when Ved walked into the room.

I've already told you that I'm not a merry, gregarious sort. But compared to Thea I'm Happy the Dwarf.

First Floor:

Both flats on the first floor were occupied by Lina Almeida, her granddaughter Kysha and an army of helpers and valets. Lina Almeida's husband had moved to their family home in Goa. No prizes for guessing why.

I spotted the Tormentor and Guide at a bedroom window, looking disapproving behind her spectacles. But then, disapproval was her default expression. It contributed to the image of the legendary school principal.

Kysha was leaning out from another window and smiling, smiling, smiling. Like the cat that got the cream. I had a fairly good idea about the identity of the cream. And I was positive that she would make the most of the opportunity that the sealing of Daisy Apartment afforded. Like her grandmother, Kysha always came out on top. Unlike her grandmother, she had purple hair, expensive silver shoes and a glittering personality.

Like her grandmother, Kysha spent her day at All Saints School. Unlike her grandmother she was not a Mentor and

Guide. She was a Grade 12 student—possibly the most unacademic, unruly one who had ever sauntered through those high-ceilinged classrooms. Nobody had expected Kysha to pass the Grade 10 board exam. That she'd managed was a minor miracle—one that saved Lina Almeida from self-combusting with mortification.

Most people disliked Lina Almeida. I disliked Kysha even more.

I don't think Kysha disliked me, she did something worse. She blanked me out. She was one of those cool girls who only notice other purple-haired, popular beings. I'm not sure why or how, but somewhere along the way she'd decided that Ved and Shanaya made the cut but that I didn't.

I hated it that her eyes always slid past me as they would slide past a patch of potholed pavement. 'Nothing of interest,' they seemed to say.

Ground Floor:

The ground floor didn't have balconies—and from the fourth floor it was difficult to see the people standing behind the window grills.

I could make out two forms at the window of the Habibullah apartment. Rashida Habibullah, the caterer, and her husband with the anxiety issues. They seemed tired and defeated, but maybe I was imagining things.

Next door, Mr Shetty was just a silhouette. An angry silhouette. But again, I may have been seeing what I expected to see.

These were the people who looked out of Daisy Apartments during that final khhrrruck of the lock.

The BMC officials were piling into their van when a voice called out in the silence. 'Sir, sir. Please. I need to ask you something.'

Daniel.

The BMC officials hesitated and looked up. Daniel had moved from his bedroom window to the balcony with its single potted palm and forlorn money plant. The balcony was scrubbed and tidy—but managed to look unloved and motherless at the same time.

Daniel was flustered. 'My father is not at home,' he called out. 'Will he be allowed to enter the building when he comes?'

The tall BMC official who had wagged his schoolmasterish finger at Baman Marker emerged from the van. 'Why didn't you tell us earlier?' he scolded in Marathi.

'I thought he would come home,' Daniel said, so downcast that my heart squeezed.

My mother seemed to feel the same way. 'That poor, poor boy,' she said. 'First his mother...and then to have to deal with such a father...it's so sad...'

'What's wrong with Daniel's father?' I demanded.

I had taken pains to hide my infatuation with Daniel from my family. Ved had figured it out, largely thanks to Shanaya's giggles and innuendoes, but my parents hadn't a clue. This was the first time my mother had ever mentioned Mr Carvalho and I was intrigued. I knew little about the man—only that he was a physics teacher. He didn't teach at a school but conducted crazily expensive tuition classes.

My mother ignored me. She was too focused on the BMC man and his rapid-fire questions in Marathi. 'We are in the middle of a lockdown,' the man seemed to be saying. 'Where has he gone? He's not supposed to go anywhere.'

'I...I...think he has gone to buy things,' Daniel stuttered in a jumble of Hindi and English. Something about the way he spoke made it clear that whatever Mr Carvalho was up to, vegetable shopping was not on the agenda.

The tall BMC man was stern. 'Phone him,' he said. 'Tell him to come back now. NOW.'

'I've been trying,' Daniel said. 'He's not answering.'

The BMC man shook his head in disgust. 'You will have to phone us when your father comes back,' he said. 'After that, we will give permission for the gate to be opened. But we need to know where he has been. When will he come back?'

'I don't know,' Daniel replied. Next to me, my mother tutted.

The Carvalhos had a cook called Florine/Florry/Flouride. She was the third member of the Sunday-evening church gang and another great friend of Alfonsa's. She probably cooked delicious fish curry. She was definitely a neat-freak and was always scrubbing the floor and washing the windows. But she was hardly desert-island-companion material—though she would keep the desert island very clean.

'What's wrong with Mr Carvalho?' I asked again, as we drifted back from the insistent sunshine into the mercifully dim living room.

'Nothing, nothing,' my mother said, assuming her my-lips-are-sealed expression.

'Please tell,' I wheedled, walking behind her and chanting, 'Please, please, please...'

After about two minutes of high-level harassment, my mother's lips unsealed a tiny bit. 'I don't know any details and it's all rumours anyway,' she said. 'But one thing I know. I would never, ever dream of sending you to that man for tuitions. Not for all the top marks in the world. Now go. Leave me in peace. I'm calling Amrita. She was looking very upset.'

My head was awhirl with questions, but plaguing my mother was pointless for the moment, so I wandered away to another corner of our 1027 square foot apartment.

6

I scrounged around the kitchen for a bit. There was only vanilla ice cream in the freezer, so I took two big scoops and topped it with peanut butter, some crushed Milk Bikis, two crumbling Polos and maple syrup that had made the journey from Canada to Mumbai sometime in the last millennium. As you can see, these were desperate times.

I was heading to my bedroom when my mother called out, 'Nandini, you remember you're making dinner, right? I'll help, but you're the head chef. Macaroni and cheese from scratch? Won't that be nice?'

Nice? Nice? It was bad enough that I was spending my summer holidays in our onion-infused kitchen instead of in a Zara—preferably a Zara in Croatia. It made things worse that my mum was acting as if I'd turned into a toddler again, and that I could be tricked into believing that a trip to the dentist was the ultimate treat.

I slammed my snack—which was not too bad, actually—onto my desk. Then I positioned my chair so that I could look out at Daniel's window and balcony. Then I called Shanaya. She didn't answer, so I called the Kapadia landline.

This time Shantabai answered. She said that Shanaya was standing on a stool and hunting for something on the loft. It was ten minutes before Shanaya called back. 'I'm literally dying,' she announced in the most alive voice possible.

'So am I.'

'I'm dying more.'

'Why?'

'My computer charger has stopped working. I've spent the last half hour looking for another charger.'

'You found one?' I gasped.

'I think so. I found an old one in the loft and it seems to be working.'

'Thank God,' I exhaled. 'You'll be okay.'

'Hardly. My mother went nuts when I said I was making toast for dinner.'

'So then?'

'I think I'll make tomato soup.'

'Huh. I have to make macaroni and cheese. Not from a box. From scratch.'

'Okay...but at least you have Ved.'

'That's exactly why I'm dying more. Because I have Ved. His awful music is pounding my brains into mashed potato.'

'You have no taste in music. I bet you like the soppy stuff that Daniel plays.'

'If you had to live with Ved 24/7, you would know...'

We'd had this argument before. I envied Shanaya her space and silence. She envied me my sibling. Like seriously!

'I'm wondering what I'm going to do for fourteen whole days,' Shanaya said. 'Unlike you, I don't like reading. I have no one outside my window to go all drooly over. I need to figure out something fun for two weeks.'

'Make buckets of soup,' I suggested. 'Go all drooly over Aashu. He's right across from you. Or hang out with Thea.'

Shanaya harrumphed. 'Yeah right,' she said. 'After which I'll adopt the Big Bum as my grandfather. I really get an off vibe from that girl. She's so closed up. Never talks. Never smiles. Always staring. Kysha says that she's hiding—'

'Kysha would,' I sneered.

Shanaya missed the arsenic in my voice and carried on blithely. 'But maybe I can hang out with Kysha sometimes. She's pretty cool. Actually.'

'Oh,' I said, suddenly wishing that I hadn't steered the conversation into this territory. I know I sound possessive, but I hated it when Shanaya and Kysha hung out together. 'Are we even allowed to leave our apartments?'

Shanaya chuckled in her most evil-dweevil manner. 'That's the only good part of this business,' she said. 'If Baman Marker obeys his own rules he won't leave his own apartment. So there won't be anyone around to scream at us. My mom won't mind, and Kysha never listens to Granny Grim anyway. Maybe Neville Khambata will hang out with us. I'm not sure but I think that Kysha has a little a crush on him. What do you think?'

'Oh yes,' I said. 'Except that it's not a little crush. It's a great big one.'

'Ohhh,' Shanaya exclaimed. 'You know something about them? I should have known you'd seen something. *You're* always spying from your window. Nandini, come on. Spill the tea.'

I winced and said in firm tones, 'No, no. I haven't seen a thing. It's just a feeling I have. You know, how she's always posting those pictures of them as kids together at the BPT garden. And of them eating ice cream at some baby birthday party and stuff.'

Shanaya chose to believe me and switched topics. 'Maybe we can watch a movie together,' she said. 'Me and Kysha and the Khambatas.'

I tried to sound enthusiastic, but truth to tell, my FOMO had kicked in. I imagined the Daisy Apartments crowd hanging out together. Shanaya, Kysha, Neville and Jeh Khambata, and maybe Daniel would join them.

Only Thea would be left out. And me.

Of course, Ved, Mini and Aashu were also stuck on the wrong side of the compound. But Ved wouldn't care. Aashu was blissfully busy with his computer stuff. And I suspected that Mini wouldn't stress too much either. After all, she had her 17,000 TikTok followers to keep her company.

For a moment I was furious that my twin and my totally best friend were so low on loyalty. That they didn't care how troubled I was by Kysha's dismissal. I was sinking into a state of sorry-for-myselfness when Shanaya exclaimed, 'I forgot to tell you.'

'What?' I asked.

'A couple of days ago...or maybe yesterday...this lockdown is making me all confused about time...' she said. 'But whenever it was, there was a huge fight on the first floor. Between Lina Almeida and Kysha. They were really going at each other. Lina Almeida was threatening all kinds of stuff. The police. Public humiliation. I'm pretty sure I heard Granny Grotesque say something about the Lord and the sins of intoxication and about going to hell...It was full on.'

'Wow,' I said, wishing once more that I lived in the happening Daisy Apartments instead of sedate Lily Apartments. 'What did Kysha say?'

'She was yelling back even more loudly than Granny Grim,' Shanaya laughed. 'Stuff like…creepy…spy…pervert. Kysha must be the only person in the world who's not afraid of Lina Almeida. I feel pretty sorry for her. It's bad enough that her parents are in Jamshedpur and that she's stuck living with Lina Almeida, it's even worse that she has to be locked down with her.'

'I guess,' I said, but I was thinking that it must be pretty ghastly to be locked down with sly, sniggering Kysha as well.

Shanaya sensed my reservations. 'You can't imagine what Lina Almeida is like,' she said. 'In school we do anything to avoid walking past her lair. She knows everything that's going on. And she sends these pale, yellow notepapers printed with the words: "With compliments from Lina Almeida, Mentor and Guide". And she writes on them in a green pen and her handwriting is all spidery.'

'Green?'

'That's her thing. When one of those notes lands up on my desk I want to pee in fright.'

'But why?' I asked. 'Nobody in my school sends notes. If teachers want to say something, they say it. What's the point? What does Tormentor and Guide write in her notes?'

'Sometimes she writes just two words. Like "Meet me". Sometimes longer stuff like, "The consequences of your action will not be good for you."'

'What action?' I asked. 'You're hardly the sort to get into trouble at school.'

'That makes no difference,' Shanaya snorted. 'When you come in from lunchbreak and find her yellow note on your table, you have no idea what you've done. And you spend hours stewing. It's worse than the actual punishment. Which can be pretty bad anyway.'

'Ugh,' I said with a shudder. All Saints School was the fanciest school in the city, but Bright Minds School was kinder. The principals retired when they were meant to retire. They didn't mutate into Tormentors and Guides who spent their days scribbling menacing messages on pale-yellow chits.

By the time I tuned in again, Shanaya had hopscotched ahead. She was giving me a detailed description of Kysha's new golden boots when I remembered that I had something super important to ask her. 'Listen,' I cut in. 'I've been meaning to check. Is there something creepy about Daniel's dad? Has your mum mentioned anything?'

'Daniel's dad?' Shanaya repeated, and I could see her antennae going sproing. 'What do you mean creepy? What's he done?'

'I don't know,' I said. 'My mum said something but then she clammed up.'

'What exactly did she say?'

'I can't remember exactly, but she hinted that he was off in some way. She said she would never send me to him for tuitions. Not that I need physics tuitions, but still…'

'Could he be a pervert?' Shanaya barked.

'Hardly,' I protested. 'We've passed him about a million times on the staircase and in the compound. He's never given out those vibes unless—'

'Not all pervs give out vibes,' Shanaya said darkly. 'You remember, right? When Daniel's mother died, people were saying all sorts of stuff…I can't fully remember but I'll try and find out.'

'Poor Daniel,' I said. 'I feel so—'

'Daniel's dad can hardly be worse than my dad,' Shanaya huffed. 'But at least I have my mom. Drippy Daniel doesn't.

And to be stuck in a sealed apartment with just that Florry woman sounds pretty terrible. Daniel doesn't seem like the sort who can manage his own groceries and stuff. He seems too—'

'I hadn't thought of that,' I interrupted. 'I hope he's managing okay.'

'Maybe you can message him and offer to help,' Shanaya suggested. 'You'll never get such a perfect excuse ever again. Just saying.'

'Ha ha. Very funny.'

'I didn't mean to be funny,' Shanaya countered. 'I think it's a seriously a brilliant idea. Write to him immediately. Now. Come on.'

'It will look really weird,' I protested, but Shanaya nagged and scolded till I agreed to write to Daniel if Mr Carvalho remained absent for another day. Or two. Or three.

Shanaya was irritated by my procrastination. 'Just do it,' she bossed. 'What's the point of all this thinking and thinking, and looking and looking? You're always so… cautious and indirect.'

'And you are always so…relentless and direct,' I laughed. 'Anyway, I bet Mr Carvalho will rush home immediately. Once he finds out that Daisy Apartments is sealed, he'll be frantic to get back to Daniel. Obviously.'

'There's nothing obvious about that,' Shanaya muttered. 'You don't know fathers the way I do. Not all dads are normalish like yours. You can't imagine…'

Shanaya's bright voice turned as dull as the monsoon sea and I knew that she would be hunching and biting her fingernails. Shanaya was masterful and calm about most things—except her father. She really disliked him. Every few months he cast a cloud over her otherwise sunny life and Shanaya turned frantic and despairing.

I'd never met the man, but I knew that he was head-to-toe despicable. Although her parents had separated before we moved into Lily Apartments, he still wanted Shanaya to live with him and his new family. He sent offensive letters and lawyers' notices saying that Amrita Aunty was an unfit mother. He watched Amrita Aunty's every move and was waiting for her smallest misstep.

He made a big deal when Shanaya did badly in her final exams, and an even bigger deal when she fractured her ankle. He got incensed when Shanaya said that biology was her favourite subject (he wanted her to study economics) and because she didn't enjoy sports (he was determined that she should play tennis).

When Murlidhar drove into a lamppost a few weeks before lockdown, Shanaya's father went mental. He had his lawyer send notices saying that Amrita Aunty was a negligent mother. Then he insisted that Amrita Aunty replace both, her six-year-old car and her driver. Amrita Aunty refused to sack Murlidhar, but she did buy a new car—just to stop the offensive phone calls.

Not that they ever stopped. 'You've done a bad job,' the father was always ranting at Amrita Aunty. 'What were you doing when this was happening? How could you allow it to happen?'

My mum and Amrita Aunty went into regular huddles over Shanaya's father's villainies. And my father was always raising his eyebrows and saying, 'Priti, don't get too involved. We really don't know the truth.'

Shanaya put a lot of energy into blocking her father. On her phone, in her dreams, in her life. She usually succeeded, except when he kicked his way through the barricades every six months or so. I was wondering if he was at it again when Shanaya sighed, 'My father has been calling and sending letters and stuff. I guess he has plenty of time because of the lockdown. Don't know what's happened exactly but my mom is really, really upset.'

'Nothing will happen,' I said in a shiny, plastic voice. 'There's no way he will get custody.'

'You think?' Shanaya asked bleakly. 'I am not so sure. I can't bear to go and live with him. And her. And them.'

'Him' was the evil father.

'Her' was the new wife, who apparently matched the father, wickedness for wickedness.

'They' were the wicked spawn of the two wicked adults.

I had no way to comfort Shanaya, so I changed the subject. I suggested we watch a movie together and, after some good-natured squabbling, we agreed to watch a mystery movie called *Knives Out* that everyone on my school chat was talking about.

Watching movies together during lockdown is different from watching movies together in regular times. Shanaya and I would both have to watch the movie in our own bedrooms, on our own computers at the same time. But we'd chat with each other while watching. It would have been way more fun to watch in the same room, on the same screen. But I guess this was the next best thing.

Shanaya had returned to her optimistic self by the time we hung up and clomped off to see what horrors our mothers had in store for us.

7

I adore whodunits. Especially if the mystery revolves around a fat, juicy murder. I like uncovering the clues, the hints, the challenges. I think I'd make a good detective, but I honestly feel I'd make a better murderer. I'm neither nervous nor squeamish. I'm not too fussed about the business of right and wrong. And I have a devious mind.

I'm the only person I know who identified the killer in *Hercule Poirot's Christmas*. If you haven't read it, you really should. After which you'll understand why I'm so proud of my detecting abilities.

Naturally then, I was really, really looking forward to *Knives Out*. As soon as dinner was done—in case you're wondering, there's a good reason why I'm not telling you how my macaroni-cheese-from-scratch turned out—I showered, slipped on my faded pink pajamas with the purple strawberries and piled a bowl with enough cheese balls to satisfy three greedy giants.

Even more naturally, I was really pissed off when Shanaya announced that she'd changed her mind. 'I'm in the mood for *Mean Girls*,' she declared when I called to tell her that I was ready with my mental magnifying glass.

'But,' I protested, 'we've watched that about a thousand times. How boring.'

'Please. I've had an awful evening,' Shanaya said in a croaky voice. 'The mixer sort of exploded when I was making tomato soup and there was liquid tomato everywhere. Like literally everywhere. On the fan, on the ceiling, in my nose, and it took me a few years to clean it up. My mom freaked and refused to help. She's in a foul mood anyway because of my bloody father and stuff.'

I was about to sulk, but Shanaya sounded unexpectedly fragile. 'Okay,' I said, trying to be a supportive friend. 'We can watch it tomorrow. Or the day after. Whenever.'

'Yes, let's ask Ved and the others to join us for *Knives Out*,' Shanaya said, regaining some composure. 'Wait. I'm putting you on speaker phone while I get into my pajamas and comb my hair. Then we can start the movie.'

'Okay,' I agreed, wondering if I should fetch more cheese balls. At some point, when I hadn't been looking, two hungry giants had come in and claimed their share.

'Horrible, horrible day,' Shanaya remarked as she moved around her bedroom opening and shutting cupboards.

'At least there was one good thing about this evening. The stuff we cooked was not posted on the chat. For some mysterious reason, even Lina Almeida didn't post pictures of Kysha's triumphs.'

'There's no mystery there,' Shanaya retorted. 'If the Almeida household actually waited for Kysha to cook dinner, they're going to bed on an empty stomach.'

'Why?' I asked. 'How do you know Kysha didn't make roast chicken or whatever she was supposed to?'

'Because I live just one floor up and can hear most things going on in the Almeida apartment,' Shanaya said as she pattered around her yellow bedroom, getting into her pajamas and brushing her hair. 'Gosh, I really need new pajamas. My red ones with the fried eggs are scandalous even by my sorry standards. They've got a new tear down the front of the left leg.'

'They're still giving Ved nightmares,' I giggled. Shanaya's red pajamas with the fried eggs were ripped in the worst possible way. The last time she'd slept over at our place about a week ago, Ved had spotted a particularly awkward hole and had turned redder than the pajamas.

'They're my lucky pajamas,' Shanaya said dolefully. 'And I really need some luck at the moment. Things are bad. That Man—'

I switched subjects before she could start talking about her horrible father. 'Tell me what's going on with Kysha,' I said.

'Major drama,' Shanaya said, reviving a little. 'Kysha spent the whole evening freaking. And Granny Grisly wasn't much better. She was tossing around words like godless and shameless and saying that she would send Kysha straight back to Jamshedpur. I heard them from my bedroom window. And while we were eating dinner, I definitely heard footsteps stamping up the stairs and doors slamming.'

'Could it have been Daniel?' I asked in sudden alarm.

'Why Daniel? I don't think he has anything to do with Kysha. It could have been Neville Khambata, but I don't know for sure.'

'You think Lina Almeida has figured that Kysha is interested in Neville? Is that enough to make her go bazooka? I mean, it's not so terrible. Hardly godless.'

Shanaya said she hadn't a clue. I actually did have a teeny weeny clue—but I kept my mouth zipped. I didn't want to feed the Nosy Nandini reputation. Then Shanaya said she was ready to start watching the film, and so that's what we did.

I'm not sure if you've seen *Mean Girls*. I have, many times. And although it's not the cleverest movie in the world, it's a bit like candy floss. Once you take the first bite, you just keep going.

I'd placed my computer on my desk, which is near my window. That way I could keep one and a half eyes on the movie, and half an eye on a certain bedroom window. I angled my chair so that I had a view of Daisy Apartments.

From where I was sitting, I could see the windows and balconies of four west-facing apartments—the Markers on the fifth floor, the Burmans on the fourth floor, the Carvalhos on the third floor and Shanaya on the second floor. I could also see some of the windows along the stairwell, but the east-facing apartments were sliced off.

Although it was just approaching 10 p.m., the residents of Daisy Apartments seemed eager for this day to end. Most had already shut windows, drawn curtains, dimmed lights. The building looked ready to say good night.

Lily and Daisy Apartments are built so that the balcony of each flat leads into a long, rectangular living room. I peered past Daniel's balcony into his living room, which was washed in a feeble, milky light. Beyond the bulky armchairs and old-fashioned cabinets, I could see Daniel at the dining table. His father didn't seem to be around. How weird.

One floor down, I knew Shanaya was sprawled on her yellow bed, with the AC set at arctic temperatures. Orange light seeped through the curtains of the bedroom window, but the rest of the house seemed asleep. I was about to look away when I noticed Amrita Aunty striding up and down the unlit balcony—a blurry, grey ghost in the gloom.

It's difficult to be certain now, but I recall Baman Marker's windows being dinner-party bright. While in the Burmans' muted living room, the billboard-sized TV screen flickered neon and sharp between the paddle-shaped leaves of the banana plants. My heart almost stopped as a bony, emaciated hand lunged across that vast screen, and a livid purple sky exploded in a splatter of scarlet.

I looked away with a shiver. The spray of blood, the light of the gibbous moon, the unfamiliar silence, cast a sinister patina over that night. Death was out and about, although I didn't know it then.

If I had, I would have done things very differently. As it is, I turned back to the movie. *Mean Girls* is about a girl called Cady, who is homeschooled somewhere in Africa before she moves to Chicago. There she lands in a regular school with a typical crowd—jocks, nerds, loners and, of course, mean girls. Somehow, Cady becomes part of this gang of bitchy, looks-obsessed girls called The Plastics and starts becoming a bit like them. I guess the movie works so well because the story is universal. There are mean girls in my class in school, there are mean girls in All Saints School, and there is one very mean girl in our compound.

Shanaya and I settled down to the movie and to texting each other on our phones. We jumped straight into our usual back-and-forth about whether Cady was pretty or not. I said she was. Shanaya said she was not. Then we talked about whether boys felt threatened by girls who were good at maths and science. Then we discussed the mean girls' clothes—which were pretty tacky, given that they were the fashion icons of their class.

We were about twenty minutes into the movie—the bit where they're all dressed in pink and at the home of the meanest of the mean girls, Regina George—when I finished my cheese puffs. I was sorely tempted to get more, but *Mean Girls* is one of those movies that make you feel seriously fat, so I decided to exercise self-control.

'Getting some raisins,' I messaged Shanaya, feeling most virtuous. 'Back in second.'

'So healthy!!!!' Shanaya replied, acting as if I was chomping on a lorry-load of spinach or something. 'Becoming the next Lina Almeida? Next you be whipping up a detox juice?'

'Hardly,' I typed.

'Going for glowing skin?' Shanaya continued. 'So you can shine across the compound at Drippy D?'

'Shut up,' I replied. 'Back soon. You keep watching. I know exactly what's going to happen.'

I darted to the kitchen with my cheese puff bowl and heaped it with black raisins and a few almonds. All that junk food was turning me into a human pudding. Still, I might as well be a pudding with good skin.

Hurrying back to my bedroom, I glanced out of the window. Amrita Aunty was still in the balcony, but now she was motionless, mantled in inky shadows. I could tell that she was wearing her short grey dress with the big billowy sleeves and looking straight ahead. I waved but she was too wrapped up in her darkness to notice. Feeling that I was intruding, I looked away.

I was about to flop onto my chair and return to Regina's mansion and Cady's problems when I saw something else. Something that gave me a pause.

On that Friday night, Daisy Apartments was as motionless as a painting. The swollen moon hanging over the roof and the two round lamps at the compound gate contributed a yellow patina to the otherwise unremarkable scene. The pattern of light and shadows was sharp, undisturbed by the slightest breeze.

Against this canvas, the sudden movement was uncanny. Someone was walking on the staircase of Daisy Apartments. A pair of legs climbing the stairs between the second and third floor.

By itself, this was not a big deal. There was always movement on the staircase of Daisy Apartments. That's what staircases were for. But there was something different about tonight. Maybe it was the thick hush, undisturbed by a single aeroplane in the sky, a single car on the road, a single passer-by yelling into a phone. Unruffled by a single salty, seaweedy breeze.

Daisy Apartments was as silent as a school during the summer holidays.

Perhaps that was why those legs felt wrong.

I continued to stare at the yellow squares along the stairwell. For a long minute nothing happened. I was almost sure that nothing was going to happen when I saw the legs again—this time through the window between the third and fourth floor. I noticed that they were wearing black pants or jeans.

There was something about the way those legs moved that was quick but cautious. Furtive even. I was puzzled. It was impossible to tell if they belonged to a man or a woman. To someone old or young. Could it be Jeh Khambata, taking his rumoured snake to the roof for an airing? Or Rashida Habibullah, carrying dinner to Mr Alimchandani as she had promised? Or Kysha, sneaking up to meet Neville Khambata on a quiet corner landing?

I'd spotted Kysha and Neville tiptoeing down the Daisy Apartments staircase a few months ago when my mother had sent me to deliver a letter to Baman Marker. I was on the fifth floor when they crept down from the roof, flushed and giggly. Another time, I'd happened upon them behind the garage. They'd been leaning against each and smoking something that didn't smell like a regular cigarette.

Did the legs belong to Kysha? Or to someone else? By now I was really curious. Grabbing my phone, I texted Shanaya, 'Someone sneaking up your staircase. Kysha to meet NK?'

'Not with GG so mad,' Shanaya replied a beat later.

'Go check!' I instructed, as the legs reappeared on the landing between the fourth and fifth floor. This time the legs were moving very, very slowly, step by step. Like an old person puffing for breath. For a moment, they stopped entirely and something pink/red/orange was placed on the steps.

'Go check,' I typed yet again. 'V suspicious. First running. Now creeping.'

'Can't,' Shanaya replied. 'In torn red pajamas. Scandal if seen. Now be quiet. My fave bit. Don't disturb.'

Glancing at my computer, I saw that the movie had reached the part where Cady's crush—a cute guy called Aaron—invites her to a Halloween party. When I looked back at Daisy Apartments, the legs had moved out of sight. Although I checked diligently for the next three minutes, they showed no sign of reappearing. Which was when it struck me that there was an obvious explanation for those legs on the stairwell.

The legs had to belong to Baman Marker. Bored without his Binaifer, the Hon Chairperson must have taken to prowling around and checking to see if the denizens of Daisy Apartments were obeying his rules. What a blah solution. And what a sad waste of my time and my little grey cells.

Disgusted, I turned back to the phone and to Shanaya's messages.

'Why did Cady dress like that?'

'I don't get it.'

'She doesn't deserve him.'

I laughed. Shanaya always said exactly the same thing, whenever we got to the Halloween scene, where Cady transformed herself into a ghastly zombie bride.

'You always say that,' I typed. 'Every one of the 8 times we've watched this movie.'

'Not 8 times!!!'

'Feels like 27.'

'2. Ok, 3,' Shanaya countered. 'Listen. What's your mom doing just now?'

'Reading, I think.'

'Can she call my mom? My mom in bit of a state.'

I leaned and peered out of the window and found the grey figure amidst the gloom. Amrita Aunty hadn't moved a centimetre.

'Of course. Back in minute,' I typed.

'Wait, wait,' Shanaya messaged urgently. 'Tell your m not to say I said to call. Explain that things messy.'

'Ok,' I agreed, before pausing the movie and dashing into my parents' bedroom on my mission of mercy. Four minutes later I was back, just in time to see Amrita Aunty walking into the living room. 'My mum calling,' I messaged. 'Why is your mother so upset?'

'Same old, same old,' Shanaya replied. 'Sick of it all. Let's watch movie.'

We hung up and restarted *Mean Girls*, but I was too preoccupied to get into it fully. I kept looking towards Daisy Apartments, but there was nothing to see. The stairwell remained free of legs in black pants. And the compound remained as inanimate as a corpse.

It was towards the end of the movie that a sound pierced the hush. It was a mundane sound—something we heard all the time on ordinary days. The dingdong of a doorbell. But today it felt unnatural, wrong.

'Is someone ringing a doorbell in Daisy Apartments?' I texted Shanaya.

'Is someone losing plot?' she texted back. 'Let me watch!!!!!'

'Ok. Ok. Will let you watch,' I replied and actually stuck to my word. We finished the movie without any more interruptions.

'Btw, DD is up and about,' Shanaya messaged after the movie had ended.

'Daniel?'

'How many other DDs do we know?'

'Doordarshan? Delhi Darbar? Donald Duck?'

'Ok. Fine. Not telling you more.'

'Tell tell tell. What is Daniel doing?'

Instead of texting, Shanaya called me. 'Donald Duck is quacking,' she laughed.

Mean Girls had clearly cheered her up. Relieved, I laughed too, as I walked across my tornado-struck bedroom to the window. 'What's Daniel doing? What could he be doing in a sealed apartment anyway?'

'He's walking around and bumping into stuff. From the sound of it he's decided to take up carpentry as a new hobby.'

'That's like really odd. His lights are all off. Almost as if everyone has gone to bed.'

'Maybe he's playing Dark Room.'

'Or maybe the apartment fuse has blown.'

'Who's turned all sensible?' Shanaya teased.

Making a rude sound I asked, 'Listen, do you know if the villainous Mr Carvalho is back? I feel horrible when I think of Daniel all alone.'

'I don't think so,' Shanaya said slowly. 'It's been seriously quiet up there. Till it became seriously noisy, that is. By the way, I asked my mom about DD's dad.'

'And???'

'She wasn't exactly in a chatty mood, but she said he used to be a teacher. At All Saints School of all places! He was brilliant, but then there was some scandal. Lina Almeida was the principal then, and because they were neighbours she hushed it up. But he lost his job.'

'What was the scandal?'

'Something about selling exam papers. My mom was vague.'

'That's terrible! For money?'

'I think so...My mom doesn't know exactly.'

'When did all this happen?'

'I think before we were born,' Shanaya said thoughtfully. 'My mom says that Daniel was a baby then and his mother was forced to go back to work immediately. She worked really long hours and the family had an awful time. Then Mr Carvalho started giving tuitions and became the hottest tuition teacher of South Bombay. Did you know that he was the one who started "Toppers United"?'

'Wow,' I exclaimed. Toppers United was one of those coaching classes that—as its name promised—produced toppers. The faces of these toppers were plastered on billboards and on the sides of buses all over the city. Loads of my cousins and acquaintances had paid hefty fees to sign up for Toppers United classes. And they all hoped—some secretly, some openly—that their faces would one day smile smugly out of the newspapers and banners on Marine Drive.

'Yeah,' Shanaya said. 'I was also zapped. I always thought he was an ordinary tuition teacher.'

We were silent for a moment while Mr Carvalho got one of those 'Before and After' makeovers in our heads. I'd always seen Daniel's father as a hunched and shabby figure—not quite as successful as the other fathers in our world. The new version of Mr Carvalho seemed straighter and more polished. And wickeder too, of course.

'My mom wonders why the Carvalhos didn't just move out of Daisy Apartments,' Shanaya said. 'You know, get a fresh start. People like Lina Almeida and Baman Marker always treat him nastily—as if he's a criminal or something. Lina Almeida acts as if he owes her big time. And my mom is pretty sure that Baman Marker—but then you know what my mom is like about Baman Marker—managed to squeeze out free classes for the jumbo, teacup-eared Baby Bums. She's also pretty sure that he was forced into helping Kysha pass her Grade 10 exams.'

'By giving her classes?' I asked.

'No. In some shady manner,' Shanaya replied. 'But remember that my mom has been in a horrible mood and that she doesn't have a shred of proof.'

'Wait a minute,' I protested, walking around my bedroom, trying to avoid stepping on poky earrings and a tangle of lacy tops. 'If everyone already knows that Mr Carvalho did what he did, then why would he let himself get blackmailed?'

'I don't know,' Shanaya said, yawning and losing interest in the conversation in her typical capricious way. 'Maybe Lina Almeida and Baman Marker have some extra-nasty details. Or maybe Mr Carvalho is afraid that it will look bad for Toppers United if the old stuff is brought up again? Or maybe my mom's jumping to conclusions.'

Shanaya yawned again and started to say bye, but I stopped her. 'Hold on a minute,' I said, as an idea emerged from my junk-addled brain. 'Selling papers that should not have been sold.'

'What?'

'Isn't that what the Big Bum wrote on the building chat this morning? It was something like that.'

'I have no idea. I don't keep checking the building chat. It's filled with rubbish about broken ovens. And my mom's too upset to tell me anything. But you think the Big Bum was targeting Mr Carvalho?'

'Who knows,' I said. 'But I just feel bad for Daniel.'

'Yes, I guess he has a reason to be drippy,' Shanaya said. 'Now do you want to say "Poor Daniel" a few more times? Or shall we carry on with our lives?'

'I'm good,' I laughed. 'But tell me what's happening at Daniel's place.'

'All silent now. He must be asleep, like most sensible people. And for once I am going to behave sensibly too. Bye.'

I said bye and dropped my phone on my desk, but I was too restless to join the sensible hordes. I pottered about for a bit and tried to twist my hair into a French braid. As usual, it flopped and, overwhelmed by a wave of self-pity, I decided that I was fated to remain Nandini Venkat with the unfashionably messy hair and the patch-of-potholed-pavement aura.

I trudged to the bathroom, brushed my teeth and headed towards my bed. On the way, I happened to glance through the window. It was well after midnight and my eyes were heavy. Perhaps that's why I was caught off guard by the second pair of legs.

Even today, I'm really not sure if I saw them running down from the fourth to the third floor. Or whether the image I have of them—ghostly limbs in flapping, translucent white—matches reality. I've revisited that night so often that I sometimes wonder if I've blurred and crumpled the memories, like a note that's been unfolded and read too many times.

As the legs flitted past, I imagined that they must be wearing white salwars. Rashida Habibullah wore salwar khameezes. So did Kavita Lamba. Maybe Mrs Burman did, though she was usually in jeans or designer dresses. But none of them had any reason to be traipsing up and down the stairs a full forty-nine minutes after midnight.

The legs did not reappear in the window between the third and second floor. Which meant what? That they belonged to someone who lived on the third floor? A Carvalho or a Khambata?

Shanaya was right. I was losing the plot. I'd had enough of Daisy Apartments and its sleepless inhabitants for one night. I was turning away from the window when Baman Marker's bedroom plunged into darkness.

The Hon Chairperson was turning in for the night.

I followed his example and crawled into bed. I wondered briefly if there was a connection between the white-clad legs and the lights being switched off just a second later. Then I decided that it really didn't matter.

8

The forty-sixth day of the lockdown began with a bizarre episode. Sir Paulash would have described it as foreshadowing. Hercule Poirot would have seen it as a puzzle worthy of his little grey cells. We, however, shrugged and carried on with our claustrophobic lives.

When I think back to our world—two sealed buildings frowning at each other across a grey cement compound—I see now what I didn't see then. That we were existing in a pressure cooker—quite like the clunky metal monsters on our kitchen counters. We had been on simmer for some time. But then the big chef in the sky decided to plop on the whistle and turn on the heat, after which there was no way to avoid the big, loud whoooooosh.

The Lily-Daisy Apartments chat became active early on Sunday morning in a most unexpected way. Mrs Kurien, Mini's mother, woke up at dawn and realized that the milk pouches had not been left outside her door. Mrs Kurien is one of those people who go nuts if they don't get their coffee first thing in the morning. The missing milk was a crisis.

Mrs Kurien peered outside the window but could not see the new night security guard. She was about to call out to him when she realized that she didn't know his name. In fact, the only thing she knew about him was that he was incompetent.

Mrs Kurien could feel the first bangs of a hammer behind her eyes. Within fifteen minutes, a whole carpenter's workshop would be pounding in her head. The easiest solution was to dash downstairs. When Mrs Kurien reached the locked gate, she saw the new night security guard dozing on the other side. She was rousing him to ask if the milk had arrived when she heard the sound.

Crrrukk. Crokkk. Discordant in the ash-grey dawn.

Mrs Kurien stopped mid-conversation and stared. Through the murk she saw that the gate of Daisy Apartments was open. Not wide, but at a sneaky, 30-degree angle that offered just enough space for a mid-sized person to sidle through. Which was when a stocky male form started emerging from the gap in the gate.

The phantasm oozed out of the blood-black doorway. Mrs Kurien couldn't see much. But she did see enough to know that the man was wearing a yellow mask, a plastic face shield, a dark long-sleeved shirt, black pants and a surreptitious air.

At first sight, it looked like Baman Marker.

'I hadn't had my coffee,' Mrs Kurien told my mother on the phone later that morning. 'It was 6.30 a.m. and my eyes weren't even focusing. But I knew there was something wrong. Daisy Apartments was sealed. Why was someone coming out? And that too at this hour of the morning? Why was the security guard allowing this person to come out? Nothing made sense.'

Mrs Kurien reacted instinctively. She yelled across the compound. 'Who IS that? We are not supposed to leave the building. Is that you, Mr Marker?'

The figure ignored her and continued into the compound past the security guard. 'Chowkidar,' Mrs Kurien shouted. 'Why are you allowing that man to come out of the building? Stop him. Stop him.'

The security guard stationed outside Daisy Apartments needed coffee way more than Mrs Kurien did. He blinked, and by the time he understood what was expected of him, it was too late. The mystery man with the yellow mask and face shield had melted into the shadows so entirely, that Mrs Kurien wondered if he was a fabrication of her caffiene-deprived brain.

'Who was that man?' Mrs Kurien called out.

'I think it was Chemmen Saab,' the security guard said. 'He said he had important work so I opened the gate.'

'Did he say he was the Chairman?' Mrs Kurien asked. But the security guard shrugged and fell back into his chair and his stupor.

Mrs Kurien shrugged as well, gathered her cold, slippery pouches of milk and headed home to make her coffee. It was only twenty minutes later, when the caffeine cleared the fog in her brain, that she realized that maybe she should say something to someone.

The problem was that she didn't know what she should say and to whom she should say it. But over her third mug of coffee, she finally made up her mind. 'Someone was spotted leaving Daisy Apartments very early in the morning,' she posted on the chat. 'It gave me quite a fright. I hope no one is ill…'

Nobody replied, which made sense in a way. Those who had been at home and tucked in bed, had nothing to contribute. And the sneaky soul who had concealed himself behind a yellow mask, face-shield and the cover of darkness was hardly going to advertise his identity and motives on the building chat.

Mrs Kurien's message was extraordinary enough to warrant a gossip-session and, while Ved and I were chewing on toast and shedding breadcrumbs, my mother made a quick call. 'Were you scared?' she asked Mrs Kurien. 'Who could it have been?'

'The person was in a mask and shield and it was quite dark,' Mrs Kurien said. 'It could have been Mr Lamba or Mr Burman or anyone…maybe not Darius Khambata or Mr Habibullah…'

'You don't think it was Baman Marker?' my mother asked. 'The way you described him I was wondering—'

'It could have been,' Mrs Kurien mused. 'Especially because he's gone silent on us. It's all so bizarre.'

'Really,' my mother agreed. 'First Baman Marker insists that we order vegetables and groceries only through him. And then, when we send in our lists, he ghosts us.'

This was no exaggeration. The Hon Chairperson had turned as silent as the bar of Rin soap that my mother needed so urgently.

At 8 a.m., my mother had decided she could wait no longer and had sent a combative message on the Lily-Daisy Apartments chat. She reminded the Hon Chairperson that she had placed an order for onions, potatoes and detergent soap ages ago. 'I need them immediately,' she had written.

At 8.07 a.m., Lina Almeida had asked when her cinnamon and Amul butter would be arriving.

At 8.23 a.m., Mrs Burman had written saying that they were out of extra virgin olive oil and asking if her supplier could leave two bottles at the gate with Day Mishraji.

At 8.40 a.m., Mrs Kurien had snapped. 'Mr Marker, are you there? Awaiting poha and sugar.'

At 9.01 a.m., Amrita Aunty had asked if her Dove deodorant had been ordered. 'Please keep in mind that I want the Cucumber and Green Tea one with the green cap. Not the one with the blue cap.'

At 9.16 a.m., Lina Almeida had asked, 'Baman?'

At 9.47 a.m., my mother had announced, 'Mr Marker, I am placing my order directly with the bhajiwala. I had informed you last night that I would need these items in the morning. I cannot wait any longer.'

At 9.48 a.m., Mrs Kurien had written. 'Ditto.'

At 9.52 a.m., Lina Almeida had written, 'Baman??? We are waiting.'

Then at 9.56 a.m., she had followed up with, 'Baman????'

At 10.08 a.m., Darius Khambata had added his voice to the clamour. 'Dear Baman. Peace to you. Last evening, I had requested you to order for us lavender essential oil and chia seeds. I woke up to your message stating that these were not essentials. But what is essential for one, may not be essential for the other. The soul is many while it is one.'

Through all this, Baman Marker remained as unresponsive as the pomfrets that arrive at Sassoon Dock on blocks of ice. I wonder now why we didn't find his silence fishy.

Meanwhile, various theories were being floated. There were those who believed that Baman Marker was enjoying a lazy morning in bed. There were others who were convinced that he was the individual who had slunk out of the building at dawn. There were still others who imagined that his phone had died.

I don't think any of us came close to guessing the real reason behind the pomfret-on-ice silence.

9

The first sign that something was amiss came just after lunch. I don't know the nitty-gritties, of course. I wasn't there. But after eavesdropping on about 300 phone conversations, this is how Shanaya and I pictured the scene.

Binaifer Marker had escaped the germy environs of Lily and Daisy Apartments and had holed up in the home of her younger daughter. Roxanne was flat-footed and teacup-eared, but I guess that has no bearing on this story.

Baman Marker had planned to decamp along with his wife, but at the last minute he changed his mind. Something had come up. Something important, but Binaifer never found out the details. All she knew was that he was fretful and kept asking if a parcel had been delivered to the house.

Binaifer didn't want to leave without her husband, but Baman Marker insisted. He intended to follow soon. The plan was that Roxanne would send him her car at 4 p.m. that evening and that he would sneak away. But then Raghunath died in hospital, the BMC arrived to seal the building and the finger-wagging official refused to leave until Baman Marker was locked into the building.

Baman Marker was trapped but not defeated. He was confident that he would be able to leave the next morning. 'Send the car as soon as I call,' he had told Binaifer. 'Now that I'm here, I might as well take care of some troublesome business.'

'Have all your immunity boosters,' Binaifer had said.

Baman Marker had promised that he would. 'Don't worry,' he had told his wife. 'It's a matter of a day.'

Binaifer Marker was not worried. Maria was in the apartment and would make sure that the dinner was cooked, the dishes were washed and that Baman was comfortable. On her part, Maria was thrilled to be in charge. She waddled by every half hour to check if Saab needed anything. The evening proceeded peacefully—in Maria's eyes, at least—till she popped into the living room at around 11.45 p.m. and started a conversation. She wanted to know if Baman Saab needed water, his phone charger, a cup of tea, a window shut, a window opened…

Baman Marker was a habitual passer of soft, hurtful remarks rather than a screamer of insults. But this time he exploded at Maria. He said that the only thing he needed was sleep, and that Maria was to stop disturbing him. He told her to go to her room and to leave him in peace. 'I don't want to see your face till morning,' he shouted. 'I don't want to hear your voice till morning.'

'Sir was talking funny,' Maria informed everyone later. 'He was shaking and he banged into a table and madam's glass cat almost fell. He told me that my voice was giving him a headache.'

Maria was offended. She pursed her lips, stalked out of the living room and decided that she would follow Baman Marker's instructions to the last letter. She went straight to her bedroom at the very back of the house, where she shut the door, switched off the lights, covered herself from top to toe with a blanket, and sank into a deep sleep. Even if she heard sounds, she didn't bother with them. They were not her business.

Soon after this, at 11.55 p.m. on Friday night, Binaifer called her husband for the last time. During the conversation he said that he was exhausted. He got shouty and aggressive when she asked him to bring along her inhaler and the two avocadoes that were in the glass bowl in the kitchen.

About twenty minutes later, Baman Marker followed up with a curt message to his wife. 'Am not to be disturbed. Will call when I wake up.'

Which is why Binaifer Marker waited till 11 a.m., before trying to contact her husband the next morning. It was also why she didn't fuss when he failed to answer the phone. Like the rest of us, she assumed that he was sleeping or sulking or that his phone battery had died. It was well past noon by the time she got jumpy.

Gradually, the jumpiness turned to worry and Binaifer Marker phoned Maria.

Maria reported that Baman Marker was still in his bedroom and that his door was latched. At which point Binaifer Marker had a panic attack and had to be put to bed. Lunchtime came and went before Roxanne called Kavita Lamba.

The moment Kavita Lamba understood the problem, she donned her white mask, sanitized her hands and climbed the three floors to the Marker apartment. Maria let her in, and together they pounded on the bedroom door.

No answer. So Kavita Lamba summoned her husband, who did some half-hearted tapping of his own. Again, no answer. At which point the Hon Secretary decided that it was time for decisive action. She sent her husband to ring a few doorbells, and she herself made some urgent calls.

Everyone was at home, and everyone was available—which is, I guess, the only advantage of being stuck in a sealed building. Ten minutes later, the Marker apartment was teeming with masked men and women, all reeking of hand sanitizer and nervous energy.

Mr Burman and Mr Lamba lurked at the fringes, Kavita Lamba and Lina Almeida issued rapid-fire instructions. Amrita Aunty made sure to grab a ringside seat. But it was the Khambatas who took charge. They were businesslike about it, as if kicking in bedroom doors was a fortnightly occurrence in their lives.

The door to the Marker bedroom looked glossy, white and solid. But the headstands and chia seeds had done their job. Neville and Jeh Khambata went into a huddle with their father, after which they went at the door. All it took was a well-aimed kick for the wood to splinter. Two more kicks and cool air-conditioned air leaked into the warm living room. Along with it came an ominous whiff—a hint of the ugliness that lay within.

There was a general backward shuffle, as the neighbours shrank away from the sagging door.

Neville and Jeh Khambata stepped aside and it was their father who gave the door the firm shove that caused it to swing open. On the other side lay the blue and brown bedroom of Baman and Binaifer Marker. Heavy blue curtains with brown swirls blocked the ferocious afternoon sun and kept the room dim and twilit. Which is why it took the neighbours a moment to process what they were seeing.

The glossy satin quilt on the wide bed was caked with vomit. A porcelain figurine lay smashed and shattered on the floor. A purple plastic folder had fallen on the brown rug, and papers were scattered across the room. A chair had tumbled onto its side and a fruity-grassy odour hung heavy in the chill air. A cupboard door was wide open. But it was the man sprawled on the bed upon whom all eyes were fixed. Baman Marker was lying at an odd angle, face-down on top of the blue quilt. He was dressed in a crumpled pant and shirt and he was very, very still.

Somebody gasped. Somebody screamed. Maria sobbed at the top of her voice. 'Is he…' Mr Burman asked, unable to utter the word that hovered in the rank, air-conditioned air.

Nobody answered.

This was the stricken tableau into which Mr Habibullah stumbled. Mr Habibullah was just about five years older than my father, but his hair was smudged with white. He had purple pouches under his eyes and his clothes drooped, giving the impression of a deflating balloon. He shuffled into the living room, speaking without punctuation or inflection. '…say I'm sorry I took so long I could not find my spectacles I don't know if it happens to you but it always happens to me…Rashida said he has only caused trouble but I must pay my respects it is not right to speak ill of the dead—'

'What do you mean?' Kavita Lamba almost shrieked. 'Why are you saying that Mr Marker is dead?'

The tone frightened Mr Habibullah who, shaking violently, retreated from the room, still talking in a monotone. Even then, nobody moved till Darius Khambata walked slowly into the blue and brown bedroom, skirting fallen furniture and porcelain shards. He leaned over Baman Marker and said in a shaky, low voice, 'He's breathing. Call a doctor. Call an ambulance. Now.'

After that, there was chaos. Everyone grabbed their phones and dialled doctors and ambulances. This was easier said than done. All the doctors and all the ambulances seemed busy tackling Covid-19. No one agreed to help.

It was a huge relief when Amrita Aunty finally got through to Dr Dilip Mirchandani. Dr Mirchandani was such a high-profile heart specialist that it took two months to get an appointment with him. He was not the sort of doctor who dropped everything to penetrate a sealed building and examine a complete stranger. It was fortunate, then, that Dr Mirchandani was married to Amrita Aunty's cousin. It was also fortunate that he—like anybody with an iota of sense—enjoyed her fiery pani puri and her pungent humour.

'Dr Mirchandani is coming,' Amrita Aunty announced finally. 'But it will take him about forty-five minutes.'

After that, there was nothing to do but to make a difficult phone call and then to wait. Lina Almeida made the call. 'You have to be strong,' she told Binaifer Marker, while the rest of the room stood at attention and Maria wailed. 'Baman is unwell. It is difficult to say how unwell, but it looks serious. We have called the doctor. Yes, it might be best if you or Roxanne come. Someone will need to take charge.'

After she disconnected, the room lapsed into an awkward silence, punctuated by the fat tuk tuk of the grandfather clock. Most of the people there had been neighbours for years. They'd attended each other's anniversary parties, complained about each other's leaking bathrooms and stumbled upon each other's secrets. But nobody felt up to chatting till Mr Burman and Mr Lamba—the relative newcomer and the perennial outsider—spoke.

'Heart attack?' Mr Burman wondered aloud, glancing at the time on the grandfather clock.

'Looks like it,' Mr Lamba said.

'Strange that we don't have a single doctor in the building. You know, Darius almost became a doctor and then the universe stepped in. There is a reason for everything,' Silloo Khambata babbled and then turned to her sons, who were looking queasy and pale. 'Neville, Jeh, you go down. No reason for you to wait.'

'You go too,' Darius Khambata said, and started steering his wife out of the room. 'There's nothing to do here. I can stay and maybe one more person?'

That served as a signal. The room rapidly emptied out till only Maria, Kavita Lamba, Lina Almeida and Darius Khambata remained. And, of course, the prone figure on that glossy blue quilt—the husk of the Hon Chairperson.

10

It was a great pity that Amrita Aunty didn't wait for Dr Mirchandani to arrive. If she had, we would have gotten an eyewitness account. As it is, we had to make do with sketchy reports that came to us in roundabout and unreliable ways.

Alfonsa got a bunch of details from Maria, and then passed on some choice morsels. To these we tacked on the whispers that Shanaya heard from Kysha, who had heard them from Neville Khambata, who in turn had heard them from his dad.

It bugged me that one of our primary sources was a notorious spotter of ghosts and spreader of rumours. And that the other was a famously eccentric wearer of batik shorts, who ambled through life in a happy haze. But as my grandmother never tired of telling us, beggars can't be choosers. And while Shanaya and I wouldn't have called ourselves beggars exactly, we were certainly scroungers. We had no option but to take the fragments that came our way and fit them into an approximate pattern.

This is the sequence of events that we came up with.

Binaifer Marker and Dr Mirchandani arrived at the gate of Daisy Apartments at the same time. Day Mishraji, who was a stickler for rules, was reluctant to allow them entry. A single bellow from the doctor changed his mind. And as the Hon Chairperson was incapacitated, there was no one to object.

Dr Mirchandani, swathed in a white safety suit, reached the fifth-floor apartment first. He strode through the crystal- and porcelain-filled living room into the bedroom, vigorously rubbing his hands with sanitizer. There, he started examining the motionless man on the bed. Lina Almeida followed the doctor but was shooed away with a firm wave.

I have no way of knowing, of course, but at this point of the story I imagine a puzzled look creeping into the doctor's eyes.

Binaifer Marker entered the apartment a few minutes later. She blinked when she spotted Kavita Lamba on the beige sofa and Lina Almeida standing outside the bedroom door. She seemed utterly dumbfounded to see Darius Khambata with one foot propped on the windowsill, immersed in a deep breathing routine.

Kavita Lamba sprang to her feet, Lina Almeida moved forward and even Darius Khambata straightened up and assumed a solemn expression. Binaifer Marker looked past them and walked purposefully towards her bedroom, as if she had returned home to fetch a forgotten handbag.

She came to a sudden halt at the door of the bedroom and stood there for a long, blank minute till Kavita Lamba and Lina Almeida lead her to the beige sofa. 'Bring some water,' Lina Almeida snapped at Maria.

The words yanked Binaifer Marker out of her daze. She straightened up, looked around and frowned. Then she started talking about a long-ago holiday in Spain and about porcelain shepherdesses. She spoke about avocadoes and metal bottles and stray dogs.

'That was a Lladro. A shepherdess,' she said fretfully. 'I collect them. I used to have six. Now I have five. I really can't understand how this could have happened. What is she doing in the bedroom even? Nobody is supposed to touch her. Everything is going wrong. I can't imagine how I forgot about the avocadoes. We call for them all the way from Ooty so I was very upset when I forgot them. Overripe bananas you can use in pancakes, but overripe avocadoes are inedible. And I can't understand what that metal bottle is doing on the table. We never use metal bottles. We use only glass bottles.'

She lapsed into momentary silence before saying with icy disdain, 'Metal bottles are…you know…very middle class. Whose bottle is it? Can somebody please tell me?'

Binaifer Marker's last question was so loud and urgent that all four pairs of eyes turned to gaze at the offending object on the round, glass-topped table. It was one of those commonplace metal bottles that are everywhere—on Amazon, in the shops that line Colaba Bazaar, in half the kitchens of Lily and Daisy Apartments. Why it should distress Binaifer Marker so much was a mystery, but Lina Almeida humoured her.

'Maria,' she said. 'Take this bottle to the kitchen. It's upsetting madam.'

'But it is not our bottle.' Maria bristled. 'You want me to wash it for you?'

Lina Almeida valued her breath too much to waste it. She merely gave Maria a dagger-sharp glare—the one that reduced entire classrooms of schoolchildren to raggedy ribbons. Maria scowled, but she did what she was told. She stomped to the table with ill grace, picked up the metal bottle and headed to the kitchen. She was too indignant to bother with the square of yellow paper that fluttered to the floor near the sofa.

Kavita Lamba bent to pick up the little note and tucked it under a crystal bowl on a small hexagonal table.

'What is that paper?' Binaifer Marker asked. 'Where are all these things coming from?'

Darius Khambata was about to examine the yellow square—or so he later told Neville who told Kysha who told Shanaya—when Dr Mirchandani emerged from the blue and brown bedroom. He looked grave and a bit peeved. 'We need to get him to hospital immediately,' he told Binaifer Marker, who had lapsed into a stupefied silence. 'We need to run some tests.'

Binaifer Marker could only swallow, but Lina Almeida rose to the occasion. 'Yes, doctor,' she said. 'But how do we get an ambulance and a hospital bed?'

Dr Mirchandani made a few calls, but it was another three hours before Baman Marker reached the hospital. He didn't occupy his bed for too long. Less than twenty-four hours after he got there, he stopped breathing.

We heard the news from Alfonsa before dinner on Sunday. 'Chemmen Saab off ho gaye,' she announced, with a sombre face and dancing eyes.

We reacted with disbelief until, just eight minutes later, Lina Almeida wrote a message on the building chat. 'Dear Baman Marker, who took such meticulous care of our buildings, has passed on. He will be sorely missed. Our prayers are with the family.'

Condolences poured in. Although none of us had particularly loved Baman Marker, everyone felt shaken and bruised. We watched in solemn silence as Maria and Binaifer Marker were driven away in the same gleaming white car that had ferried Binaifer Marker only two days ago, while her husband stood and waved.

'I've never been so shocked in my life,' my mother said as she stirred the daal for dinner. (It was Ved's turn to cook dinner tonight, but as usual the universe had conspired to rescue him. My mother was too distracted to teach him how to make hummus and salad on this most eventful of evenings.)

'So sudden,' she continued. 'Amrita says that it was probably a massive heart attack. Really, I've never been so shocked in my life.'

She had reason to repeat the exact words the very next day. And this time she really did look shocked—quite like the goggle-eyed emoji, in fact.

The forty-eighth day of the lockdown was a dreary Monday. I spent a pointless hour staring out of my window, dissatisfied and lovelorn in turn. All I got for my pains was a glimpse of an elbow that may or may not have belonged to Daniel. I couldn't even make out if his father was back home.

Then at 4 p.m., a police vehicle drove into the compound and four policemen marched up to the gate of Daisy Apartments.

Alfonsa whispered the news to Ved while he was listening to Drake in his bedroom. Ved shouted it out to me. And soon our entire family—plus Alfonsa and a persistent crow—were leaning out of the balcony. In the background, Drake continued to tell us how to Tootsie Slide.

Two of the policemen who emerged from the jeep wore regular clothes. Two wore uniforms. They strode up to the gate of Daisy Apartments and said something to Day Mishraji, who unlocked the gate with record speed.

As soon as the police stepped inside, voices from various balconies called out.

'Was that the police?'

'What has happened?'

'Where are they going?'

'They are going to the fifth floor,' Day Mishraji shouted back. 'To Chemmen Saab's house.'

'But there's nobody there,' Kavita Lamba protested.

'I told them,' Day Mishraji replied. 'They told me not to open my mouth.'

We were intrigued. 'Is it routine?' my mother asked my father. 'Surely the police don't land up every time someone dies?'

My father said he hadn't the faintest idea. The crow on the railing cocked his head. And Ved and I were clueless as well. So my mother marched back into the living room to call Amrita Aunty and we trailed behind her. 'Why do you think the police have come to Baman Marker's house?' we heard her asking. 'What do you mean you aren't sure if you should tell me? Tell me what?'

Then a longish silence and my mother asked, 'Who's DD? Oh, Dr Mirchandani. He said what? Are you serious? But you were there…was there anything to indicate? You can't be serious. I have never been so shocked in my life.'

Then silence. Then a loud gasp. 'Something like what? Some form of organic chemical? Like what? He's not sure? But still…'

'Where would one even get hold of that sort of stuff in the middle of a lockdown? When we can't even get tomatoes?'

Then a series of gasps and, 'I have never, never, never been so shocked in my life.'

By this point Ved and I were hopping and gesticulating.

'What? What?' Ved was mouthing.

'Put it on speaker phone,' I whispered.

Our mum silenced us with a dirty look. Clearly this was no ordinary gossip. It fell in that most riveting category—a Not-To-Be-Told-To-A-Soul Secret. We would need to wait till our mum could squeeze it out of Amrita Aunty before we could squeeze it out of our mum.

Ten minutes later, we were on the job. 'Tell,' we pleaded, blocking her path to the fridge and breaking her onion-chopping rhythm. 'We won't tell anyone. Promise.'

'Go away, you two,' my mother said. 'I almost cut my finger. Now I can't remember if I put salt in this pulao. If dinner is inedible, it's not my fault.'

'We don't mind if dinner is inedible,' I lied sweetly and unconvincingly.

'We mind much more that you are hiding something major from us,' Ved agreed. 'We won't tell a soul.'

My mother chose to believe us. Or maybe she just wanted to get rid of us so that she could get on with dinner. 'Dr Mirchandani told Amrita Aunty that there was something odd about Baman Marker's death,' she said, looking around to make sure that Alfonsa wasn't afoot. 'The hospital conducted tests as soon as Baman Marker got there, and apparently…apparently he died because of something he had eaten or drunk…'

'Like…food poisoning?' Ved asked.

'I'm not sure,' my mother muttered. 'It sounded more like…some chemical.'

'Chemical,' Ved and I chorused. 'What chemical?'

My mother shushed us violently, muttering about Alfonsa and her wagging ears. 'Look, you're not supposed to know a thing,' she whispered. 'Don't you dare tell a soul.'

We promised up, down and sideways, but these precautions were unnecessary. By dinnertime it was all over the building. Baman Marker had died of unnatural causes. It could have been suicide. It could have been an accident.

But the police believed that it was murder. Murder by poison.

11

I don't think anybody in Lily or Daisy Apartments did a quarter-second of work on the forty-ninth day of the lockdown. I doubt a single chapati was rolled out or a single chair dusted. Each and every one of us was too busy contemplating/shuddering/gossiping over the murder of the Hon Chairperson.

The only time my mum was not on the phone was when she paused for a loo break and a hasty lunch. Amrita Aunty was worse. She even carried her phone into the loo.

Shanaya and I spent the entire day hovering around the whispering adults. After which we did an information swap and came up with a tangled ball of maybe-facts and rumours, amidst which a few strands of truth were hidden.

The news of Baman Marker's death had cast a leaden gloom over Lily and Daisy Apartments. The news of his murder shifted the mood from heaviness to horror; from bleak disbelief to gleeful credulity.

Rumours were floated. Rumours were spread. Rumours were embraced till the next rumour came along. Mrs Kurien was the woman of the hour and everyone agreed that her mysterious stranger was the killer.

Even so, there were other theories doing the rounds:

Baman Marker had been bitten by Jeh Khambata's snake.

Baman Marker had been dispatched to the underworld by Maria, who had cooked without her spectacles and poured Clorox into his food instead of vinegar.

Baman Marker was the victim of a gang of opportunistic robbers who were preying on sealed buildings—Rashida Habibullah had heard them as they passed her door.

Baman Marker had—

Yes, we were being ghoulish. But waking up one morning and finding yourself in the middle of a murder investigation does that to you. Especially when you know the victim and might know the killer too. I honestly felt that I had gatecrashed an Agatha Christie mystery—except that there was no chance that Miss Marple would twinkle along to set everything right.

Instead of Miss Marple, we had a bumble of policemen who looked like they hadn't slept in weeks. I could see them as they tramped up and down the staircase of Daisy Apartments, wandered around the compound and investigated the two cramped garages.

Alfonsa ran from window to window, tracking them. She was convinced that the mystery was solved when the police emerged from the Khambata garage with two brown plastic cans. After that we were all pretty sure that Darius Khambata—for some unspecified reason and with some unspecified substance—had killed his cousin. Till an hour later they came out of the Burman garage with a blue can.

We were agog. Even the Lily-Daisy Kids chat, which was usually a comatose affair, woke up on that Tuesday morning. The first message was posted by the most sullen and silent person on that generally sullen and silent chat.

'My mother says we should all help the police,' Thea had written. 'She wants to know if we noticed anything unusual over the last two days.'

Thea must have hated having to send that message. With good reason. All it took was ninety seconds for Kysha to strike. 'Hey Thea,' she wrote. 'Also intresting to know wether they saw anything else of intrest. So much to see always.'

What?

Yet again I wondered how the meticulous Lina Almeida could put up with a granddaughter whose spellings were so atrocious that even spellcheck had given up the good fight. I was puzzling over Kysha's peculiar message, when Ved jumped in. 'Oh yes,' he wrote. 'I defly did see something unusual. Made famous Green Juice yesterday. But it turned out pink. Any idea why?'

'Uuuu prolly don't know diff between strabrries and spinich,' Kysha responded.

To which Ved asked, 'You do?'

This was Neville Khambata's cue to jump in with a string of laughing emojis. 'In a bit of a stew, Ky? How you going to answer that?'

'With a chalinj,' Kysha declared. 'Have best idea. Let's do Daisy vs Lily Bake Of or Juice Of or whatever.'

I followed the conversation with mounting dismay, as Kysha's jaunty messages popped on the screen.

'Neville, Jeh, Shannu and me on the Daisy team. Wanna join, Danny?'

'And Mini, Aashu, Ved and Co on the Lily team. Are all of uu up for it?'

I was not up for it. But I knew that my opinion counted for nothing. Especially when everybody else was sending thumbs ups and claps.

'We r putting on r kitchen gloves,' Mini wrote. 'We r ready.'

Ved—who had successful ducked dinner duty at the Venkat abode for four consecutive days—posted a chef emoji. But then he was part of the inner circle while I was part of the 'and Co'. Can you blame me for spending the next half hour being huffy and disgruntled?

First, I fumed over the manner in which Kysha had excluded Thea. I was sure Thea didn't want to be a part of the cooking jamboree, but the way in which Kysha had erased her was downright evil. (How could anybody be so nasty and so popular at the same time? It was *Mean Girls* all over again.)

Second, I spluttered over the throwaway remark about Ved and Co. Almost as though I was a package deal with Ved. Like one of those cheap plastic toys that they give free when you buy a box of Chocos.

Third was this stuff about Shannu. Since when had Kysha and Shanaya been on such cuddly terms? Since when had anybody in the whole galaxy called my best friend Shannu? And why hadn't Shanaya said a thing about this blossoming friendship? (By this point I was as incensed with Shanaya as I was with Kysha.)

Fourth was the niggling fear that Daniel—*Danny*? I mean *Danny*?—might join Team Daisy. (If that happened, I would give up and die. Seriously.)

I was still moping when Alfonsa popped her head into my room. 'Police are talking to everybody,' she said, beady-eyed and breathless with excitement. 'Just now they are at Shanaya's house.'

I didn't bother to ask how Alfonsa knew. I had long accepted that our once-nanny, now-inhouse-spy had her ways. Which is why I knew exactly what Shanaya meant when she sent a cryptic message twenty minutes later. 'They're here,' she wrote.

'The police?' I asked.

'No, the little green men from Jupiter.'

'Shut up. What they saying?'

'Asking what my mom was doing on Friday night.'

'Friday night??? Why?'

'Don't know. Guessing that is when killer did whatever.'

'Ohhh! When on Friday night?'

'Between 9 and 11.'

'Why then?'

'Don't know.'

'Why your mother of all people?'

'Don't know. Guess asking everyone in Daisy. Guess nobody else could have done it.'

'But the mystery man? Isn't he chief suspect?'

'Don't know.'

'What else are they asking your mum?'

'Asked if we have car.'

'A car? Why? Because you bought a new car just before lockdown?'

'I don't think so…Wait. Trying to listen. Will message.'

Shanaya vanished from my screen, leaving me twitchy. Why would the police ask Amrita Aunty, of all people, what she was doing on that Friday evening? And why precisely between 9 p.m. and 11 p.m.? And why were they asking about a car? What could someone stuck in a sealed building in the middle of a lockdown do with a car anyway?

It was not as if we could have zipped across to Waffle Wonderland or 99 Pancakes. Or to some shop that sold bottles of deadly poisons.

For that matter, what did the police imagine that Amrita Aunty could have been doing on Friday evening between 9 p.m. and 11 p.m.? At the moment, every single day was like the one that had gone before. How could we even tell one day from another? I had no idea what I'd been doing on Friday, even though it was just four days ago. I'd almost definitely spent the evening eating junk and watching even more junk. But if you asked me for details, I wouldn't have a clue.

I was saved from suspicion by the facts that I lived in Lily Apartments and I was a child. Still, I wondered what I'd been doing on Friday between 9 p.m. and 11 p.m. when, presumably, our Hon Chairperson was busy getting murdered.

Let's see. Today was Tuesday. So Friday was…Friday was... I glanced at my desk calendar and spotted the big red cross on 7 May. Lily Apartments had been sealed last Thursday, which meant that Daisy Apartments had been sealed on Friday.

Once I knew this, the fog parted slightly to allow a brief glimpse of that evening. Friday was the day I'd made mac-and-cheese from scratch. Which meant it was the day I'd watched *Mean Girls* with Shanaya. I was thinking about cheese puffs in a vague sort of way when a memory loomed through the haze. A recollection of legs on the stairwell of Daisy Apartments.

I tried to hold on to the thought but my brain had become too used to functioning at jellyfish levels and refused to cooperate. And then, quite suddenly, I had an idea.

Grabbing my phone, I went into my chat with Shanaya. Given that Shanaya and I texted each other all the time, I had to scroll back a long, long way. But I finally found what I was looking for. Our conversation while watching *Mean Girls*.

I read through the chat and gradually, Friday night acquired shape and details. The dingdong of the doorbell in that drowsy silence. The image of Amrita Aunty, pale grey in the dark balcony, as she looked out with unseeing eyes. Black-clad legs tiptoeing up a stairwell, and an orange-red-pink thing placed on the steps.

Message by message, I went over that evening. And message by message, I saw now what I hadn't seen then.

Shanaya and I had begun chatting at 9.47 p.m. We must have started watching the movie at around 10 p.m. and it was 10.26 p.m. when I told Shanaya that someone was sneaking up the Daisy Apartments staircase. In my mind, I saw those legs creeping, climbing, advancing towards the fifth floor.

I had decided that the legs must have belonged to Baman Marker. Now it struck me that the legs could as easily have belonged to his killer.

It was a disturbing idea. One that filled me with sudden frustration. If only Shanaya had listened to me, attempted a spot of investigation and figured the identity of Black Legs. If only Shanaya had worn something other than the torn red pajamas with the fried eggs. If only I had looked harder and waited longer to see if the legs climbed down again. If only I'd tried to figure out who rang that doorbell.

It bugged me that Shanaya hadn't complied. It bugged me that I'd been sloppy about my surveillance. And all of a sudden, it bugged me that my room was in such a mess. But that, at least, I could do something about.

I spent the next twenty minutes clearing up. I'm not a natural clothes-folder, pile-maker and dressing-tablerearranger. Still, I managed to scoop the clutter off the floor and chairs and dressing table and thrust it all into my cupboard.

Feeling a tiny bit calmer, I returned to my desk, my phone and my recollections of Friday night. First had come the black legs. Then had come the doorbell. Then the bumps and thumps from Daniel's house. That is where our chat had ended. But I remembered that Friday had thrown up one last riddle. Another pair of legs had appeared on the staircase of Daisy Apartments, as insubstantial as a dream. They had worn something white and flappy. And I was pretty sure that they had been running down from the fourth to the third floor before they vanished.

Pacing up and down my room, I started to join the scattered dots.

- There were two families living on the third floor of Daisy Apartment. The Khambatas and the Carvalhos.
- The bumps and thumps had emanated from the Carvalho apartment.
- Mr Carvalho had a dubious past. He had reason to dislike Baman Marker. And Baman Marker had sent a message on the building chat that could well have been a taunt aimed at the dubious Mr Carvalho.

The picture that emerged alarmed me. All this time I'd been hoping that Mr Carvalho had returned home to Daniel and to Daisy Apartments. Now I hoped for the opposite. That he had remained far away from Daniel and Daisy Apartments, so he could not be the killer.

Automatically, my eyes turned to the third floor of Daisy Apartments and my heart gave a great big whump.

Daniel was in his balcony, dressed in a black T-shirt. That disobedient lock of hair had tumbled onto his forehead again, and he was biting his perfect lips. His hands gripped the sill and he was leaning out and looking towards the compound gate. He looked very alone. Very much like he was waiting for his father to come back home.

Just then, Daniel glanced towards Lily Apartments and caught me staring. Flustered, I was about to look away, when he raised his hand and gave a quick wave. After which he flashed an even quicker smile.

Let me say it. I didn't cover myself in glory. First, I flushed, then I gawped, then I collected myself enough to attempt a half wave. But Daniel had already turned and wandered into his living room.

For a hopeful minute I imagined that he would come out again. But no. The balcony remained bare, except for the potted palm, the money plant and something that looked like a white raincoat, hanging on a corner hook. The raincoat gave the balcony an even more neglected air than usual, and my heart hurt.

For another hopeful minute, I imagined Daniel picking up his phone, scrolling through the participants of the Lily-Daisy Kids chat, looking for Nandini Venkat, and typing out a private message. But that, of course, was wishful thinking.

Still, I stayed at the window, pink-cheeked and adoring, and arrived at a decision. There was no way that I was going to lead the police to Mr Carvalho. There was no way that I was going to be the one who sent Daniel's father to Arthur Road Jail.

I was still thinking about Daniel's father when Shanaya called. She sounded bewildered, miserable and utterly unShanayalike. 'They're still here,' she whispered.

'The police?' I asked, incredulous. 'They're not done yet? It's been hours.'

'Well, 114 minutes,' Shanaya said in a wobbly voice. 'It's as if…I don't know…it's as if they think my mom had a special thing against Baman Marker. I think that they think…'

'What? What do they think?'

'They think that she really hated him.'

Okay, that was true. Amrita Aunty had really hated Baman Marker, but so had most of Daisy Apartments. And Lily Apartments. And any other corner of the world in which he had bleated and bullied and gotten his way.

'That doesn't mean that she would kill him,' I protested, jumping to my feet and striding around the room. 'They're probably harassing everyone who lives in Daisy Apartments. And anyway, why would they suspect her more than they suspect anyone else?'

'I don't know,' Shanaya said, in a voice that was barely audible. 'I bet that Kavita Lamba said something. Or that sly Thea.'

'Thea?' I choked. 'Don't be nuts. Thea doesn't talk to anyone. She is hardly going to march up to the police and announce that your mother hated Baman Marker.'

'She's creepy,' Shanaya hissed. 'She's always there whenever I open the door. And there are all sorts of stories going around about her in school. And she's always sitting in that balcony, looking out.'

'Poor thing,' I protested, immediately defensive. 'Looking out of your balcony is hardly a crime.'

'You should hear what Kysha says—'

I really didn't want to hear what Kysha had to say. About Thea, or about anything else.

'Shanaya, listen,' I interrupted. But Shanaya didn't listen. She was now wondering if Lina Almeida had said something to the police.

'Shanaya, stop,' I tried again, and then jumped. I'd stepped on something small and sharp. I looked down and saw a metal earring shaped like a flower. One of the petals was embedded in my foot, which was bleeding. I really, really needed to sort out my room. But first I needed to soothe Shanaya.

'There really isn't anything to worry about,' I said so loudly that Shanaya stopped speaking and actually listened.

'You were at home with your mother the whole time,' I hurried on. 'Maybe you don't remember, but Friday night was when we were watching *Mean Girls*. I clearly remember looking out of the window a couple of times. Your mother was standing in the balcony for ages and ages. And after that she had that long chat with my mum. She could hardly have been running up and down the building, killing Baman Marker.'

'Are you sure?' Shanaya asked, suddenly hopeful. 'Are you absolutely positive? How did you figure all this out?'

'Check our chat for Friday night,' I suggested. 'It will all come back. But basically, Amrita Aunty has a proper, proper alibi. Which is probably more than Mr Burman or Darius Khambata or whoever else has.'

'But do you think the police will believe us? They seem so…so…out to get her…'

'Of course, they'll believe us. My mum and I will tell them if necessary. And I don't even think it will be necessary. I think they're talking to everyone.'

'Okay,' Shanaya said.

'Anyway,' I continued, 'the killer has to be the mystery man. Why else was he hanging around in a sealed building for hours and hours? And why else would he have slunk away in the morning?'

'I guess,' Shanaya trailed off.

'He had to have entered Daisy Apartments before the building was sealed. Do you think he was hiding in somebody's house? Or somewhere on the staircase or—'

Shanaya interrupted, 'Listen, I've got to go, the police are calling me. But thanks, Nandini. I feel much better.'

'Call me when they leave. Tell me what happens,' I said. But I was talking into a void.

12

Wondering if your crush's father has killed someone is not a good feeling. Wondering if the police suspect your best friend's mother of the same crime is even worse. Especially when the mother in question is Amrita Aunty, who is such a warm, vibrant presence in our lives.

This really could not be happening. And yet it was.

I imagined two large policemen sitting on Amrita Aunty's pale grey sofa and staring at her abstract paintings, with their slashes of mustard and black-green. I wondered what they thought of the twisty metal sculptures that dotted the low tables. They were lethal objects with many heads and many limbs. Crazily pricy but not entirely…cosy.

For a panicky second, I wondered if Baman Marker had been whacked on the head by a heavy object. But, of course not. None of the eyewitnesses had mentioned a gaping wound on his head and everybody knew he'd been killed by some mysterious poison. This was a relief because, truth to tell, I could imagine Amrita Aunty getting enraged and cracking someone's skull with a heavy, murderous sculpture. It was also a relief that we had a convenient trespasser as a convenient suspect.

Again, I wondered why the police weren't out and about, hunting for the trespasser. Why, instead, were they parked on Amrita Aunty's expensive leather sofa? Did they know something that we didn't?

It was about 5 p.m. when, seeking reassurance and salt, I drifted into the kitchen where I found my mother, Alfonsa, and a packet of jalapeno-flavoured nachos.

Once again, my mother had been too preoccupied to bully Chef Ved into making dinner. Once again, I wondered how Ved had managed to be born under a lucky star while I had not. After all, we were twins. I was younger than him by ninety measly seconds—which was hardly enough time for a lucky star to vamoose.

My mother was making a pesto sauce in our grumbling mixer-grinder. Alfonsa was washing a bowlful of cherry tomatoes. The nachos were sitting in a brown packet in the kitchen cupboard.

First, I grabbed the nachos. Next, I concentrated on protecting my bounty from Ved, who had a sixth sense about junk food and landed up in time to demand his share. Finally, I turned to my mother. 'The police have been at Shanaya's house for hours,' I said. 'And they're asking Amrita Aunty loads of questions.'

'Really?' my mother frowned. 'Poor Amrita. She has enough to deal with already. But it's probably just a formality.'

'They must be interviewing everyone,' Ved agreed. 'But have they even figured how Baman Marker died? I mean, how he was poisoned?'

My mum didn't know. But Alfonsa did. Of course.

'Juice,' she said in a low, spy-in-a-trenchcoat voice. 'He was killed with juice. They found a note and everything.'

'How juicy,' Ved quipped.

My mum and I quelled him before giving Alfonsa the respect she deserved. 'Juice?' my mother asked. 'He was killed with juice? What juice? How do you know, Alfonsa?'

'Maria told me,' Alfonsa said smugly. 'Maria has come back to Chemmen Saab's house. The police said the house can be cleaned up, so madam sent her. She will be staying here only. Poor Maria is scared. It's not good to stay in a house where someone has been murdered. Spirits…'

Alfonsa shuddered, crossed herself repeatedly, and clutched the silver crucifix dangling from a chain around her neck.

'But how was Baman Marker killed by juice,' I asked hastily. Once Alfonsa wandered into the realm of the supernatural, there was no leading her out again. 'What did Maria say?'

'The police asked Maria lots of questions.'

My mother was trying to push ahead with the pesto and salad, but her heart was not in it. 'What questions?' she asked Alfonsa.

'They kept asking her about a steel bottle. It was on the round glass table in Chemmen Saab's living room.'

'A steel bottle?' I asked, befuddled. 'So what if there was a steel bottle on the table?'

'The bottle doesn't belong to Binaifer Madam,' Alfonsa explained. 'Binaifer Madam likes only glass bottles. She likes the ones with flowers from Westside.'

'But then whose bottle was it? The steel bottle, I mean,' my mother asked, almost slicing her fingers along with the tomatoes. 'Why was it on Baman Marker's round glass table?'

'That's what the police kept asking Maria. Whose bottle is this? Why is this bottle in the house? What was in this bottle?'

'Poor Maria,' my mother tutted. 'I hope the police aren't troubling her. How can she know anything?'

'Of course, Maria knows everything,' Alfonsa retorted. 'Who do you think poured the juice out of the bottle for Chemmen Saab? Maria only.'

'What juice?' my mother asked, trying to make sense of these random nuggets. 'What was the juice in the metal bottle? Where did it come from?'

'It was that same green juice that Almeida Madam always makes,' Alfonsa said. 'Maria says it's very thick and smells of grass. Almeida Madam used to send it to Chemmen Saab all the time.'

We stared at Maria with open mouths. I was the first to recover. 'Green Glow Detox Smoothie!!!' I squawked. 'Baman Marker was killed by Green Glow Detox Smoothie? But how? It's supposed to be healthy.'

'Maybe he suddenly turned allergic to celery or kale,' Ved said, shuddering. 'I don't blame him.'

'Or maybe acute food poisoning?' my mother pondered. 'Maybe the leafy vegetables weren't washed properly. Lina Almeida must be feeling terrible. Finally, things are starting to make sense.'

Except that they didn't.

'If he died of allergic reaction or food poisoning, why are the police hassling Amrita Aunty?' I asked. 'I mean, wouldn't they just say Accidental Death and end it?'

My mother turned back to Alfonsa, who had now wandered to the window on the pretext of shooing a pigeon. 'What exactly did Maria say?' she asked.

Alfonsa took her time. 'Maria said that Chemmen Saab only had a sandwich for dinner because he was busy talking to many people. After that she watched her show on TV, had her dinner, cleaned the kitchen and then spoke to her sister in Goa. At around 11 o'clock, Chemmen Saab called her. The bottle of juice was on the table and he asked her to get his big mug. She got the mug, poured half the juice and went back to the kitchen to watch TV.'

'Okay,' my mother said. 'After that Maria went to bed?'

'No, no. After that Madam phoned. She told Maria to pack some mangoes and things for when Chemmen Saab would go to Roxanne baby's house. After that Maria went to ask Chemmen Saab if he wanted anything…' Alfonsa trailed off with a salacious gleam in her eye.

'And?' Ved asked.

'Chemmen Saab shouted at Maria,' Alfonsa said. 'He said she was disturbing him. He told her to go away. Maria says that Chemmen Saab was talking funny. And walking funny.'

'Funny?' we chorused.

'As if he had been drinking,' Alfonsa smirked.

'Wow,' Ved goggled. 'This is getting stranger and stranger.'

Alfonsa smirked some more. 'Chemmen Saab told Maria to go away, so she went away. Why should she stay when he didn't want her?'

Alfonsa paused and we nodded. 'Then?' I exhaled.

'Then she went to her room, locked her door and went to sleep,' Alfonsa said.

'But what about the juice?' I asked. 'What happened to that?'

'Chemmen Saab must have drunk all the juice,' Alfonsa said. 'The bottle was empty in the morning. It was on the table.'

'Maria left the bottle there?'

'Yes,' Alfonsa said. 'Maria decided she would only do what Chemmen Saab told her. Why should she do extra work, and then be insulted?'

We nodded sympathetically for a few seconds before my mother stopped grating the parmesan cheese to ask the big question. 'Why does Maria think the juice killed Baman Marker? It sounds like it could have been anything.'

'The police took away the glass,' Alfonsa explained. 'They also took away the steel bottle. And they also checked the glass table. Then they called Almeida Madam upstairs and they asked her many, many questions.'

My mum sighed, 'Poor Lina Almeida. I detest the woman, but this is awful luck. She was trying to do a good turn and look what happened. She must be feeling miserable.'

'No, no,' Alfonsa snorted. 'Almeida Madam is not feeling sad. She screamed and shouted and called Maria a liar. She said that she didn't send the green juice. She said that Maria must have made the juice. Poor Maria cried and prayed to God. And then God listened to Maria's prayer.'

'How?' we chorused. 'What happened?'

Alfonsa was the queen of the cliffhanger. She paused for maximum effect before announcing, 'Then the police found the note.'

'What note? What note?'

'The note that came with the juice bottle. It was a small yellow piece of paper. It had Lina Almeida's name on it. God listened to Maria's prayer.'

There was silence in the kitchen while we absorbed this last bit of information. 'Wait,' I said finally. 'Let me understand properly. Somebody brought a metal bottle filled with juice and gave it to Baman Marker? But Maria must know who brought the bottle of juice.'

'No,' Alfonsa said triumphantly. 'Nobody knows. The bottle was left outside the house. That is what Chemmen Saab told Maria.'

'Okay,' my mother said, trying to piece the elements together. 'A metal bottle filled with juice was left outside Baman Marker's house. It came along with a note that had Lina Almeida's name on it. Baman Marker thought that Lina Almeida had sent him Green Glow Detox Juice. He called Maria and asked her to pour it into a glass. Then later he became sick. The police think that he became sick because of the juice. Then Lina Almeida said that she had not sent the juice in the first place. Is that right?'

'Yes,' Alfonsa said. 'Then God heard Maria's prayers and the police found the yellow note with Almeida Madam's name on it.'

'If Lina Almeida had not sent the juice, how was the note there?' my mother asked.

'Must be forged,' Ved suggested. 'Somebody else could have written it and signed her name.'

'No,' Alfonsa interjected. 'The police showed the note to Almeida Madam. She said she had never seen the bottle in her life. But she said that the note paper belonged to her. Her name was printed on it and everything. And the writing on the note was her writing. But she didn't know when she had written it.'

'I don't understand. Did she write the note?' I asked, giddy with confusion.

'Yes,' Alfonsa said. 'But she said she must have written it a long time ago. Maybe she had written it in school. She did not know more.'

Once again, we contemplated this twist in perplexed silence. 'I don't understand,' I said again. 'How would a random person get hold of a note that Lina Almeida had written? And if Lina Almeida did not send the juice, who did?'

'The killer obviously,' Ved said. 'The whole world knows that Lina Almeida sent smoothies to Baman Marker. Then Lina Almeida posts the recipe for Green Glow on the building chat and gives someone an idea. The killer uses the recipe to make the smoothie and then leaves it outside the door. With an original Lina Almeida note.'

'Except that the killer tweaks the recipe a little,' I said. 'And adds a slug of poison.'

I've told you before that I'm not a fearful, queasy person. But on that Tuesday in May, I was spooked. Rattled by the way in which death had slipped into our world as quietly as a mouse. The way it scuttled in and out of our lives—elusive but real.

13

On the fiftieth day of the lockdown, I turned detective. This is how it happened.

Wednesday started early. At least early by teenagers-during-lockdown standards.

Shanaya called a few minutes after 9 a.m., yanking me out of a dense sleep and frightening me half to death. Through the lockdown, Shanaya had slept till 11 a.m. at the very least, after which she had to be cajoled out of bed. She needed plenty of hot liquids and chocolate before she was prepared to walk, talk and generally function.

Only something huge would induce her to call me at 9.03 a.m. 'Shanaya, what?' I said in a panicky-groggy voice. 'What happened? Are you fine?'

The minute I heard her hoarse whisper, I knew that she was not fine. 'They're here again. Searching our house. And our car. And…I am really scared. Nandini, you need to tell them what you saw that night. About my mom being in the balcony while we were watching the movie.'

Shanaya's voice was faint and echoey, as if she was sitting in a coffin. This alarmed me as much as what she was saying. 'Shanaya,' I asked. 'Where are you? Why are you sounding so odd? What are the police saying? What do they think?'

'They keep asking my mom what she was doing between 9 and 11 that night,' Shanaya whispered. 'I told them everything. That I had made tomato soup for dinner and the mixer exploded. That my mom said that she and Shantabai would not help me. That I had to clean the kitchen myself. Then my mom was mad because everything got late. You know she likes to have dinner at around 8 o'clock because of her diet. But we started dinner just before 9 o'clock, I think.'

'And after that?'

'After dinner, my mom and Shantabai cleared up. It took ages because the kitchen was still messy. The tomato soup had splashed onto the recipe books and the fruit basket. Then Shantabai went to her room. But after that my mom says she doesn't know what she was doing. She says she has no clue. And the police are just refusing to believe her.'

'I'm pretty sure she was in the balcony for a long time,' I interrupted. 'I'm pretty sure she was there the whole time till my mum called her. And then they talked forever. They were still talking when I went to bed, ages after midnight.'

Shanaya was silent and I heard a thumping sound in the background. 'Where are you speaking from?' I asked. 'It almost sounds like you're underground.'

'That's not important,' Shanaya snapped. 'I called because I need you to do something. Are you properly awake?'

'Listen. Let me brush my teeth,' I said, trotting towards the bathroom. 'I'll call you back.'

'Better not,' Shanaya replied. 'I'll call you later. But I want you to google something. Will you remember? I want you to google Ethylene Glycol. Okay?'

'Ummm...what?'

'Ethylene Glycol. Write it down somewhere. You will never remember otherwise.'

'Okay,' I said, locating a pen and grabbing the red, plastic-covered copy of *Crooked House* that I'd checked out from Metsons Library a few days before lockdown. Turning to the last page, I scribbled the words 'Ethylene Glycol'. 'Okay. Got it. I'll do it right away and call you.'

'No,' Shanaya said firmly. 'Don't call. I'll call. This is not urgent. Do it whenever.'

Shanaya disconnected the phone, leaving me confused and dopey. I put the red paperback on top of my computer and wondered if I should go back to bed. But I was distressed by the thought of strange men pawing through Amrita Aunty's shoes, peering into the fridge and messing with Shanaya's dried leaf and seeds collection.

Finally, I brushed my teeth, washed my face and scooped my slippery, straight hair into a ponytail. To get away from the ugly thoughts, I hurried to the living room where my parents were eating toast and re-enacting a familiar squabble. 'Amrita's very well-connected,' my father was saying. 'She knows all the top people in Mumbai. They are there to support her. I really don't see why you're getting so involved. You get too, too influenced by her.'

'She's my friend.'

'A friend who doesn't always behave as she should.'

'Why? Because she likes the occasional drink? Because she doesn't act like her life is over just because her marriage is over? You have double standards. That husband has gone and married again, had children, done what he wanted and that's totally fine. But Amrita—'

'Priti, we really don't know what happened. Either in that marriage or on the night that Baman Marker was killed. Amrita is capable of—'

'Say it. Say it. Capable of what?' my mother challenged as she stalked off to the kitchen. She returned with two mugs of tea and banged them on the dining table. 'She's one of my best friends. Kavita Lamba and Lina Almeida are, are...vindictive witches. They are deliberately pointing the police towards Amrita. They are trying to implicate her in a murder that she did NOT commit. For me, the interesting question is why? Whom are they trying to protect?'

My father took a sip of tea and made a face. 'Cold,' he complained. 'For the record, I think that Amrita is more than capable of murder. And it really makes no sense that Lina Almeida and Kavita Lamba would try to influence the police.'

My mother snorted and looked quite capable of murder herself. 'If the police land up to talk to us, please keep your bloody views to yourself,' she hissed. 'And just look at the facts. Lina Almeida routinely sends her juices and smoothies to Baman Marker. Then one fine morning, she decides to post her recipe for Green Glow Detox Smoothie on the building chat. That same evening, a bottle-full of smoothie lands up outside Baman Marker's house. Along with it is a note—a genuine note, mind you—from Lina Almeida. To me at least, Lina Almeida looks like the chief suspect. So why are they harassing Amrita?'

What she said made perfect sense, but my father remained unconvinced. He got up from the breakfast table, shaking his head. 'The police don't owe you an explanation, Priti. I'm sure they're searching other houses and other cars as well. Though why they're obsessed with cars in the middle of a lockdown, I have no idea. Anyway, I have an important meeting now. Don't disturb me.'

My mother didn't deign to answer. She turned to me and remarked, 'You're up early!'

'Shanaya called. The police are searching their place.'

'I know,' my mother sighed, passing the Chocos and muesli to me. 'Amrita called me.'

I poured muesli into a bowl, splashed some milk on it, and said, 'Amrita Aunty could not have killed Baman Marker. I remember Friday night clearly. Shanaya and I were watching *Mean Girls*. We started around 10 o'clock and I distinctly remember seeing Amrita Aunty in the balcony. She seemed upset. She was standing there for ages without moving. Then Shanaya asked if you could call and talk to Amrita Aunty. Remember?'

My mother looked up with interest. 'It was *that* evening?'

'Yes.'

'Are you sure?'

'Yes. Shanaya and I were chatting over WhatsApp the whole time during the movie. The entire conversation is on my phone. And I actually saw a pair of legs climbing up to the fifth floor a little after 10 o'clock.'

'Why didn't you tell me all this before?' my mother demanded.

'Tell you what?' I asked. 'That someone climbed the stairs of Daisy Apartments? I mean, I hardly knew that Baman Marker was being murdered at the same time. I only started figuring it out yesterday and there's no way we can be sure that the legs belonged to the killer…'

'What exactly did you see? This could be really important. Tell me slowly. In detail.'

My mother looked so serious that I was seized by foreboding. Between spoons of muesli, I told her what I could remember about Friday night. I told her about the person in black pants who had climbed the staircase to the fifth floor. About the pink/orange/red object that the person had placed on the step. About the doorbell that had pierced the silent night. And, finally, about the legs in white salwar/pajamas/palazzos that had dashed down from the fourth to the third floor and then vanished.

I was finishing up when Ved entered the living room, collapsed onto a chair and popped two slices of bread in the toaster. 'What's the deal?' he asked. 'Alfonsa woke me up by screeching in my ear. She's all excited because the police are in the Burman's balcony, looking for something.'

'The Burmans?' my mother and I yelped. 'That's a relief.'

Ved yawned, stretched, and took a grateful sip of tea from his 'No Drums, No Band' mug. Then he tuned in to what we were saying. 'Why are you thrilled that the police are harassing the Burmans? Have the Burmans done something to us? I didn't know they were the enemy.'

'No, no. It's not personal,' my mother said. 'We're just relieved that Amrita is not the only suspect. This probably means that the police are searching every single flat in Daisy Apartments and that we're overreacting.'

Ved gaped at us. 'Wait. What? Amrita Aunty is a suspect? For the Baman Marker murder? How come nobody tells me anything? Why would the police suspect Amrita Aunty? I don't get it.'

I didn't get it either, but I told Ved what Shanaya had told me. Then I ended up telling him about Friday night—not that I expected him to help untangle the knots. My twin is not that smart at the best of times, and this was not the best of times.

Sometimes, though, it's the obvious questions that cut through the clutter and lead to the obvious answers. I guess this was one of them.

Ved is a master at the art of the obvious. He crunched loudly on his toast before doing his thing. 'So 9 p.m. to 11 p.m. is the important period?' he asked. 'Basically, that's when the killer delivered the smoothie to the fifth floor?'

'I guess,' I said. 'Maria says she poured the juice at 11 p.m., so the juice had to have been placed outside the door before then. And the police have been asking Amrita Aunty what she was doing between 9 p.m. and 11 p.m. So that seems to be the critical time.'

'Why 9 p.m.? What happened at 9 p.m.?'

'No clue.'

Ved drummed on the table with the butter knife. 'So what are you saying? That the black legs could have belonged to the killer?' he asked. 'The doorbell and the white legs were later, right? So they're irrelevant.'

'Probably,' I agreed. 'But the black legs could have belonged to anyone in Daisy Apartments, right?' Ved continued, 'There was nothing about them to say that they belonged to a man or a woman. Or to someone on the first floor or the fourth floor?'

'It could have been anyone. But—' I stopped short.

'But what?' my mother asked. 'But what? Have you remembered something else?'

'The thing is,' I said, 'I saw the legs climbing from the second floor to the fifth floor. The legs could have started from the ground floor. Or the first floor. Or from the second floor. But it's highly unlikely that they belonged to anyone living on the third or fourth floor.'

'But why?' Ved asked. 'It could be absolutely anyone in Daisy Apartments.'

'Not really,' I replied slowly. 'Just imagine, if you wanted to deliver a poisoned drink to your victim on the fifth floor, what would you do? You would go there as quickly and quietly as possible, leave the juice and rush back to your own apartment, right?'

I stopped. Both my mother and Ved nodded their agreement.

'But suppose the Burmans were the killers. They live on the fourth floor. Why would they climb all the way down to the second floor and then turn around and climb up to the fifth floor?'

'It wouldn't make sense,' Ved agreed. 'So what does it mean? If Black Legs was the killer, then the killer lives on the ground, first or second floor?'

'Ground, first or second,' my mother echoed as she pulled herself up from her chair and checked the clock. 'Oh God! It's already 10.30 and I haven't started cooking yet. I just can't function. This murder business is too upsetting.'

She moved towards the kitchen, but paused when Ved asked, 'So that means who? Mr Shetty and the Habibullahs from the ground floor, Lina Almeida from the first floor. The Lambas and Amrita Aunty from the second floor?'

'I guess,' I said in a shaky voice. The killer of my imagination was a monstrous being, cloaked in evil. It frightened me that the hood might fall away to reveal a familiar face.

Ved, though, lacked imagination. He continued drumming on the table and mulling over the matter. 'Then it could be Amrita Aunty, right?' he asked.

'Noooo,' my mother and I protested.

'Why?' Ved asked.

My mother and I tried to explain that Amrita Aunty could never be a killer. But Ved dismissed our objections. 'I'm not talking about whether she killed him or not,' he said. 'I'm just saying that if the person that Nandini saw was the killer, then Amrita Aunty is on the list of suspects.'

'Actually, she's probably the only person in Daisy Apartments with an alibi,' I protested. 'Shanaya cooked dinner and managed to explode the mixer while making tomato soup. There was a major mess and it was around 9 p.m. when they got down to dinner. Then Amrita Aunty and Shantabai cleaned the kitchen again, which took loads of time.'

'Oh, yes,' my mother said. 'Amrita was livid. Even the fan was splattered with tomato.'

'After that, Amrita Aunty was in the balcony for ages and then she and Amma talked on the phone for hours,' I said.

Ved, though, was not impressed. 'You can't be sure,' he said.

'Sure about what?'

'Sure that Amrita Aunty came straight from cleaning the kitchen to the balcony. You can't be sure that she was in the balcony all the time. It would take her less than five minutes to run up to the fifth floor, put down the bottle, and run down again.'

'Well, she definitely could not have been Black Legs,' I retorted. 'She was definitely in the balcony while those legs were climbing up.'

'How can you be certain?' Ved asked again. 'You were watching a movie. You were chatting with Shanaya. Then you noticed some black legs climbing. And you also managed to keep tabs on Amrita Aunty at the same time? It sounds a bit…'

Put like that, it did sound far-fetched, but I had an ace up my sleeve. 'Amrita Aunty was definitely not Black Legs,' I insisted. 'She was wearing her grey dress. The short expensive one with the big, puffy sleeves.'

'So?'

'So she was wearing a dress. She was not wearing black pants.'

'Maybe she was wearing black pants with the grey dress?' Ved suggested, but his voice lacked conviction. You could believe many things about Amrita Aunty. You could believe that she would bludgeon a man to death with a metal sculpture or stir poison into his detox smoothie. But you could never, ever believe that she would commit a fashion faux pas. You could never imagine that she would pair her designer grey dress with black pants—not even if she was in the middle of a deadly crime.

Shaking her head, my mother picked up her phone and started checking her messages. Ved slouched away to his bedroom, his drums and his not-music. I was trailing behind him when my mother stopped me. 'One minute, Nandini,' she mumbled. 'I was wondering, has Shanaya said anything to you?'

'About?'

'Ummm…you know…about why the police are focusing so much on Amrita?'

'No,' I said surprised. 'Is there even a reason? I thought that it was Kavita Lamba and Lina Almeida being witches. Why? What reason could Amrita Aunty have—I mean other than the fact that she hated him—to kill Baman Marker?'

'No reason,' my mum mumbled again, careful to keep her eyes on a wooden Ganpati.

My mum is not a mumbler or an eye-averter. Her shiftiness was as disturbing as Shanaya's early morning phone call. For the first time I wondered if Amrita Aunty was in serious trouble. Did the police have a genuine reason to suspect her?

And what if Amrita Aunty was taken away? What if Shanaya was banished to the Italian-marble-lined apartment on Altamount Road where her father lived? How would she survive?

As importantly, how would I?

The possibility filled me with liquid despair. I had friends at school, of course. But the space they occupied in my life was the size of a chia seed. The gaping hole that Shanaya would leave behind was unimaginable, unfillable, unbearable.

It could not happen. It would not happen.

I knew that Amrita Aunty was innocent. Now all I had to do was to convince the police. But how? The answer came to me on a deafening drum roll. There was only one way to make the police believe me. I had to find the real killer. Once I figured that bit out, I felt much calmer.

14

I wished Shanaya would call so that we could get down to some hardcore detective work. But the phone remained stubbornly silent and my brain remained sluggish and uncooperative. Finally, in an attempt to make time inch along—I started cleaning my room. Again.

I picked up about 200 tiktik clips, scrunchies and dismembered bits of jewellery from the floor. Some I tossed into the bin, some I sorted into pretty cardboard boxes. The clips went into a pink cardboard box that had once held lotions with names like Cactus and Cucumber. The rubber bands and scrunchies went into a blue box that had held carved soaps from Thailand. My anklets went into a red-checked tin that had once held buttery shortbread biscuits from Scotland.

Most of these boxes were from Amrita Aunty, who went on regular trips with her gym gang and her school gang. Shanaya stayed with us when her mother was away, and Amrita Aunty always brought along heaps of indulgent gifts nestling in beribboned boxes. 'Just to say thank you for your love and hospitality,' she would write on the card.

Thinking about kind, generous Amrita Aunty, I was overcome with tearful helplessness. Why was I wasting my time clearing the mess in my bedroom? It was much more important to tackle the mess surrounding the murder of the Hon Chairperson.

'I have to do something,' I fretted, as I headed to my desk and my laptop. Which was when I spotted the red copy of *Crooked House* and remembered that I had unfinished business at hand.

Scolding myself for having forgotten Shanaya's request, I switched on my computer. Then I gazed out of the window while the MacBook Air flashed to life. The compound was blanketed with the sort of summer heat that brings along mangoes, prickly heat and a spike in AC sales. In his balcony, Neville Khambata was striding around in a skimpy pair of blue-checked shorts. Nothing else.

The heartthrob of Daisy Apartments was talking on his phone with a wide, white smile, and I tried to catch his words. I was not the only eavesdropper at large. Kysha was in her balcony, her body angled and alert, and her expression savage.

Thea, too, was at her bedroom window. I wondered if she was eavesdropping on Neville Khambata but it was difficult to tell. She was leaning on the sill staring fixedly across the compound at Lily Apartments.

Unaware that he had as many listeners as 94.3 FM, Neville guffawed into his phone. 'Love you,' he exclaimed. 'No, no…all that is only to pass the time…only you…I promise, only you.'

The words were clear and sharp in that empty, sun-dazzled morning. I heard them across the compound. I'm not sure about Thea, but Kysha heard them as well. Before my eyes, her smooth face twisted and her mouth contorted. She looked like a feral cat, about to scratch. A feral cat with deadly nails.

Shanaya would have pooh-poohed at my observations. But then Shanaya belonged to that vast majority that looked at Kysha and saw an attractive face, fashionable clothes and cool-girl aura. I belonged to that tiny minority that looked at Kysha and, like an x-ray machine, went right past skin, bone and smile. Beyond the polished purple façade and glittering silver shoes to a heart that was cold, hard, manipulative.

It was lucky for Neville Khambata's girlfriend that Kysha was stuck in a sealed building. It was not so lucky for Neville Khambata that he was stuck in the very same sealed building.

So far, however, Neville Khambata was oblivious to what he'd set in motion. He strolled back into his living room, which didn't seem to help Kysha's mood. She paced up and down her balcony before flinging herself on a wooden chair, grabbing her phone and stabbing at it with a vengeful finger.

Kysha's anger was a hot, dangerous force, and I ducked away from the window, unwilling to stand in its path. I was tempted to call Shanaya but she had policemen crawling all over her home, so I turned to my laptop and did what I should have done ages ago.

I plugged 'Ethylene Glycol' into Google and waited.

I really didn't know what I was looking for. Google seemed to know even less. It took me to a website which informed me that Ethylene Glycol was 'the simplest member of the glycol family of organic compounds' and that it was 'commonly used as an antifreeze in automobiles'.

Yawn. Yawn.

I had thought that nothing could make today drabber and then Ethylene Glycol had tootled along and proved me wrong. My eyes glazed as I scrolled past line after line of pointless information—gas compressors...polyester fibres...packaging film...And then suddenly, mid-yawn, I spotted words that made me sit up. Ramrod straight.

Ethylene Glycol Poisoning.

By the time Shanaya called two hours later, I knew exactly how Baman Marker had died. And that Ethylene Glycol had played a big role in the Friday-night horrors.

First, Ethylene Glycol was a colourless, odourless, sweetish chemical, easily masked by the flavours of fruits and vegetables. (Green Glow Detox Smoothie was the perfect camouflage.)

Second, in the early stages of Ethylene Glycol poisoning, victims behaved as if they had consumed too much alcohol. As if they were drunk, in short. Which was exactly how Baman Marker had acted with Maria. (After this stage came nausea, convulsions, a stupor and then—if the poison went undetected and untreated—a general collapse of body organs. This fit with what had happened to our Hon Chairperson. I actually felt sorry for him when I read about the cardiac failure and respiratory distress. It sounded like a grim way to go.)

Third, Ethylene Glycol worked as a poison only in certain circumstances—and those circumstance had been in place on Friday night. The murderer was either very intelligent or very lucky. (Think about it. If it had been a regular evening at the Marker household, Binaifer would have noticed that something was wrong. But Binaifer was away and Maria had taken herself off to bed. Baman Marker had decided that his discomfort was because of too much sun and work.

So, instead of raising the alarm, he'd locked the bedroom door and gone to bed.)

Fourth, it was easy to get hold of Ethylene Glycol even in the middle of a lockdown. Ethylene Glycol is the main ingredient in many car coolants. The coolant is the liquid that you put into your car to make sure it doesn't overheat. Look in your storeroom or your car boot and you will probably find a dusty, forgotten plastic bottle sloshing with the stuff. (The fact that Ethylene Glycol was not some esoteric, difficult-to-find poison complicated matters. Almost anybody in Daisy Apartments who had access to a blender, a metal bottle, a bunch of green vegetables and a cupful of coolant could be the killer. Which was pretty much everyone.)

Fifth, it explained why the police were not stuck on Mrs Kurien's mystery man as the killer. If the murder weapon had been a gun or a knife, the intruder would have been the chief suspect. But this culinary weapon pointed towards an insider.

The question was, which insider?

To commit this crime you didn't need to be particularly brave or particularly strong. You didn't need to possess extensive knowledge of arcane poisons. In fact, Ethylene Glycol was such an easy and obliging murder weapon, it was amazing it wasn't used more frequently.

Or maybe it was. I don't know. Just putting it out there.

15

The police searched four flats in Daisy Apartments on that humid Wednesday.

One team took apart Amrita Aunty's tasteful, art-filled home on the second floor. Another went at the Burman's hi-tech flat on the fourth floor.

Later on in the day, the policemen walked down to the peeling, faded apartment belonging to the Habibullahs. Then, in the evening, they shocked everyone by swarming into the bare, medicine-infused home of Mr Alimchandani on the fourth floor.

Like the rest of Lily Apartments, I spent a chunk of the day gawking at Daisy Apartments. It was a waste of time. However intently I gazed, Daisy Apartments continued to look like just another square, squat, mustard Mumbai building. There was nothing new to see besides a pair of black pants draped on the clothes rack of Mr Alimchandani's balcony. And a wide, round basket that had materialized in the Khambatas' balcony.

What else? I spotted a couple of policemen through Shanaya's bedroom window. In the Carvalho apartment on the third floor, Florry/Florine/Flouride scrubbed and dusted. She spotted a white raincoat thing hanging from the hook and snatched it with brisk movements, rolled it into a tight bundle and tucked it under her arm. Then she took a long time adjusting the two battered wooden chairs so they sat at an angle of precisely 60 degrees while I watched with whole-hearted respect.

I was trying to concentrate on *The Shining* when Shanaya finally, finally called. She said that the police had left some time back. That everything was where it shouldn't be. That Amrita Aunty was having a meltdown and insisting that every metal sculpture and green bean be put back in its place in the next thirty seconds.

'The house is in a mess, but the police weren't too bad,' Shanaya said in a rough, tired voice. 'Whatever they were looking for, it was something biggish. I thought that they would go through my underwear and slash the mattresses and things, like on TV. But they were more interested in the bathroom and the kitchen and the fridge. And in my school stuff. They went through my schoolbag and pencil box twice, which was so weird. I can't even imagine what they wanted.'

I was about to agree that it was bizarre, when I realized that maybe it wasn't. 'Do you have any notes from Lina Almeida with you?' I asked abruptly. 'You know the ones you were telling me about? The little yellow ones with her name printed on them?'

'Blank notes with Lina Almeida's name printed on them? Of course not,' Shanaya replied. 'Listen, I can't talk for long. My mom's in a state. I'll call you after she's calmed down.'

'Shanaya, wait,' I said urgently. 'I'm not talking about blank notes. You said that Lina Almeida kept writing notes to kids in school. Could you have any of those lying around?'

I was hoping that Shanaya would answer with a resounding 'No way. I tossed each and every chit in the bin at school.' Instead, she hesitated. 'No…yes…I don't know,' she said. 'Why? I used to get so many notes from her, there could be a couple lying around. In my school bag or mixed with last year's books. Or under my bed. Or anywhere. I even use them as bookmarks sometimes. Why?'

I took a deep, dismayed breath and started explaining. 'You know, right, that a small yellow note was found in Baman Marker's house? It was delivered along with the smoothie. The note was from Lina Almeida. On her printed yellow paper and in her handwriting.'

'But that means that Lina—'

'No, it does not mean,' I huffed. 'Lina Almeida is the most obvious suspect. But somehow she's managed to convince the bloody police that she's as pure as ghee. She admitted that it was her notepaper and her handwriting, but she says it must be an old note. Something she wrote ages ago. So the police are probably checking if anyone has her notes lying around.'

'Well, I certainly don't have a note from the Tormentor and Guide that reads, "Dearest Baman, do drink this healthy green smoothie. Take care. Lina Almeida",' Shanaya said after a pause, through which I could hear Amrita Aunty screaming and heavy objects thumping and clattering.

'I don't know exactly what that note said.'

'Even if they found a couple of notes in my school bag, that's hardly a big deal. Half the world has notes from Lina Almeida. That's what she does at school. All day. Every day. Any kid who's put a toe in All Saints School will have collected a fat stack. Thea, Jeh Khambata, Kysha…'

'Jeh Khambata?' I said. 'Wait a minute. I didn't know that Jeh studied in All Saints School. How come not Neville?'

'Apparently by the time Neville was old enough to go to school, the Khambatas had lost faith in regular schools,' Shanaya said, erupting into a sudden chortle and I realized that I hadn't heard her laugh in a long time. Ever since the police had driven into the Lily-Daisy Apartments compound, the colour and energy seemed to have drained out of her. I really missed the old Shanaya.

'The Khambatas decided that they wanted something more connected with the universal soul,' Shanaya was still explaining. 'A school that encourages you to get your hands dirty. You know what I mean.'

Her rude laughter warmed me, but the feeling of wellbeing was short-lived. There was something I needed to know urgently. 'Listen, Shanaya,' I said. 'Do you have a can of coolant in your house?'

'What?' Shanaya asked, sounding suddenly hassled. Again, I could hear Amrita Aunty saying something in the background.

'Coolant,' I repeated. 'Remember you asked me to google Ethylene Glycol?'

'Oh yeah,' Shanaya said. 'That thing. I asked you to look it up because Dr Mirchandani told my mom that Baman Marker's death could be a case of Ethylene Glycol poisoning. Did you find it on Google? What is it even? You think the police were looking for bottles of this Ethylene Glycol stuff in our house? We definitely don't have bottles of poison lying around so they must be pretty disappointed.'

'Are you sure?' I demanded. I had to know before Shanaya hung up. 'Ethylene Glycol is not an obvious sort of poison. It's the stuff that's used to make coolants. You know, the liquid you put into a car to keep the engines from getting too hot? The stuff that comes in big plastic cans?'

'Murlidhar handles all of that for us,' Shanaya replied. 'But you mean this coolant thing can actually kill?'

'Apparently,' I said. 'It tastes sweet, so can easily be mixed into drinks. And if the quantity is largish and if it isn't detected in time, it can do all kinds of horrible things to the body. And ends up killing the person.'

Shanaya was silent while I showered her with Ethylene Glycol trivia. 'This woman in the US killed not one, but two husbands with Ethylene Glycol,' I said. 'There's even a movie about her. But do you know if they found coolant in your house?'

'They took a few things away,' Shanaya snapped. 'But Nandini, I don't know what this stuff even looks like. I'm not Neville or Jeh Khambata. And anyway, my mom is banging drawers, slamming cupboards and generally being totally OCD. I have to go.'

'Call me when you have time.'

'Yes, yes, I—'

Shanaya disconnected mid-sentence, and I didn't blame her. The thought of Amrita Aunty in a drawer-slamming mood was scary. Still, I wished that we could have finished our conversation. I hadn't had a chance to tell Shanaya about my big decision of the morning—that, one way or another, I was going to solve this murder.

'Call as soon as you can,' I messaged. 'Urgent.'

Then twenty minutes later, I messaged again. 'Triple urgent.'

Shanaya, though, was too busy putting sauce bottles and paperback novels in their appointed places to check her phone. So now, what?

I was restless. Too restless to binge on Instagram even. Which, as you will agree, is another level of restless. I walked around my room, but there's only so much energy you can shed by striding around an XXS Mumbai bedroom that's strewn with single socks and ratty pajamas. After four minutes of this, I went to check on Ved. He was on a Zoom call with his bandmates, so I drifted into our balcony and looked down. Absentmindedly at first, but then with quickening interest.

Staring at the two garages, I remembered Shanaya's throw-away remark about Jeh and Neville Khambata. And I began to wonder.

No, no. I didn't wonder whether Jeh and Neville Khambata were the killers. They may have been experts on coolants, but they also loved animals, were into vermiculture and tended to a herb garden. Say what you will, composting and murdering simply don't go hand in hand.

What I did wonder about were the ingredients that had gone into the murder of the Hon Chairperson of the Lily-Daisy Cooperative Housing Society. And about which residents would have access to these ingredients. Hurrying to my room, I sat at my computer and created a Google Doc which I called—well okay, this is a bit embarrassing—'Little Grey Cells'.

I shared the document with Shanaya and started to type at a feverish pace:

1. Who would have had
   Access to Coolant?
   Access to note written by Lina Almeida on yellow paper?
2. Who could be Black Legs?

3. Who has motive?

4. Who threatened Baman Marker recently?

After this, I made a list of all the possible suspects, starting with Mr Shetty on the ground floor and ending with Maria on the fifth floor. To this I added the nameless trespasser who had faded into the dawn on Saturday morning.

This was the easy bit. The tedious part came next. I was hard at work when Ved slouched in and flopped on my bed.

Ved is not usually welcome in my room. Over the last year he has used my red wedge heels from Zara (Rs 3,290), my shiny purple pen from London (4 pounds) and my silver bangle from Colaba Bazaar (Rs 2,300) to experiment with new beats and rhythms. I'm still upset about the silver bangle, which now has an amoeba-like air about it.

It was a sign of how topsy-turvy the world had become that I didn't shoo my pesky twin away. I actually pulled up a chair so that he could read the Google Doc. By the time Ved was done I was jiggling with impatience. 'Whatdyouthink? Whatdyouthink?' I asked, after he'd gone through the document. 'Do any names pop out at you? Who are your top three suspects?'

'I don't know,' Ved said.

'There's nothing to know,' I countered. 'Just say from the top of your head.'

Ved nodded. 'Okay,' he said. 'I guess my top three are Mr Burman. Amrita Aunty. And if Mr Carvalho is back in Daisy Apartments, then him as well.'

'Are you serious?' I scowled. Ved's answer upset me because it confirmed my worst fears. The two people I really wanted to protect were the two people who looked guilty.

'You don't agree?' Ved asked. 'Then who are your top suspects?'

'Lina Almeida,' I declared. 'Everything, everything points towards her. And she's not even on your list?'

Ved tilted the chair so far back that he almost fell. 'Everything points to her except motive,' he said. 'She's the only person in all of Lily Apartments and Daisy Apartments who truly adored Dear Baman. Why would she kill him? And that too, in a way that points a finger directly at herself? She's not that stupid.'

Ved had a point, but I was too pig-headed to admit it. 'It may be a sort of smoke screen,' I sniffed. 'Exactly to make people feel the way you do. In a way it's the perfect crime. Actually genius if you think about it.'

Even I knew I'd gone too far. Ved, who had tilted his chair again, burst into such explosive laughter that he fell backwards and banged his head on the floor. 'Owww, bloody owww,' he spluttered, still laughing. 'Nandini, I know you love books with twists and shocks. But even you can't imagine that Lina Almeida, with her silk saris and her God-loves-me-best aura, is a criminal mastermind. It's a bit much.'

'But…' I started.

'There has to be a reason for a Mentor and Guide to kill someone,' Ved insisted. 'Hey, by the way, you forgot to add mixer.'

'What?' I asked.

'The killer would need access to a mixer. To make the Green Glow Detox Smoothie.'

'I bet every kitchen in Daisy Apartments has a mixer!'

'The Habibullahs don't. At least they haven't for the past twenty days. Theirs has conked out. Don't you remember?

For some reason Amrita Aunty decided that I was the right person to fix it and I was sent across with a screwdriver. I'm hardly an expert, but even I could see that it was totally dead.'

'Like Baman Marker.' The thought popped into my head, but I bit it back—one must not be flippant about the dead and all that.

'Listen, share the doc with me too,' Ved said as he stood up. 'Let me see if I can think of anything.'

'You know how to think? I'm impressed.'

Ved was taking his revenge by drumming on my head with his phone when my mother hurtled into the room. 'Stop it both of you,' she said automatically and charged to the window. 'I think the police have wrapped up for the day. Amrita is planning to contact her school friend, whose sister is a top lawyer. And Sheela Jagtiani is going to complain as well. She's absolutely livid. I simply cannot understand why they would search poor Mr Alimchandani's house. He's too weak to leave his bed. What were the police thinking?'

Ved started telling us about a film he'd watched, in which a wheelchair-bound man starts exercising and doing weights and secretly learns to walk again. He then commits a murder but escapes suspicion because everyone thinks he's still paralyzed.

I approved of the twist. My mother did not. 'Are you hinting that Mr Alimchandani is pretending to be old and weak and bedridden?' she asked coldly. 'This is not a game, you know. Terrible things are happening. Somebody has died, and more lives are being destroyed.'

My mother walked away from the window and sat on my bed. For the first time since lockdown had begun and Rakhi had stopped coming in to sweep, dust and tidy the house, my mother didn't criticize the state of my room. I would have liked to think this was because I had done such a brilliant job, but it was probably because she was so agitated.

We soon found out why.

The police had spent almost four hours searching Shanaya's house. They'd checked the fridge, the bathroom cupboards, the bookshelves. They'd looked under the beds, in pencil boxes and in waste paper baskets.

The police had spent seventy minutes in the Habibullah apartment. They'd begun their search in the kitchen and were sceptical when Rashida Habibullah told them that her mixer grinder had stopped working weeks ago. Once the neighbours backed her story, the three policemen lost heart and searched the rest of the house in a perfunctory manner.

They spent even less time in Mr Alimchandani's apartment. This was partly because Mr Alimchandani was so clearly unwell, and partly because Sheela Jagtiani threatened legal action from her window across the compound.

The police spent two hours in the Burman flat, after which Mr Burman insisted that they leave. He had called his lawyer, who made some calls of his own and the policemen quickly retreated.

None of us said it, of course, but more and more it was looking as if Amrita Aunty was the chief suspect.

16

On Wednesday night, Kavita Lamba sent a message on the Lily-Daisy Apartments chat. 'The police will be visiting the residents of Lily Apartments over the next two days. They want to know if you noticed anything unusual on Friday night. Please cooperate.'

My mum read out the message in a neutral voice at dinner, between carrying batches of chilly-cheese toasts and cinnamon toasts onto the table. But the minute my father left the room, she got into whirling-dervish mode.

'We have to convince the police that it could not have been Amrita,' she said, speaking fast, stalking around the living room, straightening chairs, rearranging the metal boxes, turning off lamps and plumping cushions. 'Tell them about those black legs. And about the doorbell and the white legs. And the thumps and bumps that Shanaya heard in the Carvalho house. The more I think about it, the more I'm wondering about that Mr Carvalho.'

I didn't like the direction this was taking. 'But,' I said, 'how can we randomly point the police towards someone else? Just like that?'

'We aren't pointing the police towards Mr Carvalho,' my mother countered. 'We don't even know if the man's back in Daisy Apartments. We're just showing the police that there was a lot going on that night. We're just telling them that there were people walking up and down the staircase and ringing doorbells. We are just telling them that they need to look beyond Amrita.'

'Okay,' I said. 'But will they even believe me?'

'They'll believe at least some of what you say,' Ved said, as we carried our plates and sauce bottles back to the kitchen. 'Because you have the chat with Shanaya to prove it. Good thing you didn't delete it. And pity you didn't mention Amrita Aunty being in the balcony on the chat, but still…'

I was hurrying to my room, hoping to catch Shanaya on the phone, when my mum stopped me. 'Hold on for a second,' she said. 'Nandini, I want to know exactly what you saw that night. Everything. Was there anything, any small detail, that could help us to figure out who Black Legs was? Or whether Black Legs is the killer?'

I perched on one of those bestselling chairs that my mother had fashioned out of old suitcases. Ved sprawled on the sofa, while my mother stood near a side table and clutched a clay Ganpati for luck. The lights in the room were dim and all three of us were wearing battered grey T-shirts—which was pretty much our lockdown uniform. We made a dreary picture.

'I've told you,' I said. 'They were just legs wearing black pants or jeans. First they climbed fast, then they climbed very slow. And at some point the person put down something that seemed pink or orange or reddish.'

'Are you sure about that?' Ved asked. 'You haven't mentioned that bit in your chat with Shanaya.'

'I'm sure,' I said. 'I totally remember it.'

'I wonder what it was,' my mother remarked. 'You couldn't make out at all?'

'Look,' I said, exasperated. 'I saw it across the compound, through a small window. At that point I had no idea it was important. It could have been anything. A bag. A bundle of clothes. A cushion.'

'So something lumpy?' my mother persisted. 'Something with an irregular shape?'

'I think so,' I said. 'It could have been a biggish, softish bag. What puzzled me is why the person needed to put it down.'

'Could it have been something heavy?' Ved asked.

'Maybe,' I replied. 'But if Black Legs was the killer, it must have been a bag with a metal bottle full of poisonous Green Glow Detox smoothie. Which is hardly heavy.'

'Then why did Black Legs need to put it down?' Ved asked. 'It doesn't make sense.'

I was about to reply when another thought struck me. One that made me yelp. 'Wait a minute. Wouldn't the killer have left the metal bottle outside the door in a bag? I mean, nobody would plonk down a bottle on the staircase landing just like that, without a bag. And if the killer left the metal bottle in a bag, then...'

We looked at each other with widening eyes. 'Then two people would have known what the bag looked like,' Ved said. 'One of them is dead. But the other is Maria. And if Maria knows then...'

'Then Alfonsa knows,' my mother completed his sentence as she dashed towards the kitchen.

Ved and I followed at a more dignified pace, and arrived in time to overhear my mother simper and wheedle, 'Thank you so much. Please call and ask her.'

Looking all chuffed and prima ballerina-ish, Alfonsa strutted to her little room behind the kitchen. We heard a string of Konkani punctuated by exclamations, before she sailed back into the kitchen. One look at her triumphant face and we knew that we would get the information, but we would have to work for it.

Alfonsa headed to the kitchen sink and attacked a spoon with a sponge and single-minded purpose. After thirty seconds of this my mother intervened. 'What did Maria say?' she asked. 'Was the bottle left in a bag?'

'Yes.' Scrub, scrub. Rinse, rinse.

'Does she remember what the bag looked like?'

'Yes.' Clitter clatter, wipe wipe.

'What does it look like? What colour is it?' I asked a bit too loudly.

'The police asked Maria about the bag today,' Alfonsa replied in her oblique way.

'And?'

'She gave it to them. They took it away.'

'What kind of bag was it?' Ved tried this time around.

Alfonsa ignored him and devoted her attention to a glass for three unending minutes. Then finally she relented. 'Maria had put the bag away in the drawer,' she said over her shoulder. 'With all the other plastic bags and paper bags.'

'But—'

'When the police asked for the bag Maria was worried. Because they have two or three of the same bags, but then she remembered that she had put this one right on top of the pile.'

'But—'

By this point my head was hurting. I knew exactly how those poor fellows felt in that story about the blind men in the grotty corners of the compound and gobbled her treats in a frantic, furtive manner).

What I'm trying to say is that there were always people strolling into our compound with jaunty orange bags packed with deliciousness. Maybe the only thing that the residents of Lily and Daisy Apartments—young and old—agreed upon was that Waffle Wonderland was bomb.

On last Friday night, though, the Waffle Wonderland bag was packed, not with deliciousness, but with death. I wonder if I'll ever feel the same way about my favourite shop again.

and the elephant. You know the one I mean, right? The story in which each blind man is able to feel a small part of the elephant and has no way of knowing what the whole animal looks like.

I was sick of seeing only the tail of the story. 'So what colour was the bag?' I snapped.

My mother gave me an imperceptible shake of her head. Being stuck in a sealed building with Alfonsa-in-a-sulk was worse than being stuck in a crypt with a toe-shedding ghoul. Mercifully, Alfonsa was too occupied with her revelation to notice my rudeness. She bustled to a corner cupboard, rummaged a bit, and pulled out a sturdy, familiar paper bag.

It was orange, with hot pink swirls and mauve lettering that spelt the words, 'Waffle Wonderland...packed with deliciousness'. She held it up with a flourish and announced, 'This bag.'

I took one look at it and exhaled. 'Of course.'

Waffle Wonderland is my favourite eatery in the whole, entire world. As its name suggests Waffle Wonderland sells waffles. All kinds of waffles: dark chocolate waffles and peanut butter waffles; vanilla waffles and vegan waffles. To these already magical creations, the happy customer can add any topping known to mankind—whipped cream, marshmallows, butterscotch kisses, salted caramel sauce, granola, cherry jam. Pomegranate, even mini jalebis and little til laddoos.

There's a Waffle Wonderland a ten-minute saunter away from Sassoon Dock. It was a saunter that Shanaya and I undertook often before lockdown. As did Kysha, Mini and Neville Khambata. And Thea (though she didn't saunter, sh scurried along with hunched shoulders, and then huddl

17

Shanaya, Ved and I spent Wednesday night working on 'Little Grey Cells'. We typed, we debated, we agreed and we disagreed. At around midnight we did a group call. Although we were pretty sure that Black Legs was the killer, we tried to keep an open mind.

It took a lot of digging. The three of us had never been that interested in the adults with whom we shared our compound. We had no idea, for example, that Mr Habibullah used to run a lace and buttons business before his problems began. Or that old Mr Alimchandani had been a builder. Or even that Mr Carvalho's first name was Ronald. (Ronald? Like Ronald McDonald? That my adoration for Daniel didn't wobble by half a centimetre proved that it was True Love.)

My mother supplied us with most of these tidbits. My father provided a few sketchy details about Mr Burman and his financial shenanigans. I didn't understand the nitty-gritties, but it did sound like Mr Burman had broken a lot of rules.

A quick read-through of the Lily-Daisy Apartments chat also helped us to organize our ideas. This is what the doc looked like at the end of Wednesday. (The comments in brackets are my thoughts and not a part of the document.)

LIST OF SUSPECTS—Means, Motive and Rating

1) Mr Shetty:
Around 70
Retired engineer
Never married, does social work

Means:
No car so coolant might be tricky
No access to yellow note

Motive: Upset about treatment of Raghunath—not proper motive for murder

Black Legs: lives on ground floor so possible

Suspicion quotient: 2; no motive, no means

2) Rashida and Tahir Habibullah:
Around 50
Caterer and former owner of lace shop
One son at university in North Carolina, Mr Habibullah has anxiety issues

Means:
No mixer
Have a van but not parked in compound—not sure about access to coolant
No connection with All Saints School so access to note difficult

Motive: Endless harassment and destruction of catering business by Baman Marker

Odd detail: Mr Habibullah acted as if Baman Marker was dead when neighbours went up on Saturday afternoon—could he have known something?

Black Legs: They live on ground floor so possible

Suspicion quotient: 5; motive, but no means

3) Lina Almeida
Around 65
Tormentor and Guide at All Saints School
Lives with granddaughter Kysha and retinue of helpers.

Means:
Two cars parked in compound, so access to coolant
Easiest access to yellow note

Motive: Nothing obvious

Odd detail: Lina Almeida sent Baman Marker healthy smoothies every week, so easiest for her to commit the crime

Black Legs: Lives on first floor so possible

Suspicion quotients: Separate scores because of disagreement
Nandini: 10
Shanaya: 8
Ved: 3; has means, but no apparent motive

4) Kavita and Rajesh Lamba
Around 45
Corporate jobs
Kavita Lamba is Hon Secretary of society. Daughter Thea is strange. Rajesh Lamba is even stranger, talks to no one.

Means:
Car parked in compound so access to coolant
Thea student at All Saints School so access to yellow note

Motive: Nothing obvious (though husband could be nursing secret hatred—he looks the sort)

Black Legs: Live on second floor so possible

Suspicion quotient: 4; means, but no obvious motive

5) Amrita Kapadia
42
Runs online art gallery
Divorced. Lives with daughter Shanaya.

Means:
Shanaya student at All Saints School so access to yellow note
Car parked in compound so access to coolant

Motive: Frequent disagreement with Baman Marker, but hardly motive

Black Legs: Lives on second floor so possible

Suspicion quotient: 6; has means but little motive (Simply cannot understand why police think she is chief suspect)

6) Darius and Silloo Khambata
Around 60
Yoga teachers
Two sons, Jeh and Neville. Animal lovers, vegans, eccentric

Means:
Sons always fussing over motorcycles and car. Own one of the two building garages, so might have plenty of coolant
Jeh attended All Saints School many years ago but why would they preserve ancient notes?

Black Legs: Unlikely as live on third floor

Motive: Disliked Baman Marker and harassed by him, but not a real motive

Odd details: Posted baffling message on the building chat—'Only kindness works at times like this. Remember that old joke from our childhood? When you point one finger at others, there are three fingers pointing back at you? Let us be mindful of this.'

Also note that second pair of legs—wearing flapping white pants—stopped on third floor
Darius happens to be cousin of Baman Marker

Suspicion quotient: 5; both means and motive are middling

7) Ronald Carvalho
Around 47
Tuition teacher, founder of Toppers United
Wife died last year. Lots of gossip. Lives with one son, Daniel
BUT—don't know if he was in Daisy Apartments on Friday night

Means:
One car parked in compound so access to coolant
No direct connection with All Saints School. But works with students from many schools, so may have access to yellow notes

Black Legs: Unlikely as lives on third floor

Motive: May have felt threatened by Baman Marker and his message on building chat on Friday morning—'In most cases one knows how it will End. When Money is moved that should not be moved. When Papers are sold that should not be sold. When Plants are bought that should not be bought. Then we know it can Only end Badly.'

Odd details: The second pair of legs stopped on third floor
Thumps and bumps from dark apartment on Friday night Mr Carvalho is a man with A Past.

Suspicion quotient: 9 (if he was in Daisy Apartments on Friday night); has both means and motive

8) Mr Alimchandani
Around 80

Used to be a builder
Unable to leave the house. Spends day in bed or wheelchair. Daughter Sheela lives in Lily Apartments

Means:
No car or access to coolant
No access to note
Unable to walk. Unable to check he is even having right medicine. So no way he could have instructed his helper to make detox smoothie and spike it with coolant

Black Legs: Unable to walk so impossible

Motive: Horrible scene involving Sheela on Thursday where she implied that Baman Marker was blackmailing family in some way

Odd detail: Sheela Jagtiani predicted that something ghastly would happen to Baman Marker. Less than 36 hours later, it had

(Theory suggested by Shanaya—that Sheela could have instructed the helper over the phone, got him to make smoothie and spike it with coolant. But not very plausible. Firstly, the helper is not an old, dependable employee who could be trusted to commit a crime and stay silent. Secondly, where would the helper find coolant and a note signed by Lina Almeida? Not even Agatha Christie would have risked a murder that tangled.

For me the big question was why the police searched the house of a complete invalid. Because Sheela Jagtiani freaked? There had to be some other reason that we didn't know about.

I discounted Shanaya's theory. Shanaya is a collector of leaves, seashells and designer sneakers. She's determined to become a marine biologist, which means she will become a marine biologist. I, on the other hand, collect murder mysteries and wish I could become a detective. What I'm trying to say is that my sleuthing skills are sharper.)

Suspicion quotient: 1; no means, even if some motive

9) Ranjit and Aparna Burman
Around 35-40
He runs small but success financial company; she has high-flying public relations job
No children, seem super rich

Means:
Own three cars and the second garage, so easy access to coolant
No connection to All Saints School so access to yellow note difficult

Motive: Rumours that Ranjit Burman involved in financial misdeeds. Baman Marker was his CA and might have figured things out—definite motive

Black Legs: Live on fourth floor so less likely

Odd details: Baman Marker's message on building chat might have targeted Mr Burman as well as Mr Carvalho. Especially the bit about money.
Mr Burman publicly threatened Baman Marker while Lily Apartments being sealed.

Suspicion quotient: 8; strong motive

10) Maria
56
Housekeeper
Never married. Believes in ghosts and mermaids. Totally runs Marker house.

Means:
Access to coolant difficult
Access to notes difficult

Motive: Can't be fun to work for the Markers but not a real motive

Black Legs: Lives in same house as Baman Marker; only wears dresses so unlikely to be Black Legs

Suspicion quotient: 3; no means and little motive

11) Mrs Kurien's stranger
Age: ?
Profession: ?

Means: ?

Motive: ?

Odd detail: The stranger must have entered Daisy Apartments before it was sealed on Friday evening. Difficult to imagine that he landed up, along with a metal bottle full of Green Glow Detox Smoothie in the afternoon, then hung around till night and left the smoothie outside the door.
Also difficult to understand how he entered at all. Day Mishraji swears that not a single stranger entered Daisy Apartments on Friday morning.

Suspicion quotient: 4; stranger as mysterious as ever, but not as suspicious as initially appeared to be.

Conclusions and questions:

- Could an outsider be the killer?
- (Unlikely)
- Could there be any way that Black Legs might belong to the third or fourth floor, but needed to go down for some reason and up again?
  Could perhaps have dropped something?
  Could perhaps have an accomplice on a lower floor?
  (Possible, but...)
- Most apartments have house-help staying with them. Could one be the killer?

There are at least eight members of staff—like Mr Alimchandani's helper and the Carvalho's housekeeper—in Daisy Apartments at the moment. None are on the building chat so would not have had access to the Green Glow Detox Smoothie recipe.
Also, Lina Almeida note would have been a challenge.
(Most unlikely. I know I sound like South Bombay brat full of biases, but to me at least this feels like a rich person crime.)

Things to follow up on:

- Ask Aashu if he saw anything odd that night—Ved
- Ask Mini if she saw anything odd that night—Ved (reluctantly)
- Find out if Mr Carvalho is back—Nandini (Shanaya insisted with evil chuckle)
- Read building chat of Thursday and Friday to spot threats, tell-tale remarks—Nandini
- What exactly did the Lina Almeida note say? Maybe that would help us figure where it came from—Shanaya to ask Kysha if she knows
- Why did police focus on Amrita Aunty, the Habibullahs, the Burmans and Mr Alimchandani?

I should have felt all pleased and Junior Miss Marple-ish after creating this Google Doc. Instead, I felt vaguely sick.

I've told you before that I love mathematics. We'd started Set Theory at school and these are the sort of problems that we'd tackled: In a club, 30 girls play hockey and 40 girls play football. There are 55 girls in all. How many play both?

This is how we went about such problems. If the girls who play hockey belong to one set and the girls who play football are part of another set, the ones who play both games are the intersection of the two sets.

Sorry, sorry. You really don't need to know all this. It's just how my mind works.

Anyway, these were the three sets I created:

Means: All the people who have the means
Black Legs: All the people who could have been Black Legs
Motive: All the people who had a motive

This is what I figured:

The intersection of Means and Black Legs was—Lina Almeida, Amrita Aunty, the Lambas.
The intersection of Means and Motive was—Amrita Aunty, the Khambatas, Mr Carvalho, the Burmans.
The intersection of Motive and Black Legs was—Amrita Aunty and Rashida Habibullah.

Only one person fell in the intersection of all three sets—Amrita Aunty.

I knew, of course, that while Black Legs was creeping up with a metal bottle filled with poison, Amrita Aunty was standing in her balcony in a grey dress and grey mood. I knew with unwavering certainty that she was not the killer. Which offered little comfort.

The police might well choose to ignore the words of a nosy teenager, and swoop down on Amrita Aunty anyway. Or, if they chose to believe the nosy teenager, they would swoop down on their next suspect. Who could very likely be Mr Carvalho.

18

On the fifty-first day of the lockdown, I did something foolhardier than sharing a bowl of soup with a coronavirus super-spreader. On the fifty-first day of the lockdown, I messaged Daniel.

This is how it happened.

I had spent the night in that awful 0-watt-bulb zone between wakefulness and sleep. A bunch of worries sat on my chest, but one squeezed harder than the rest. I was terrified that, in the process of trying to protect Amrita Aunty, I would incriminate Mr Carvalho.

The police might land up today. Before I said anything to them, I needed to find out whether Mr Carvalho had returned to Daisy Apartments in time to do away with Baman Marker. How to find out?

I could ask Alfonsa to ask Florrie/Flouride. Or I could ask Daniel.

I'm a roundabout person. Someone who takes the crooked side streets, rather than the four-lane highway. Someone who would choose the Alfonsa-Flouride route, even if it involved a twenty-minute detour into Florrie-Flouride's bunions and migraines. So I'm really not sure what compelled me to pick up my phone, look for Daniel's number and type a series of messages.

'Hi Daniel. This is Nandini Venkat from Lily Apartments.'

'My mum and I were wondering if you were fine.'

'Is your dad back home?'

'If not, we can help organize groceries and stuff.'

'Let me know.'

I hit 'Send' for the last time. Then the enormity of what I'd done hit me. I dropped my phone and followed it onto the bed with a thud. I stuck my flaming face into my hands. I was pretty sure that, at this very moment, Daniel was texting the rapacious girl with the bright, tight tops, and that they were laughing at my clumsy overtures. 'What have I done? What have I done? What will he think of me? What is wrong with me?' the questions ran through that long, sweaty morning like a news ticker.

I needed to tidy my cupboard; I needed to go through the Lily-Daisy Apartments chat once more; and I needed to trap the thoughts flapping about just beyond my range of vision. Instead, I mooched around, checking my phone and wondering, 'What have I done? What have I done?'

I was checking my phone for the 417th time when Ved burst into my room. 'Have you spoken to Shanaya,' he demanded. 'Have you seen? Have you heard?'

Ved models himself on an ice cube. That he should be running and yelling frightened me half to death. 'What?' I asked with a sandpaper-dry mouth. 'Have the police arrested someone? Not, not...Amrita Aunty?'

'No, no,' Ved said. 'This is something else. Kysha has posted something on Instagram. On her private account. Something big. If it is what I think it is.'

'What?' I asked, affecting indifference. Kysha had two Instagram accounts. I followed her public one. The private account was strictly for friends and—as I've told you before—I didn't make the cut, although Ved and Shanaya did.

Ved was about to answer when my phone rang. Shanaya.

'You'll never guess,' she yelped. 'You will just never guess.'

'Guess what? This Kysha business?' I asked with an irritable inflection. What was it about Kysha? She couldn't spell to save her life. She smushed more chemicals into her hair than those polluting factories dumped into the Ganga. But still she managed to win friends, influence people and be the centre of fascinated attention.

'Isn't it horrible?' Shanaya demanded. 'She's said that she will be posting more details. She said that it all ties up with something bigger…I'm really wondering…'

'Wait a minute, Shanaya,' I said. 'I don't know what this is about. Ved just came to tell me.'

'Put me on speaker phone so we can all chat,' Shanaya instructed. I put Shanaya on speaker phone while Ved went to the door of my bedroom and peered into the corridor. Watching him shut the door with silent deliberation, I felt apprehensive all over again.

'Can one of you please tell me what the hell is going on?' I protested.

'Ved, show Nandini,' Shanaya's voice rose from the phone on my bed. 'Are you showing her?'

'Yeah,' Ved said and held out his iPhone with the thrice-cracked screen. I took it from him and started reading. It took me a little while to understand what the hysteria was about. But once I did, I was pretty hysterical myself.

Kysha had written a series of posts for her Instagram story. She had started the posts late last night—but had only got to the OMG bits this morning. This is what she had written:

> So it isn't easy to speak out. Especialy when your speaking out against someone close. But I cld not stay quite any longer.
>
> So the thing is that this guy is a freind. But he is harming others. He doesn't know where to stop. And now I am woried and afraid.
>
> So I have known him all my life. He is 2 years older than me. When we were kids we went to the garden together. He was like my big brother.
>
> So a year ago I notised that he was using. You know what I mean. So it started with a girl he's dating. I think she introdused him to it.
>
> So it started with the not so bad stuff. Just to feel melow. Then slowly more scary stuff. tHe got others onto it. He tried to get me onto it. Before the lockdown I realized he was deEling.
>
> One day someone found out where he hid that stuff.
>
> Then something terible happened. To that person. What if my friend did it? I really don't know what to do. What wld you do?
>
> I need to think about it before I say more.

I read the posts in stunned silence. Then I read them again. All the while, Shanaya talked and talked from the phone on my bed. And Ved talked and talked from the chair near my desk. I wished they would shut up for a second. I needed to think.

Could Kysha really be saying what I thought she was saying?

'Wait a minute,' I said, so urgently that both Shanaya and Ved stopped. 'What's she hinting at?'

'That Neville Khambata does drugs, obviously,' Shanaya said. 'But what about—'

'Not just does drugs,' Ved corrected her. 'He does more. He deals in drugs and he has a stash somewhere. And he's actively trying to get others to use.'

'Yes, yes, I get all that,' Shanaya said impatiently. 'What I don't get is what she means by the last bit. That stuff about "worst thing that a person can do". What's that about? It almost sounds like…'

'Yes,' I agreed. 'It almost sounds like…'

The thing about being absolutely, totally, forever best friends is that sometimes, half a sentence can convey as much as a chapter. Ved, though, was not a part of this telepathic sisterhood. Looking exasperated, he said, 'Can you guys please stop doing that mindreading business. It almost sounds like what?'

'Like Kysha is saying that Neville killed Baman Marker.' Shanaya's voice was matter of fact. Almost as if she found the idea…not believable exactly…but not absurd.

'That's what I thought too,' Ved said, equally placid. 'But I don't know.'

'What do you mean you don't know?' I asked. 'Surely you know that's impossible. I mean, we're talking about Neville Khambata. He rescues puppies. He grows rosemary and oregano in his balcony.'

'But he also smokes dope,' Shanaya interrupted. 'I've seen him. And once I saw him outside the gate, buying something from a scarily shady guy. I told you about it.'

'I've heard things about him too,' Ved said. 'And just imagine. If he was a dealer and he was hiding drugs somewhere and Baman Marker saw him, wouldn't that be a perfect motive?'

'But how can you assume all this without any evidence?'

'We know he smokes dope,' Shanaya countered. 'And if the police start investigating him, maybe they'll stop troubling my mom. They want to talk to her again. Today or tomorrow.'

'But, Shanaya,' I started. 'We need to find the real killer—'

'No,' Shanaya said, wrathfully. 'We need to make sure that they stop hassling my mom.'

'But we can hardly throw Neville Khambata under the bus…'

'I thought you cared about us, Nandini.'

'Of course I care,' I retorted. 'It's all I'm thinking about. But we can't jump to random conclusions. How will that help?'

'Maybe it's not that random,' Ved said. 'Neville Khambata goes to Waffle Wonderland. He's the Coolant King of Daisy and Lily Apartments. And he smokes weed.'

'Kysha goes to Waffle Wonderland,' I replied. 'She hangs out with the Coolant King. And she has the best possible access to Lina Almeida's notes. And—'

Shanaya and Ved protested loudly but I spoke even louder. 'And if smoking weed is the thing then Kysha does it too. I've seen her with Neville near the garage, smoking together. The thing is, it's a big leap from doing dope to being a drug dealer to being a murderer.'

'Why would Kysha lie?'

'I know you don't like Kysha, but she would never lie about Neville Khambata. That too on Instagram.'

'She says she will be posting more. Maybe she will give more details then.'

Ved and Shanaya spoke on top of each other. Once again I wondered how they could be so blind, but my I-don't-believe-you-guys face was wasted. Shanaya couldn't see me because she was in her yellow bedroom in Daisy Apartments. Ved could see me, but he never noticed anything that wasn't written in block letters and accompanied by a drumroll.

'Loads of people are reposting Kysha's story,' Shanaya said. 'Everyone's wondering who and what she's talking about. Kysha's crazy about Neville. It must have really been difficult for her to do this.'

I rolled my eyes, even though eye-rolling doesn't come naturally to me and always ends up giving me a headache. 'She's done it because she has a crush on Neville,' I snorted. 'Neville is ready to flirt and smoke with Kysha when no one else is around. But he's not about to dump his well-behaved, grammatically-accurate, sweet girlfriend for Kysha. That bugs Kysha. Actually, it would bug me too.'

'You're just guessing,' Shanaya's disagreement leapt up from the bed. 'Neville Khambata's always had girlfriends. He's been dating that Tara girl for ages. For a year, at least. Kysha's not suddenly going to turn psycho.'

'Actually,' I started to say but then clamped my mouth shut. I could have told Shanaya and Ved about what I'd seen from the balcony yesterday—about Neville Khambata's ill-timed conversation with his girlfriend, and about the vengeful eavesdropper. But what was the point? It was not as if Kysha had waved a sword and announced, 'I will have my revenge.' She'd merely looked like she wanted to pluck out Neville Khambata's liver and stamp on it.

'Let's see what Kysha does next,' I said. 'If she has something definite, she'll tell the police. If not…'

There wasn't anything left to say and we dispersed. Shanaya had an online art class. Ved wandered away for an unhealthy snack. Usually I would have followed him into the kitchen, but today I had work to do. I went looking for my mother and found her at the dining table, surrounded by sheets of paper and incomplete drawings. 'I'm busy,' she said, without glancing up. 'We've suddenly got a big order. Huge house in Lonavala.'

'Seriously?' I exclaimed. 'Who on earth furnishes their weekend home in the middle of a lockdown?'

'Rich people don't care what's happening outside their windows,' my mum replied, measuring her sketch. 'Not that I'm complaining. They have ghastly taste. But again I'm not complaining. At this point all work is welcome work. Now leave me alone for an hour.'

'Okay. But can I have your phone?' I asked. 'Just for ten minutes. I want to read the Lily-Daisy Apartments chat once more. To see what was going on during the day on Friday. Before…'

'Didn't you check the chat yesterday?' my mother asked. 'But okay, take the phone and vanish. Now I've forgotten my calculations. Don't come near me till lunchtime.'

For once it was easy to play obedient daughter. I did exactly what my mother wanted, took the phone and vanished.

19

Back in my bedroom, I made my way to the Lily-Daisy Apartments chat.

Yesterday I'd been looking for a specific post—that menacing message that Baman Marker had sent about moving money and selling papers. Along the way I'd noticed a message that'd made me pause and think, 'Oh really?' before it slipped away. I wanted to retrieve that elusive detail.

With the help of my mother's phone, I travelled backwards in time. The Lily-Daisy Apartments chat had turned graveyard silent on Monday evening, after the police marched into Daisy Apartments and the word 'murder' entered our conversations for the first time. I guess no one wanted to risk sharing a joke and a confidence with a killer.

Up until Monday, though, the chat had been hyperactive. On Sunday, we'd gotten news of Baman Marker's death. Naturally, there'd been many aghast messages.

On Saturday, Baman Marker had been rushed to hospital and in the early morning, Mrs Kurien had spotted the interloper. That had been a talkative day as well.

Friday was the day that Daisy Apartments had been sealed and Baman Marker had received his nasty surprise in a metal bottle packed in a Waffle Wonderland bag. That was the day I had planned to return to, but I scrolled too far back and found myself in the midst of a spiky conversation that had taken place on Thursday night.

The conversation had started with a message posted by Mrs Doshi, who lived on the ground floor of Lily Apartments. Mrs Doshi wanted to know where the Hon Chairperson had found the new night chowkidars. She complained that the man stationed outside Lily Apartments had been burping for the last half hour. She had tried to scold him from her window, but the burper had ignored her and continued to burp. 'Mr Marker,' she had asked. 'Have these men come with recommendations?'

Baman Marker had ignored the question. Ruby Vaz had not. 'That sounds most unpleasant,' our Hon Treasurer had written. 'Now especially, we need to be able to trust the people around us. It would be good to know if these men have come with credentials. Do put our minds to rest, Mr Marker.'

Minutes later, Amrita Aunty had leapt in, guns blazing. 'Couldn't agree more,' she'd written. 'Information about employees, details of contracts, the reasoning behind decisions, financial facts, building expenditure should be available to all residents. Transparency is our right, and something we demand.'

Another prolonged silence, then Baman Marker had responded, 'I have chosen these men personally and they come with excellent testimonials.'

Amrita Aunty had replied with a single word. 'Really?'

After which the chat had remained silent till kind Mr Shetty added his postscript. 'The two new guards have been living on just one meal a day since the lockdown. One of them is suffering from a digestive problem. I have given him Digene. I hope it will help.'

Okay. This is where I need to make a confession. When I'd begun reading this exchange on the chat, I'd experienced a surge of hope. Could these nameless, faceless security guards be the killers? To me that was the easiest, happiest solution.

Mr Shetty's words made me feel foolish and ashamed. An impoverished man living on a single meal a day would hardly whip up an upmarket smoothie, pack it in a Waffle Wonderland bag and add a yellow Lina Almeida note for good measure.

There was, of course, the possibility that one of the new security guards had played the role of accomplice. Perhaps he had opened the gate to allow a smoothie-bearing killer to creep into Daisy Apartments. But the more I thought about it, the more unlikely it seemed. Opening the metal gate of Daisy Apartments was a loud, bad-tempered business. It involved groans and krrrchhhaks that generally made it impossible for anyone to slip in and out unnoticed.

Still, I added a question on our Google Doc. 'Could the two new night watchmen be involved in any way?'

Then I returned to the chat.

Friday morning had started out on an uncommunicative note. Lily Apartments must have been sulking about its new status as a sealed building. And Daisy Apartments must have been squeamish about its proximity to a sealed building. The first message of the morning had come from Baman Marker. 'A parcel for Me was delivered Last

Night,' he had written. 'It was in a brown Envelope and very Clearly addressed to me. It was delivered to the Wrong apartment. If it was inadvertently delivered to you, inform Me Immediately.'

The missing parcel. That was it. The detail that had snagged my attention yesterday. I made a note of it in the Google Doc and returned to my mother's phone.

The next message was a video from Mrs Burman about the importance of washing hands to escape the virus. Then a joke posted by Mrs Kurien. After which Kavita Lamba had written her unkind message about Mr Sevnani—the one that had triggered the angry exchange that I remembered so well.

I made a brief note of all the messages on the Google Doc.

- Rashida Habibullah, Amrita Aunty protest about naming and shaming of Mr Sevnani.
- Darius Khambata writes: 'Remember that old joke from our childhood. When you point one finger at others, there are three fingers pointing back at you? Let us be mindful of this.'
- Baman Marker replies: 'In most cases one knows how it will End. When Money is moved that should not be moved. When Papers are sold that should not be sold. When Plants are bought that should not be bought. Then we know it can Only end badly.'

  (What had then seemed like a mad rant had now revealed itself as a poison-tipped dart. Ranjit Burman had, presumably, moved money where it should not have been moved. Mr Carvalho had sold papers that should not have been sold. Neville Khambata had bought plants—or drugs—that should not have been bought. Examined in this light, Kysha's accusations didn't seem all that absurd.)

- Chat turns routine.
  Complaints about the new security guards.
  Questions about repairman for dead mixer (Rashida Habibullah)
  Question about whereabouts of misplaced parcel (Baman Marker—again)
  Question about whether plastic shops in Colaba bazaar are open (Ruby Vaz)

  (Then a lull, while people were probably cooking, cleaning and hunting for lost parcels. And Binaifer Marker was packing her bags and getting set to sneak out of Daisy Apartments and into her daughter's white car.)
- Amrita Aunty asks where Binaifer Marker has gone.
- Baman Marker replies: 'Her family knows where she is. She is not in Banyan Tree Resorts in Phuket. She is not in an apartment in Worli. Thank you.'

  (I remembered feeling uneasy when I read this message on Friday, and I felt uneasy again. Something squirmed deep in my memory. I made a note to ask Ved and Shanaya if 'Banyan Tree Resorts in Phuket' or 'an apartment in Worli' made sense to them. For the moment, though, I continued reading through the chat.)
- Lina Almeida proposes cooking scheme. Posts recipe for famous/infamous Green Glow Detox Smoothie.
- Baman Marker sends third message about parcel. 'I have reason to Believe that my parcel was delivered to Another Flat in Daisy Apartments. The night watchman will be able to Point out the apartment to which he delivered it. I can only Hope that the parcel is returned before things turn Ugly and I am compelled to Contact the Authorities.'

  (The Hon Chairperson sounded pretty frantic about this parcel. He had sent three messages in an increasingly hysterical manner. My first assumption—that the parcel contained organic avocadoes or oat milk or sun-dried raisins or something—seemed faulty. But what could the parcel possibly have contained? Where had it vanished? And could it be connected to the murder?)

Turning back to the chat, I noticed that Baman Marker's final message about the missing parcel had been posted at 4.02 p.m. on Friday afternoon.

Soon after that, the BMC officials had arrived and sealed not just Daisy Apartments, but the fate of its Hon Chairperson.

20

I know exactly what you're thinking, but no. I hadn't forgotten about Daniel. I was giving the universe time to work its magic.

This was way easier said than done. Usually, I check my phone as automatically as I breathe. My mind will be thinking about nachos or the red boots on sale in H&M, while my fingers pick up my phone, click, swipe, click. Shanaya, the Bio Queen, had once described it as an involuntary muscle action.

Still, I had managed to avoid WhatsApp all morning. After lunch, though, my self-restraint crumbled. I know I sound like one of those zombie teenagers who are the target audience for Social Media Addiction workshops. But I challenge you to be stuck in a messy, poltergeist-infested room in a sealed building—with only a drummer brother and a book about a haunted hotel for company—and survive without your phone.

Honestly, it took me more energy to stay away from my phone than it would have taken to levitate a dining table. Especially on that suffocating afternoon, swaddled by air as hot and stifling as a rubber sheet, when absolutely nothing was moving. Not a speck of dust. Not a leaf. Certainly not our investigation.

Ved had called Aashu and Mini. Aashu hadn't seen a thing on Friday night. That wasn't surprising. Aashu rarely saw anything that happened beyond his computer screen. Mini hadn't seen anything either. She'd been online, playing Pictionary with Kysha and three of their friends from Cuffe Parade. The game had started around 9.30 p.m. and had lasted a couple of hours. Mini had no idea if anyone had stepped away for a few minutes—and anyway, why was Ved was asking these bizarre questions?

I was hugely grateful when my phone rang at 3.03 p.m. It was Shanaya, sounding like she'd slugged a gallon of Lina Almeida's Sweet Potato Energy Shake. 'I have news for you,' she announced. 'I think DD's dad is around. I can hear footsteps and regular sounds.'

'Oh,' I said, snapping to attention. 'Really? I actually sent Daniel a message asking him if his dad was back. Just so that I could put it on the Google Doc.'

'Yes, of course,' Shanaya said in full sarcastic mode. 'Just so you could put it on the Google Doc. Obviously. I believe you. When did you message Daniel?'

'In the morning.'

'Why didn't you tell me? Did he answer? What did he say?'

'I haven't checked my phone for some time.'

'Why? What're you doing that's so important? Never mind. That doesn't matter. Check your phone now,' Shanaya instructed.

'Okay. Let me check,' I said. 'I'll call you back.'

Shanaya told me not to disconnect the call, but I did it anyway. The last thing I wanted was an audience for my heartbreak. Even if it was an audience of one.

You don't need to know precisely how hard my heart was banging, or how wildly my hopes were zigzagging. All I will say is that the monster roller coaster at Ferrari World in Abu Dhabi was a restful experience compared to this. There, at least, you're only worried that the rollercoaster will fly off the rails with a crash smash. Here, I had a big list of possibilities:

a) That Daniel hadn't written back.
b) That Daniel had written back with a stand-offish 'Sorry? Nandini who?'
c) That Daniel had written back with the information that his father was in Daisy Apartments and had been so all along. Which would promptly take the shady Mr Carvalho all the way up to 'Suspect No 1'.

I checked my messages with fumbling fingers and saw that seventy-one WhatsApps had arrived in the four hours that I'd stayed away so that the universe could work its magic. I only bothered with the three that were from Daniel.

This is what they said:

'Hi. Of course, I know you. Nandini Venkat from next door. I attended your birthday party when we were kids. You had a cake shaped like a book. Your brother had a cake shaped like a guitar.'

'Thank you for offering to help. Really kind of you and your mother. A family member fell ill so my father was taking care of her. He was away for six days. He got back this morning.'

'How has the lockdown been for you?'

It was a good thing that I wasn't standing. My legs wouldn't have held up. Amazement had robbed me of all my abilities—except the ability to call Shanaya. So that's what I did.

Shanaya answered immediately. 'Did he?'

'Yes.'

'And?'

'He said that his father was away for six days. But he got back this morning. I guess Mr Carvalho could not have been the killer.'

'I told you it was quiet in their house,' Shanaya said, but I could hear faint disappointment in her voice. I didn't blame her. I too wanted a suspect in place of Amrita Aunty. I just didn't want it to be Daniel's father.

'But what else did Daniel say?' Shanaya asked. 'Did he seem interested? Happy to chat?'

'Don't know,' I said, and I was being totally truthful. I'm great at analyzing 'The Road Not Taken' and 'Caged Bird'. Sir Paulash's star student, in fact. But it's much tougher to read the hidden meaning in three short WhatsApp messages sent by a boy across the compound.

'What do you mean you don't know? Wake up, Nandini.'

'He was sweet in a neighbourly way.'

'Neighbourly!' Shanaya choked. 'Are you confusing him with Mr Sevnani or Mr Shetty? Teenage guys don't bother with neighbourliness.'

'Mr Sevnani doesn't bother much with neighbourliness either,' I said, and we both gurgled till we remembered that our elderly neighbour was still unwell and that our world was in shambles.

Shanaya instructed me to read out the messages and listened carefully, with the lofty silence of an expert. (Shanaya's had two boyfriends. She usually acquires them just before the All Saints School Social—in the same way that she would get new shoes or earrings. Then she sheds them a few weeks later. She's definitely more into the new shoes than the new boyfriends. Still, she's had two more boyfriends than I've had.)

Shanaya made me read out the messages twice before she made her pronouncement. 'He's interested,' she said.

'How do you know?' I asked. 'How can you assume such a thing?'

'Isn't it obvious?' Shanaya replied. 'He remembers your birthday cake from what? Four or five years ago? I can't remember my own cake from last year.'

'Maybe he's just really into cake,' I quibbled.

Shanaya ignored me. 'Also, he's asked you a question at the end. That's a big giveaway because it means he wants to carry on the conversation. Doesn't that tell you anything?'

'It tells me that he's super polite. Or maybe just lonely,' I said.

'So good, na?' Shanaya said. 'Makes it easier for you.'

'I guess…'

'How are you going to reply?'

'I don't know.'

'What do you mean you don't know? Why are you sounding so pathetic and helpless all of a sudden?'

I didn't know that either. For a generally can-do person—even if not quite as can-do as my bossy best friend—I was behaving disgustingly limp. 'I'm scared I'm looking fat,' I said, coming up with a random answer. 'I've been junking like crazy. Am I looking fat?'

'I haven't seen you for a week,' Shanaya replied. 'And given that you're sitting in a sealed building and communicating over WhatsApp, I really don't think it matters. Just be enthusiastic when you write to Daniel. Start a topic of conversation. Talk about…talk about… music. Or some movie.'

'How can I suddenly start talking about music, or a movie,' I protested. 'I'll sound deranged.'

'Then talk about something else,' Shanaya said. 'About the murder. Anything.'

'Actually,' I admitted, 'that's not a bad idea. It'll kill two birds with one stone. For all you know, Daniel might have seen something. Or heard something.'

'Yeah fine. Then throw the stone. Hurry up. And tell me what happens.'

I took some time figuring out a stone/tone that was the right mix of casual and inquisitive, but I finally sent my message. 'Last week was horrible,' I wrote. 'But worse for you, I guess. With your father away. Must have been creepy to be alone when you knew that someone in the building is a killer.'

Daniel was online and replied in a couple of minutes. 'Definitely creepy. But I'm still hoping it isn't someone from the building.'

'Who else could it be?' I typed. 'Did you see something that night?'

'No,' Daniel replied. 'Haven't thought much about it.'

This boggled me a bit. Daniel hadn't thought about a murder that had taken place just two floors over his head? How was that even possible? For a disloyal moment I wondered if Shanaya was right after all and Daniel was a tiny bit drippy. But his next message both reassured and confused me.

'What about you?' he'd written. 'Do you have any theories? Did you see anything that night?'

I paused and tried to figure out how honest I could be. I obviously couldn't tell Daniel that I viewed his father as a potential murderer. But could I/should I tell him the other stuff? About Black Legs and the Waffle Wonderland bag? About coolants and yellow notes? I was still dithering when Daniel sent another message.

'Florence says you solved the case. Says it's common knowledge that you and Shanaya know who did it. Florence has been known to exaggerate. But asking anyway. Did you see something?'

Oh dear. Florence—that was her name, at least one mystery had been solved—was an integral part of Alfonsa's gang. What rumours had Alfonsa been spreading in the wider world? Why hadn't we been more careful when she was lurking? And, most unnerving of all, what would happen if these rumours reached the wrong ears? The ears of a killer who didn't want to get caught?

I wasn't worried for myself. Two sturdy, creaky metal gates stood between me and the murderer. I was safe, but Shanaya was not. For a sick minute I imagined a doorbell ringing in Daisy Apartment and Shanaya opening the door in a distracted way. I imagined Mr Burman standing outside, wearing a genial, crooked-financial-wizard smile. And then his arm swinging, a flash of metal, a spray of blood, a short cry.

The thought was so distressing that I forgot that I was messaging The Boy of My Dreams. Or rather, I forgot to be tongue-tied and shy. The rumours needed to be squashed. Immediately.

'Florence exaggerates as always,' I typed, adding a string of laughing emojis so that I didn't come across as a Mini Mentor and Guide. 'I only saw a pair of legs on the stairwell that night. Very little proof to link them to the killer. I honestly don't know a thing.'

'Who did they belong to?' Daniel wrote back in an instant.

'No clue. All I know is that they were dressed in black.'

'The word on the street is that you have it figured out.'

'No, no. The word among Alfonsa, Florence and gang is that I have it figured out. Remember that they have also spotted mermaids at Sassoon Dock and ghosts in the garage. So…'

Daniel replied with a string of laughing emojis and a question. 'You really haven't?'

'No,' I insisted. 'If I had, wouldn't I tell the police and end this nasty business?'

Daniel finally believed me. 'Okay,' he wrote. 'But what did they do?'

'What did who do?'

'The legs.'

'Climbed the stairs.'

'And it wasn't Mr Marker?'

'It could have been anyone. Why Mr Marker?'

'Just wondered. Because he was going up and down the building that night. Talking to people.'

Really? I frowned and read Daniel's message again. Baman Marker had been wandering up and down Daisy Apartments on that fateful Friday night? How come nobody'd mentioned this before?

'Are you sure?' I demanded.

'Yes,' Daniel replied. 'He came to my place.'

Perplexed, I shook my head at the phone. Why had Baman Marker gone to the Carvalho apartment on the night that Daisy Apartments was sealed? Why would a man who was so afraid of infection wander about the building? Once again, I realized that I was seeing only a small part—perhaps the tail, perhaps the trunk—of the elephant. I really needed to understand the entire beast. With fumbling fingers I typed, 'Why? What did he want? When did he land up?'

I pressed Send, then reread my message and worried that it was a boyfriend repellent. I was finding it impossible to play captivating girl next door in the middle of the murder investigation and kept slipping back into tough detective mode.

Fortunately, Daniel didn't seem to mind. 'Before dinner sometime,' he replied after loads of typing. 'Maybe around 9. He asked if some parcel had been delivered to our place by mistake. He refused to believe that it hadn't. Insisted on asking Florence as well. Then insisted that he wanted to talk to my father. He seemed upset about the parcel, whatever it was.'

'He kept asking about the parcel on the building chat too,' I wrote back.

'He did? Don't know. Am not on that chat. My father is, but never tells me what's going on.'

'Why did Mr Marker think you had the parcel?'

'Not sure. I think he messaged my father, who didn't reply. So Mr Marker came down.'

'And then?'

'He acted like I was lying when I said I didn't have his parcel. After he left, I heard him going to other apartments too. Wait. Let me just call you.'

I'd barely registered the last sentence when my phone rang. Daniel's name flashed on the screen and threw me into fat-fingered confusion. This was what I'd been dreaming about for six whole months. But now that the dream had solidified into miraculous reality, I was unprepared. Reluctant even. My mouth was gluggy and my tongue felt swollen and clumsy.

'Hi. This is Daniel,' Daniel said most unnecessarily. I guess he had no way of knowing that I'd saved his number on my phone a full five months ago.

I'd managed to text Daniel with nonchalance. But talking to him was another matter altogether. My brain seemed unable to go beyond OMG, OMG, OMG, and my mouth had turned into a tub of Fevicol. It took loads of willpower to utter a glutinous, 'Hi.'

'Hi. Is it okay that I've called? I thought this would be easier,' Daniel said. His voice was higher and lighter than I'd imagined, and, for some reason, that wobbled me even more.

'It's fine. Wow. So Baman Marker came to your house on Friday night. That's seriously something...' I babbled, sounding all Barbie and fake-bright.

Daniel handled it well. Maybe he thought this was how I always sounded. 'I think he went to a couple of other apartments as well,' he said. 'I heard him ringing other doorbells.'

'And then? Did you hear anything?' I asked, still plastic and peppy.

'I was about to shut the door when I heard voices,' Daniel said. 'Someone...not shouting exactly...but talking loudly. Sort of aggressively.'

'Who was it?' I asked, curiosity replacing the simper in my voice.

'I think it was Mr Burman,' Daniel said.

'Mr Baman? Baman Marker? I don't think I've ever heard him shout. He must have been seriously stressed about that parcel.'

'No, no. Not Mr Marker, Mr Burman.'

'Oh, I thought you said Baman…' I trailed away.

Baman. Burman. I'd never realized how similar the names were. Or how easy it would be for a new security guard to confuse 'Baman Saab' with 'Burman Saab'. I didn't have time to chase the thought, though, because Daniel was talking.

'He was saying that he would not put up with more harassment. Then he said something weird…I can't remember exactly…but something about having…I can't remember the word…not guns, not weapons…'

'Ammunition?' I asked.

'Ammunition!' Daniel exclaimed. 'Yes. How did you know?'

'Lucky guess,' I tittered. 'Uhhh…uhh…did you tell the police?'

'I told them some of it. But I don't know how seriously they took me. I think they saw me as a kid. They were more interested in meeting my father.'

'But your father wasn't around.'

'I guess they'll talk to him today. Though there's nothing he can tell them. He wasn't even here.'

'Yes,' I agreed. 'Did Baman Marker say what was in the parcel?'

'No, but it had to be something small,' Daniel supplied, 'Mr Marker said it was packed in a brown envelope. And he kept asking if it could have fallen behind a table or been forgotten under a book. Not sure why, but I imagined it the size of a…I don't know…a KitKat chocolate or something.'

'That tiny? What on earth could it be?'

'No idea. I'd forgotten about the parcel till just now. I didn't think it was important. I thought it was the usual Marker stuff.'

Daniel laughed and I laughed too. Not because anything was funny, but because I was struck by a sense of giddiness. OMG, Daniel knew I existed. OMG, he had actually called me. OMG he was chatting with me as if it was the most natural thing in the world. OMG we were actually laughing together. OMG...

Lucky for me, then, that the boy of my dreams stepped into the breach with utmost gallantry. (Sorry, sorry. I promise not to gush again.) 'You still haven't told me what you saw,' he said. 'Florence is convinced that you saw the killer committing the crime. You should see how excited she is.'

'What rubbish,' I laughed again, but not quite so giddily. 'I was watching *Mean Girls* with Shanaya that evening. My computer is on my desk so I happened to catch a few glimpses of Daisy Apartments. That's all.'

'But what did you see?'

'I told you. I saw a pair of legs climbing.'

'But...did the legs do anything? Why were they of special interest? When was this?'

'I saw them climbing from the second floor to the fifth floor. At around 10.25 p.m. The legs were wearing black pants and they weren't doing anything suspicious. Except that the person was carrying something orange and pink. Maybe a Waffle Wonderland bag.'

'That's it?' Daniel asked. 'I imagined something...much more...suspicious...'

'What? That I had seen someone adding poison to a bottle full of smoothie and then force-feeding the Hon

Chairperson?' I asked. This came out in my normal, sardonic-Nandini voice and I didn't blame Daniel for hesitating and stuttering.

'No, not really,' he said finally, while I worried that he might prefer the fake tee-heeing Nandini to the real, acidic one. 'What smoothie? Why is a Waffle Wonderland bag suspicious?'

'The bag is suspicious because the poisoned Green Glow Detox Smoothie was delivered to Baman Marker in a Waffle Wonderland bag,' I said, trying to be a Nandini in the middle.

'What Green Glow Detox Smoothie? How do you know all this?'

'How do you *not* know all this? Your Florence is part of the Gossip Girls of Lily-Daisy Apartments. Hasn't she told you anything?'

'She told me that you witnessed the crime,' Daniel pointed out. 'And she told me that Mr Marker was poisoned. That apparently someone left juice in a bottle outside his house. I don't know the name of the juice and I don't know the name of the poison. And I definitely didn't see the killer.'

'Seriously? You don't know any of this?'

'Seriously. I think Florence is right and you did see it all firsthand,' Daniel half-joked. 'How come you know more than anybody else? Probably even more than the police? Rashida Aunty had called to check on me yesterday. She doesn't know any of this, either. Can you tell me everything from the beginning?'

'Okay,' I said, and told Daniel the entire story—the sprinklies and chocolate sauce version. I told Daniel about how Baman Marker died, and about all that I saw and heard on that ugly night. The black legs, the doorbell, the flapping white legs that seemed to run through the sleeping building like a wisp of a dream. I told him about Ethylene Glycol and its horrendous side effects. And about the little yellow note that had gone along with the spiked smoothie. I told him that the police believed that the poisoned drink had been delivered between 9 p.m. and 11 p.m. on Friday night.

'I guess it finally makes sense,' I said. 'Baman Marker was wandering around ringing doorbells and fighting with his neighbours at around 9 p.m. And Maria poured the drink at 11 p.m. So the smoothie must have been delivered some time in that period.'

Daniel heard the story from beginning to end. Then he asked a bunch of questions about Black Legs and White Legs and the ingredients that go into Green Glow Detox Smoothie.

'Why?' I teased. 'Are you planning to become a chef? I strongly recommend that you look for more attractive recipes than a drink made from spinach, kale and celery.'

'No,' Daniel replied, all earnest. 'I want to do something connected with music. That's the only thing I've ever wanted to do. I'm not that great with academics...'

I was wondering how to respond when Daniel spoke again. 'I have a sort of dyslexia. With numbers. So I had to drop maths and some of the sciences in Grade 8. It really, really upset my father.'

Once again, I floundered for a response, but finally settled on fake-cheery. 'Ved's also much more into music than academics,' I said, ignoring the bit about dyslexia and Daniel's obnoxious father. Next time I would be more prepared.

If there was a next time.

The conversation had started to splutter but I didn't want to hang up. What if Daniel never called me again? What if I'd wasted my only chance to charm him? 'Listen,' I said, trying to keep the connection alive. 'Will you call me if you think of anything else that happened on Friday night? Or if you have a brainwave about the parcel?'

Daniel promised and we said bye. Outside the window, the golden May evening had tarnished at the edges and I realized with astonishment that it was almost dusk. We'd been chatting for more than an hour.

I stared at the darkening sky and thought about Daniel. About how his voice was flimsier than I'd imagined and about how his sense of humour was so different from mine and how he was not great with academics. And how none of it mattered.

Even when the sun went down, my evening continued to glow. I drifted through the hours leading to bedtime. Shanaya called a couple of times and messaged many more times. 'Did you talk? What happened?' she wanted to know.

I wrote back, telling her that I would call the next morning. I told my parents that I had a headache and hurried back to my bedroom after dinner. I didn't check the Google Doc. I didn't watch Netflix. I didn't attempt to tidy the clutter in the room. Instead, I spent the evening hugging my happy secret to myself.

21

You know, when you catch a flight, there's that painful bit when you're stuck in the aeroplane and nothing much happens? The plane is parked in one place for ages, after which it taxis around listlessly? Then, just when you've given up hope of ever getting anywhere, things get businesslike. The plane reaches the runway and pauses for breath. The engines roar, the aircraft picks up speed and before you know it, you're up in the air.

This investigation was like that. For the longest time, nothing progressed. But then, on Friday morning, I reached the runway and things started moving at a bone-rattling, mind-scrambling speed.

Soon after breakfast on the fifty-second day of the lockdown, I wandered into Ved's room. A coppersmith was tuk-tuking away on a leafy branch outside the window, and Ved was tap-tapping on his phone inside the room. I sat on his high, narrow bed and checked my messages. There was nothing from Daniel, which was disappointing but hardly surprising.

Ved's bed was neatly covered with a blue striped bedspread and there wasn't a single anklet, sock or bra strewn on the floor. I hated to admit it, but Ved's room was in much better shape than mine. The moment Ved hit send, I asked the question that'd been tickling me for hours. 'Have you ever noticed that Baman and Burman are really similar names?' I demanded.

Ved looked puzzled. 'No…yes…no…I guess so,' he said. 'But why?'

'I've been trying to figure out where Baman Marker's lost parcel went,' I said. 'And I'm wondering if it landed up with Mr Burman.'

Ved glanced at his phone in a distracted manner. 'Why are you so hung up on that parcel? It must have been some typical Baman Marker thing. A pumpkin seed cake or organic wildflower honey or something.'

'You really think so?' I asked. 'The parcel was handed over to the new watchmen on Thursday night. Through the next eighteen hours, Baman Marker asked about it three times on the Lily-Daisy Apartments chat. By the last time, he was freaking. Then at dinnertime on Friday, he went marching around Daisy Apartments, ringing doorbells and asking people if they had the parcel. Would he do all that for a bottle of honey, even if it came from the most organic bees and wildest flowers in the world?'

Ved looked up from his phone and finally focused. 'Baman Marker actually went up and down Daisy Apartments confronting his neighbours?' he asked. 'And risked getting coronavirus for this parcel? Wow. It must have been important. But hold on. How do you know all this? Who told you?'

This was the question I'd been hoping to avoid. 'Daniel told me,' I said in my most no big-deal voice. 'He said that—'

My strategy failed. Ved was clear that this was a big deal. He goggled and yelped and bashed his snare drum and sprang up from his stool and generally made a ruckus. 'Daniel told you?' he yelped. 'Since when have you and Daniel been talking to each other? When did this happen? How come you never told me?'

'Stop shouting,' I said, trying to shush him. 'I messaged Daniel to find out whether his father had come back to Daisy Apartments. Remember it was on my list of things to do? Anyway, he ended up calling me.'

'When did this happen?' Ved demanded.

'Just yesterday.'

'Oooh,' Ved crowed. 'Just ended up calling? Ooooh. So romantic.'

This went on for a bit. I waited till Ved got all the wisecracks and hoots out of his system before continuing. 'What do you think?' I asked when he quietened down. 'Could a new night watchman confuse Baman with Burman? Suppose someone came with a parcel and said, "This is for Baman Saab", do you think the night watchman might think he meant Mr Burman?'

Ved pondered over this and tried out the two names in a variety of accents. Then he nodded. 'It's easy. In fact, I'm pretty surprised nobody's confused them before. I guess that's because everybody referred to Baman Marker as Chairman Saab.'

'Chemmen Saab,' I corrected Ved. 'But that would make it even more confusing if an outsider came along with a parcel and said, "This is for Baman Saab". I think—'

My mother marched into the room before I could complete the thought. 'So Ved, what are you making for dinner tonight?' she asked with a militant air.

Ved was ready with his answer. 'Sandwiches,' he said, all smug-bug-in-a-rug.

I opened my mouth to whine. I mean, making sandwiches was hardly cooking. But my mother got there first. 'Lovely,' she said, sweet as a raspberry lollipop. 'In that case, I expect you to make some green chutney for the filling. I can tell you how to grate the coconut. Yes?'

Ved looked crestfallen but he agreed without protest.

'And Nandini,' my mother continued, 'I'm sure the police will land up today. Be clear about what you're going to say.'

'Okay. But I'm pretty nervous. I hope I don't end up making things worse for Amrita Aunty.'

'Not sure it can get any worse for her,' my mother muttered, and her mood seemed to shift from grey to charcoal. 'Things are really messy.'

Shaking my head, I repeated the question that I'd asked at least a dozen times. 'But why? Why are the police so determined to pin this on Amrita Aunty? What is her motive? People don't go around murdering their neighbours just because they squabble about parking spots and leaking walls…'

My mother looked away and again I felt a twinge of disquiet. What was she not telling me? I was about to probe when Ved started expounding on my Baman-Burman theory. 'What do you think?' he asked my mother. 'Do you feel the parcel is super-important? And that it could have landed up with Mr Burman?'

'Possibly,' my mother replied. 'It's a good theory but where's the evidence? And how do we know that Baman Marker was all that desperate to find the parcel?'

'Daniel told me some stuff,' I mumbled, trying hard not to blush. 'Baman Marker went up and down Daisy

Apartments on Friday night, asking people if they had the parcel. Daniel actually heard Baman Marker talking to Mr Burman. And apparently Mr Burman was being aggressive and saying odd stuff.'

'Odd stuff like what?' my mother asked.

'Something like "I don't need to be afraid any more…"' I said, careful to avoid looking at Ved, who was making a series of hideous kissy faces in the background. 'I can't remember the exact words.'

'Naturally,' Ved said in ghastly falsetto. 'But you can always ask Daniel again.'

I glared at Ved, but it was my mother who detonated. 'Ved,' she hissed. 'What was that? Do I now need to start worrying that you are troubling Daniel as well? That poor boy is already having a rough time. I will not let you add to his problems. Do you hear me?'

My jaw fell. Literally. I gawped at my mother. Then I gawped at Ved. 'What do you mean?' I asked. 'Troubling Daniel as well? Who else has Ved been troubling?'

'Ved can tell you if he wants,' my mother huffed. 'A lot of things happened after you went to bed last night. It was a great shock to both Appa and me. We can only hope it isn't true.'

I gawped again. One day, one measly day, I had decided to play the lovelorn maiden and I had missed a full-fledged family drama. 'What?' I asked Ved. 'What's this all about? What's happening?'

Ved looked mutinous and crossed his arms. 'Nothing,' he said.

'What nothing?' I persisted.

'I wasn't involved,' Ved persisted.

'Involved in what?'

'Nothing.'

'What the hell,' I yelled. 'Just tell me.'

My mother stepped in. 'Okay,' she said. 'It's all a bit complicated and it took me a long time to understand what was happening. But in a nutshell, this is it. Kavita Lamba called me soon after dinner last night. Apparently, Lina Almeida's granddaughter—I've never liked that girl—posted something on Instagram about the Khambata boys. I'm still not sure about the details but I think she said that they did drugs and that they were actually drugs pushers—'

'Nandini knows that part,' Ved interrupted.

'Naturally, the Khambatas are upset,' my mother continued. 'Especially with the allegation that the boys are selling drugs and forcing their friends to try them. Darius Khambata says that the Almeida granddaughter—I can never remember her name—is no innocent bystander. That she actually begged the Khambata boys to buy weed for her.'

'I totally believe that,' I said. 'Kysha is a witch. I've always felt that. But wait a minute. What I can't understand is why Kavita Lamba called you. Because she is the Hon Secretary?'

'No,' my mother snorted. 'Because she is Thea's mother. Darius Khambata called Kavita Lamba with a request. He said that Thea had often seen the Almeida granddaughter with the Khambata boys. He wanted to know if Thea was willing to tell the police what she had observed. Am I making any sense?'

'Jeh and Neville Khambata certainly haven't forced Kysha to use drugs. I've seen them too,' I blurted out without thinking. After which I wished I'd kept my mouth taped. My mother wasn't handling my revelation too well.

'You're also involved in all this?' she groaned, lurching across the room and collapsing on a three-legged chair. 'Nandini, why?'

'I'm not involved in anything,' I tried to explain. 'I've only seen them. You remember that day when my schoolbag ripped and my books fell down in the compound? And when I came home I couldn't fine my biology jotter? So I went down again and was looking all around the compound? That's when I saw Kysha cuddled up with Neville Khambata. They were in that little passage between the compound wall and the garage and they were smoking something that didn't seem like a regular cigarette.'

This didn't comfort my mother one bit. 'I can't understand what's going on,' she moaned. 'Till a week ago we were ordinary people living in an ordinary building. Then the building gets sealed and things fall apart. Within one week we have a murder, drugs, drug peddlers, and Other Things.'

The Other Things had clearly upset my mother more than the murder, the drugs and the drug peddling put together. 'What other things?' I asked.

'I'm getting to that,' my mother snapped. 'After Darius Khambata phoned her, Kavita Lamba tried to talk to Thea. For a long time, Thea insisted that she hadn't seen anything. Then suddenly she had a complete meltdown. It turns out that she's being viciously bullied by that Almeida granddaughter. What's her name again?'

'Kysha,' I supplied.

'Oh yes, Kysha,' my mother said. 'Thea had spotted Kysha and the Khambata boys smoking together a few times. Kysha warned Thea not to say anything to anybody. She claimed that she had photographs of Thea. Photographs in which Thea looked fat and ugly and was partially undressed. She warned Thea that her every move was being monitored and photographed.'

'Photographed?' I asked, glancing at Ved. 'Photographed how?'

'I'm not sure,' my mother replied. 'Kysha warned Thea that those pictures would be circulated on all the All Saints School chats. Poor Thea is extremely conscious about her weight. And she's already shy and withdrawn. For a girl like her, the thought of being humiliated in school must have been unbearable.'

'Poor, poor Thea,' I agreed. 'I've been wondering why she's always staring at Lily Apartments. And why she's started looking…haunted. But wait a minute. Why did Kavita Lamba call you?'

My mother looked bleak. 'Thea thinks it could be Ved.'

'Thea thinks what could be Ved?' I asked. 'She thinks that Ved has been watching her and been photographing her from across the compound?'

'I haven't taken photographs of Thea,' Ved snorted. 'I'm not such a loser. Do these pictures even exist? Has she even seen them?'

'Thea doesn't know who it is,' my mother replied, giving Ved a nasty glare. 'But she told her mother that Ved, Mini and Aashu were often whispering and giggling together with Kysha. She said it could be any of them. And how does it matter whether the photographs exist or not? What matters is that Thea thinks they exist and that she has been living in terror.'

My mother stared at us, her mouth downturned and her eyes hard. 'What matters,' she said, as a parting shot, 'is that somehow my children are involved.'

On that dramatic and rather unjust note, my mother flounced out of the room. I waited for her to go beyond eavesdropping range before I turned to Ved. 'Did you?' I demanded.

'No.'

I waited. Then I waited some more while Ved went to his drums, sat on his stool and began to bang away. The noise gave me a headache, but I didn't budge till Ved sighed and said, 'No pictures.'

'But?' I asked. Don't ask me how I knew there was a but. Twins always do, even twins as unidentical as us.

'But sometime before lockdown, Kysha asked me to stare hard at Thea whenever I passed her in the compound. It was a bloody joke, nothing more. I did it a couple of times, then I forgot.'

Ved returned to his drums. I returned to my room, my phone and nineteen impatient messages from Shanaya. I didn't call her immediately. Instead, I picked up a few pairs of shorts and T-shirts from the floor and squished them into my cupboard while I tackled an unpleasant idea. Had Shanaya also been a part of the plan to torment Thea?

I hoped not, but I couldn't be sure.

22

When I finally called Shanaya, it felt like we hadn't spoken for a century. We talked for so long that the phone turned warm and moist in my hand and the morning slipped into lunchtime. We broke for a quick, distracted lunch and returned to our sweating phones and looping, unproductive discussions.

We talked about Daniel, and my chat with him. (Shanaya crowed and said, 'I told you he was interested' about three dozen times.)

We talked about Kysha and Thea. (Shanaya said she hadn't been a part of the nastiness. I don't think I believed her. I was realizing that Shanaya and Kysha were much friendlier with each other than I had imagined. I was realizing that I didn't know my best friend and my twin quite as well as I had imagined.)

And finally, we talked about Baman-Burman. (Shanaya agreed that my theory made total sense and decided that Mr Burman was now our Chief Suspect. She suggested we tell the police. Once again, I was confused. If Mr Burman had taken away the parcel meant for Baman Marker, wasn't it more likely that the enraged Hon Chairperson would kill his pesky, thieving neighbour than the other way round?)

We backed and we forthed, and we forthed and we backed. I came up with many ideas, but Shanaya was in a pessimistic, heavy mood and squashed every suggestion. She sounded sad and stressed, which made me sad and stressed in turn. Somehow, we had to sort this mess out soon—I really, really wanted my clever, energetic friend back.

We were exhausted when we hung up. Shanaya planned to take a nap, but I crossed my fingers and checked my phone. The crossed fingers were useless. Daniel hadn't sent me a message.

I looked past my curtains with their pink and yellow dots. Daniel's window was an empty oblong and there was nothing to see besides curtains that must have begun life as a rich maroon but had turned anemic because of copious amounts of sunshine and Surf powder.

The curtains flapped as wind whisked through the compound. The wide, green leaves of the Burmans' banana plants paddled in the afternoon air. A fat grey cloud sailed along the bleached sky, a teaser for the monsoons that would blow in soon. Suddenly, things were moving.

Feeling optimistic for no real reason, I went to Ved's room, settled on his blue-and-white striped bed once more and started chatting. Ved was more energetic than Shanaya, which is probably why we had our big breakthrough.

'I guess the question is, why was the parcel so important?' Ved asked for the twentieth time. 'What do you think was in it?'

'Daniel said it was small,' I replied, also for the twentieth time.

'How small exactly?' Ved asked, veering a little from the script.

'As small as a KitKat chocolate, according to Daniel. What could be so small? Could it be money?'

'Maybe a credit card?' Ved suggested. 'Or jewellery? Maybe an invaluable Parsi heirloom. Maybe diamond earrings that cost a bomb. The earrings land up at Mr Burman's house and he decides to keep them. Then Baman Marker figures out that Mr Burman has stolen the earrings. He threatens to tell the whole world. Mr Burman panics and kills him.'

This might have worked as the storyline of a Bollywood blockbuster, but it didn't work as well in a real world inhabited by conniving, cautious varieties like Baman Marker.

'Why send invaluable jewellery anywhere in the middle of a lockdown?' I scoffed.

'Who knows?' Ved said. 'Maybe the diamond earrings had gone for repairs and the jeweller wanted to return them to the Markers before he went to his village. Maybe—'

'But if Baman Marker knew that something so precious was on its way, wouldn't he go down and wait for the parcel? He knew the delivery man wouldn't be allowed upstairs. He knew that the earrings would be left at the gate with two new, burping night watchmen. Why would he risk—wait a minute—'

An idea had suddenly tapped me on the shoulder. Blocking out Ved's questions and the coppersmith's tuk-tuk, I examined it carefully. A bit like that make-believe jeweller must have examined the diamonds in those make-believe heirloom earrings. Then I muttered, almost under my breath, 'There may be a way to find out what was in that parcel.'

'How?'

'All we need is a little luck.'

'HOW?'

'The Compulsory Register.'

'What?'

'Remember the register that's kept at the gate?' I asked with exaggerated patience. 'Remember that everyone who comes to the building has to put down their name and number and why they've come to the building? Salman of Citypoint Vegetables is always complaining. He says it's a big pain.'

'So?'

'Just think, Ved,' I snapped. 'The person who brought the parcel for Baman Marker probably had to write his name in the register. That was the rule laid down by the Hon Chairman. The security guards were paranoid about following every rule laid down by Chemmen Saab. They were totally afraid of him.'

'So, what are you saying exactly?'

'We know that the parcel was delivered on Thursday evening after 7 p.m. because the night watchmen were already on duty. Hardly anybody comes here in the evenings because of the lockdown. If we check the register, it will be pretty easy to find the name and phone number of the person who brought the parcel. Does that make sense?'

'Yes,' Ved whooped. 'Let's go and check right away.'

'The only problem is, how to do it? Night Mishraji will be seriously zapped if we go downstairs and ask to look at the Compulsory Register. He will start throwing the rules at us. What we need is a proper excuse.'

'More than an excuse, we need an adult. Let's ask Amma.'

We found our mother at the dining table, bashing away at her laptop and talking to Ramesh Bhai, her carpenter, on speakerphone. She waved us away with a forbidding scowl, so I returned to my bedroom. I wished that Daniel would send me a message. I wished the killer would get caught and that this smog of uncertainty would dissipate. I wished that Shanaya would return to being her bright, funny, tough self. I wished that my waist was smaller.

I decided to tackle my wishlist one item at a time. I would start with my waist. I'd recently read an article about fun ways to lose weight, and hula hooping seemed the best solution. (Ten minutes a day for six weeks, and you can shrink your waist by 3.4 cm. Actually.)

Today might as well be Day 1. I found my blue hula hoop under the bed and got busy. There was just one hitch. I was incapable of keeping the hoop up and going for more than forty-three seconds. After three frustrating sessions of forty-three seconds, I needed a break, so I returned to the living room where my mother was staring at her computer with white-lipped concentration. 'Can I talk to you for a minute?' I asked. 'I know you're working but it's important.'

'What now?' she groaned.

'It's about the parcel that went missing,' I said, speaking fast. 'I'm almost positive it had something to do with the murder. And I was thinking that maybe the delivery man who came last Thursday night with the parcel might have written his details in the register downstairs.'

'Okay,' my mother said, swivelling back to her computer.

'But I'm not sure that Night Mishraji will show me the register,' I said. 'I think we might need an adult and a plan.'

My mother sighed, torn between her work and Amrita Aunty. 'Okay, let's go downstairs quickly,' she said.

'Worst comes to worst it'll have to be Maggie noodles for dinner again.'

'I thought Ved was making dinner tonight,' I whined, losing no chance to play slimy sibling. 'It's his turn.'

'Yes, yes,' my mother said. 'But that will be even more time-consuming for me. You get Ved. I'll think of an excuse for Night Mishraji.'

Two minutes later, my mum, Ved and I marched out of the door, masked and purposeful. Alfonsa hovered, trying to guess where we were going. As we climbed down the stairs, I wondered if there was someone across the compound in Daisy Apartments, puzzling over the three pairs of legs trotting down the stairwell of Lily Apartments.

Night Mishraji was more than puzzled when we reached the ground floor and stood behind the locked metal gate, like creatures risen from the dead. He actually flinched when my mother hailed him, and he shambled up to us with great reluctance.

My mother decided that peremptory was the way to go. 'Show me the register,' she ordered.

'The register?' Night Mishraji looked stricken. 'I will have to ask Secketry Madam if I can show the register to anyone.'

'I'm in a hurry,' my mother said. 'I need to know if Salman of Citypoint Vegetables delivered vegetables for me last Thursday. He has sent me a bill of Rs 1200 but no vegetables reached me. I need to know what happened to the vegetables. Is he lying? Or did Somebody Else take those vegetables? Rs 1200 is a lot of money.'

The accusation in her voice was unmistakable. Night Mishraji heard it and quailed. 'I always bring everything upstairs,' he protested. 'Nobody else has ever complained.'

'Just bring me the register,' my mother said.

Night Mishraji looked around nervously to confirm that neither the Hon Secketry nor the ghost of the Hon Chemmen was lurking in the vicinity. Then he shuffled to the table positioned in the middle of the compound and returned with a dog-eared notebook featuring a snow-capped mountain. He handed it to my mother through the grills of the gate.

Ignoring Night Mishraji and his unhappy gaze, my mother flipped the pages of the book till she reached Thursday, 7 May. 'I can't make out a thing,' she said in a low tone, indicating a page filled with illegible scrawls.

'The parcel was delivered after 7 p.m.,' I suggested. 'Start from the bottom of the page.'

My mother's finger moved down the page and hovered over the last entry. 'Got it, I think,' she said. 'There's only one entry after 7 p.m. And it's written in a decent handwriting. Mr Kenneth Fernandes. Parcel for Baman Marker. Mr Fernandes belongs to something called… something called…Wide Eye?'

She angled the book towards us so that I could take a photograph. On the other side of the gate, Night Mishraji was getting fretful, but none of us cared. I checked that my photograph was clear and slid the notebook back to him, after which we climbed back to the fourth floor, jiggling with glee and questions. 'Wide Eye?' my mother asked as we climbed the steps. 'What on earth is that? I hope I read it right. Nandini, did you get a clear photograph of the entry? And of Kenneth Fernandes' phone number?'

'Wide Eye sounds like an optician,' Ved said. 'Hope we don't find out that Baman Marker's spectacles broke and he ordered a new pair. And that the reason he was desperate to find the parcel was because he needed the spectacles so badly. That would be a real let down.'

Ved and my mother continued talking, but I had zoned out. I was focusing on the two words. Wide Eye. I had seen them somewhere. Small white letters on a shiny black surface. I had seen them often. I just didn't know where.

The answer came to me in a flash between the third and fourth floor. 'CCTV,' I yelped, startling my mother and Ved, who were a few steps ahead of me. 'Isn't Wide Eye the company that's installed the CCTVs in the compound? I always feel spooked when I walk under the cameras and see the word Wide Eye on them. It sounds so…so…greedy and watchful.'

We entered out apartment, took off our masks and sanitized our hands before my mother spoke. 'Nandini,' she smiled. 'I honestly think you're more observant than any CCTV camera.'

I smiled back in a distracted fashion. Being nosy came with advantages, but the murder of the Hon Chairperson had demonstrated that it also came with some serious disadvantages. More and more I was getting the feeling that Baman Marker had been dispatched to the hereafter because of his nosiness. And nastiness, of course.

My mother echoed my thoughts. 'Baman Marker collected the secrets of others,' she said as she headed to the kitchen to make herself a cup of tea. Ved and I followed her and ripped into a bag of chivda. Alfonsa followed us and started washing a fork in slow motion, while she listened with glinting eyes.

Reaching for the tea leaves, milk and sugar, my mother continued, 'Baman Marker knew all kinds of things about people. Not secrets, exactly, but small, dirty details. He knew if your apartment had an illegal bathroom. He knew if you had an alcohol problem. He knew if you'd been involved in some long-ago traffic accident. All the four CCTV cameras were connected to his phone. I'm starting to wonder if he actually sat and watched the footage from the cameras.'

'And that while watching he saw something…' I intoned.

'Something that got him killed,' Ved said through a mouthful of chivda.

'Maybe he didn't manage to save that particular bit of footage,' my mother guessed, as she poured the tea into her red mug. 'Or maybe he didn't realize that what he'd seen was significant. When he realized that he needed it, he contacted Wide Eye and asked for the footage.'

Ved and I nodded in unison. It made sense, a lot of sense. Now all we had to do was find out if our theory matched reality.

My mother agreed to make the call to Kenneth Fernandes of Wide Eye. 'I just hope he isn't a halfwit with a memory problem,' she grumbled as she punched the number. Then she put the phone on a green coffee table, next to a pair of wooden Ganpatis and took a deep breath.

For the next minute, the Ganpatis, Alfonsa, my mum, Ved and I were regaled by Kenneth Fernandes's ringtone—a lush, instrumental version of 'Somewhere Over the Rainbow'. The song had reached the 'Where trouble melts like lemon drops' bit when Kenneth Fernandes answered with a rich, plummy 'Hello'.

'Hi, is this Mr Fernandes of Wide Eye?' my mother asked.

'Yes, Kenneth speaking. May I have the pleasure of knowing with whom I am speaking?'

The orotund voice belonged neither to a halfwit nor an amnesiac and my mother brightened perceptibly. 'I am Mrs Venkat from Lily Apartments near Sassoon Dock,' she said in her dinner-party-at-Bombay-Gym tones. 'Mr Baman Marker, our Chairperson, had contacted you on my behalf. He had requested some…some material that I needed. I think you delivered it on Thursday but then on Friday evening you know…the tragedy…'

Mr Fernandes sucked in his breath. 'Terrible, terrible business,' he thundered. 'Such a polite, soft-spoken man. And so knowledgeable about security issues. In fact, he contacted me just a month ago to say that he wanted to install two more cameras in your compound. His passing is a real loss.'

'Yes,' my mother agreed.

'The police contacted me yesterday,' Mr Fernandes continued. 'They wanted all the CCTV feed of last Friday and Saturday. I helped them immediately. My duty as a citizen.'

'Good, good,' my mother said. 'One must do one's duty as a citizen. That was really good of you. I was actually wondering if you could help me as well.'

'Of course, madam. It is my duty.'

My mother clutched one of the Ganpatis for moral support and jumped in. 'Mr Marker never managed to pass on that material to me. Mrs Marker is staying with her daughter right now, so there is no way for me to get hold of it. Do you think you could send me a duplicate?'

Kenneth Fernandes was silent for a long moment and I was overcome by sudden panic. What if we'd got it all wrong? What if my mum had said something that had made him suspicious?

Then Kenneth Fernandes spoke and I could breathe again. 'Are you referring to the pen drive that I left at your building last week?' he asked. 'The one that Baman Sir said was extremely urgent? The one with three days' footage from the CCTV camera?'

'Yes, yes,' my mother said. 'Could you please...would it be possible to give me a duplicate?'

'Do you remember the dates?' Kenneth Fernandes asked.

'Uhhh...uhhh...' my mother stuttered. 'I will have to—'

'Hold on. I have them written in my diary. I am a big believer in diaries. Old-fashioned, but old is gold. Here we are. You requested footage from the front gate CCTV camera for three days? 1 February, 16 February and 20 February, is that correct?'

'Yes, yes.'

'You are lucky. When Baman Sir called me last Thursday afternoon, I really wasn't sure that I still had the footage. We usually delete it after two months.'

'Oh really?' my mother said.

Kenneth Fernandes launched into a detailed explanation about Wide Eye and their 2703 CCTV cameras installed across the city. Apparently, the footage was kept for two months. Under normal circumstances, all February footage would have been deleted on the 1st of May. But given the lockdown and the reduced staff at Wide Eye, this hadn't happened on schedule.

'Baman Sir was very relieved,' Mr Fernandes said. 'He asked for the footage immediately. I offered to share the files online. But Baman Sir was an old-fashioned gent. And he was so worried about the vandalism in the building that I agreed to drop the pen drive at the gate. After all, customer is king.'

My mum thanked Kenneth Fernandes fulsomely and said that she could view the footage online. Mr Fernandes agreed to share it on Google Drive and requested my mother to keep Wide Eye in mind for any future security requirements. My mother promised—and she meant it. I was pretty sure that as soon as lockdown was done and Reincarnations reopened, the store would be sporting a Wide Eye CCTV camera.

The link to the files arrived soon after dinner. Till then I mooned over Daniel and phoned Shanaya. Sadly, Daniel remained invisible—both on my phone and at his window. And Shanaya remained gloomy and monosyllabic, even though she did offer to help with the CCTV footage. 'You do 1 February, I'll do 16 February and Ved can do 20 February,' she said.

'Okay,' I agreed. 'Listen, Shanaya. I have a really good feeling about things. I'm sure this will end soon.'

'Maybe,' Shanaya said darkly. 'But the question is, how will it end?'

Shanaya's anxiety was contagious. I'd planned to go to bed soon after dinner, but found myself too jittery to sleep. Instead, I decided to get a head start on the footage. Positioning myself at my desk, I clicked on the link that took me to 1 February. Then I stared at the screen and clutched my head.

The CCTV camera that had been installed on the front gate gazed at an uninviting patch of road and pavement, as well as a stretch of driveway that led into the Lily and Daisy compound. Kenneth Fernandes had told us that the CCTV camera came on when it sensed motion. The problem was that in those bustly days of February, before coronavirus became a Thing, there was constant motion near the gate.

There were hours and hours of footage to watch, and none of it was Netflix material. Dreading the task that lay ahead, I looked out of my bedroom window. And froze.

In the stairwell of Daisy Apartments I saw legs. Legs climbing the stairs.

Something clicked in my head and, in that moment, my theories and my world fell apart.

23

On the fifty-third day of the lockdown, I woke up early with a pounding head and puffy eyes.

I lay in bed and refused to do the things I normally did. I didn't look across the compound at a certain window with faded, once-maroon curtains. I didn't check my phone. I didn't even worry about whether I was looking fat. There was no point. If my theory was right—and I was pretty convinced that it was—then I was the saddest person alive. Literally.

Sorry, sorry. By now you're probably wondering if I plan to whine for the next forty-eight hours. Let me just get this over and done with.

This is what happened on Friday night—exactly one week from the night that the Hon Chairperson drank the contents of a metal bottle filled with Green Glow Detox Smoothie and Ethylene Glycol. Exactly one week from the night that his lungs and heart started collapsing as he lay alone in a blue and brown bedroom. Exactly one week from the night that a soft-footed killer struck.

My father was expecting a call at 9 p.m. so we'd had an early dinner. Maggie noodles, in case you were wondering. Ved's lucky star had come through yet again.

Amrita Aunty called while we were clearing the table. Amrita Aunty rarely called these days. She rarely answered when my mother called. And even when she did pick up the phone she was distracted, prickly, cold. Naturally then, my mother rushed to take the call. 'Amrita,' she cried. 'How are you? How are things? I haven't spoken to you in ages.'

Then silence and another exclamation. 'Poor man. Naturally they will have to allow a doctor to enter the building. Poor, poor Sheela. It's seriously only bad news these days.'

Three minutes later, Ved and I returned from the kitchen with our haul of Bourbon biscuits and found our mum in the balcony. 'Mr Alimchandani seems to have had a stroke,' she said. 'Rashida Habibullah went up with his dinner and realized that he wasn't responding. A doctor will be coming soon. Poor Sheela is freaking out.'

We watched from the balcony for some time, but there was no sign of the doctor and we drifted away. My mother to her computer. Ved to a Zoom call with his school friends. And I to my bedroom and my worries about Shanaya. I was exhausted, but I knew I would never be able to sleep. Which was why I sat at my desk with my computer and the CCTV footage.

I glanced out of the window about ten minutes later. The Carvalho house was quiet, but the compound was not. A car had driven in and a man had emerged from the driver's seat. He slipped on a whitish safety suit while the night watchman opened the groaning gate of Daisy Apartments.

The doctor stepped into Daisy Apartments and my eyes turned once more to the Carvalho balcony. I spotted Florence on yet another one of her neatening sprees. I saw her folding a newspaper, picking up a mug and rearranging the two chairs exactly as she had a few days ago. Tuesday? Wednesday? I couldn't remember when, but I did remember her efficient bustle as she scrubbed and dusted and yanked a raincoat from a hook.

Her task complete, Florence disappeared into the bowels of the dark apartment. I was about to return to my computer screen when my eyes slid to the windows that looked into the staircase of Daisy Apartments—squares of yellow light set against darkness. Which was when I experienced a flash of déjà vu so sharp that my breath caught.

A pair of legs was climbing the staircase from the third to the fourth floor. The doctor, on his way to see Mr Alimchandani, dressed in a white safety suit that flapped around his ankles.

It was at that moment that I knew.

I knew with cold certainty that the second person that I had seen last Friday night had worn neither a white salwar nor white pajamas. He or she had worn a white safety suit. Or something that looked very like a white safety suit.

Once I saw this, I saw other things.

I saw the flurry of activity on Friday afternoon, when Daisy Apartments was being sealed. I saw the BMC men in their white safety suits swarming through the building. And I thought about how safety suits granted the wearer both anonymity and the right to wander at will. After which I thought about how a translucent raincoat could so easily be mistaken for a safety suit.

Then I saw all the unanswered questions that had remained at the periphery of the investigation. Suddenly, they came together in an insistent chorus. I had no option but to hear them out, one at a time.

When Lily Apartments had been sealed, no BMC official had entered our flat. Or Mini's flat or Aashu's flat. So then why, on that afternoon when Daisy Apartments was being sealed, had I spotted a man in a safety suit walking through the living room of the Carvalho apartment?

Why had a man in a safety suit gone all the way up to a roof that was hardly ever used? Why, when I had definitely counted five people in safety suits from my balcony that afternoon, did I have a feeling that only four had driven away in the BMC van after Daisy Apartments was sealed?

What had happened to the fifth man?

What had caused the mysterious bumps and thumps in the Carvalho apartment? What had happened to the white-clad legs that I had seen so fleetingly? Where had they gone after they reached the third floor?

And finally, why would anyone take out a long, whitish raincoat in the middle of a sunny, dry day in May and hang it on a hook in the balcony?

There was one answer that worked for these questions. You may have figured it out yourself, but I'll say it anyway.

Mr Carvalho was the killer.

The brilliant physics teacher with a dubious past had created a brilliant alibi for himself. He'd managed to fool everyone—the neighbours, the BMC, the police, nosy Nandini Venkat from next door. He'd achieved this with a sleight of hand. And with some help from his son.

Daniel.

This is how it must have happened. When the BMC arrived to seal Daisy Apartments, Mr Carvalho had executed a trick worthy of a conjurer. He had put on his mask and his translucent raincoat. Then, pretending to be a harassed BMC official, he'd hurried out of the apartment and vanished onto the roof of Daisy Apartments.

Meanwhile Daniel had announced—to the BMC officials and the world at large—that his father was not at home.

Mr Carvalho must have hidden on the roof and, later in the evening, must have returned home to whip up a poisoned smoothie. At 10.20 p.m. he must have tiptoed up to the fifth floor with his deadly gift. After midnight, he must have crept upstairs again to make sure that the Hon Chairperson had accepted his offering.

After that, Mr Carvalho must have holed up in his apartment and waited for dawn. Then, around the time that Mrs Kurien went to fetch her milk, he must have slipped out of Daisy Apartments and melted into the soupy, grey Saturday morning.

All this I saw with sickening certainty a week later, while a doctor in a whitish safety suit climbed the stairs of Daisy Apartments.

I didn't mind that Mr Carvalho was a killer. But I did mind that Daniel had lied to me. That he had acted friendly and chatty only so that he could find out how much I knew about the murder of Baman Marker. No wonder he hadn't called or messaged again.

Do you blame me for being devastated?

Eventually I went to bed, where I tossed and turned and sniffled. Again and again I went over the details that did fit. And the details that didn't. The baffling fact that although the Carvalhos lived on the third floor, I had first spotted Black Legs though the window between the second and third floor.

The puzzling fact that Mr Carvalho had shed his raincoat when he delivered his deadly parcel at 10.25 p.m. but had worn it again during his midnight sortie.

The fact that Mr Carvalho had whipped up a poisoned smoothie in Florence's kitchen. (I couldn't imagine Florence being part of the plot. If she had, Alfonsa would have known and made sure that we knew too.)

I was still confused when the sun rose and streaked the night sky with watery violet and septic yellow. But it was while brushing my teeth that I made up one part of my fragmented mind. I didn't know what I was going to do about Mr Carvalho, but I did know what I was going to do about his son.

I was going to make him regret messing with Nandini Venkat from next door.

24

I called Daniel about twenty minutes after Florence whisked aside the anemic maroon curtains and opened the bedroom windows to the summer glare. He answered on the second ring with a smile in his voice. 'Nandini Venkat from next door!'

Despite everything, my heart hula hooped.

I had planned to confront Daniel with icy fury. But the warmth that rushed through the phone flooded me with inconvenient tenderness. Daniel was asking how I'd been and what I'd been doing. Ignoring his friendliness, I held onto my rage and said what I had planned to say.

'I know.'

The words came out poky and hard. Daniel missed a couple of beats before he said, 'Know what?'

'I know that your father was in the building last Friday night.'

Although I'd spent the last six months thinking about him, I didn't know Daniel at all. I was prepared for lies, bluster, indignant denial, anything. Still, Daniel managed to catch me off balance.

After another pause, he said, 'Okay.'

Okay? That's all? Your father has just been exposed as a murderer and all you say is 'okay'? All the sneers and speeches I had planned shrivelled on my lips. I was still gaping when he spoke again. 'Do you know anything else? About what else happened?'

This time, I was angry enough to speak. 'What do you mean?' I asked. 'What exactly are you asking me? Are you asking me if I have proof that your father killed Baman Marker?'

'Something like that,' he said in a strangled voice, and in my mind I saw Daniel standing in a cheerless bedroom, biting his perfect lips and clenching his beautiful hands.

I pushed the image aside. 'I may not have proof,' I said curtly. 'But I have a pretty good idea about how it happened. And I'm sure that the police will find proof once they're pointed in the right direction.'

'Do you know…what I mean is…are you sure that my father did it? I'm not asking about proof. I'm just asking if you're sure.' There was no challenge in Daniel's voice. Only quiet dread.

'Don't you know?' I taunted.

'No,' Daniel cried, and then quickly lowered his voice. 'I don't know. That's why I'm asking you, Nandini. Because you seem to know—'

'I don't believe you,' I said baldly. 'You've already lied to me.'

'Yes, and I'm sorry,' Daniel said. 'I didn't want to lie to you, but I didn't know what else to do. Ever since I heard that Mr Marker was killed on Friday night, I've been afraid. I really wanted to know who, what, how… Then Florence told me that you knew everything…and then you messaged…and I felt I had to find out if my father…'

'Why didn't you just ask your father?' I snarled. 'You'd have gotten a nice, first-person account.'

'I did ask,' Daniel replied in an empty voice. 'He denied it. Which doesn't really mean anything. If a person can kill someone, then that person can lie.'

It was bad enough that I had started the morning with puffy eyes and a non-functioning brain. This bizarre conversation was making my head spin. Either Daniel was an Oscar-level actor, or he was telling the truth. I was too disoriented to decide which.

'Look, Nandini,' Daniel said suddenly. 'I am not saying that my father didn't do it. He hated Mr Marker. And he had good reason to hate Mr Marker. But there are things I don't understand. My father left the house in such a hurry on Friday afternoon, he only had time to take his wallet, his phone—and, of course, that raincoat. So how did he get hold of that green juice, and that coolant? And that note written by Aunty Almeida?'

All this time I'd refused to succumb to Daniel's untrustworthy charm but I couldn't ignore his doubts—partly because they echoed my own. 'Your father must have made the smoothie when he came downstairs again,' I said. 'After the BMC men left.'

'You don't understand,' Daniel said. 'He didn't come down till much later. Can I explain exactly what happened?'

'Okay,' I said, not because of the entreaty in his voice but because I really wanted to know.

'My father had been upset for a couple of days,' Daniel explained. 'He gets into these moods. Then something happened that morning, to make him go almost crazy. When the BMC came to seal Daisy Apartments he started shouting and throwing things. He said that there was no way he would be stuck in a sealed building. He had things to do, and he would do them. When my father gets into his rages he is uncontollable. He smashed two plates that day. And threw a small table across the room. Then suddenly he calmed down and had an idea. He told me to tell the BMC people that he was not at home. He grabbed his raincoat and left. I thought that he had left the building. I tried to call him, but the phone was switched off.'

'Then?' I prompted.

'Then sometime after 11 o'clock on Friday night, the doorbell rang,' Daniel said. 'It was my father. He told me that he'd been hiding on the roof. The only reason he'd come down was because he needed to use the loo. He'd been careful to wait till Florence went to bed, and he left the building before she woke up the next morning.'

'What sense does that make?' I asked. 'Why didn't he just leave the building around the same time as the BMC men? Wasn't that his original plan?'

'Yes. But he got nervous. Mr Marker was standing in the middle of the compound, and my father was afraid of being recognized. So he went up to the terrace instead. To hide.'

'I don't understand. Why would he spend hours and hours on the terrace?'

'He was determined to get out of the building,' Daniel explained. 'He didn't dare come back to the apartment because he didn't want Florence to know that he was still around. So he remained on the terrace, waiting for a good time to get out.'

'So he was the mysterious man that Mrs Kurlen saw?'

'Yes.'

I thought about what Daniel had said and alighted on an inconsistency. 'But I saw those white legs climbing down much later at night,' I pointed out. 'After midnight.'

'Yes,' Daniel said, and for the first time his voice wavered. 'My father came down to use the loo after Florence went to bed. But he went up again because he'd forgotten his phone on the terrace.'

'Okay,' I said, wondering what Daniel wasn't telling me.

I didn't have to wonder for long. 'He was upstairs for almost an hour,' Daniel said in a rush. 'That's why, when I heard that Mr Marker had been murdered…'

'You thought there might be a connection,' I supplied, recalling that just seconds after the white legs had run down to the third floor, Baman Marker's bedroom had been plunged into darkness.

'You must be wondering how I could suspect my own father,' Daniel said. 'But it's always been complicated in our house.'

'Okay,' I said and then, because it seemed so inadequate, I added, 'Why did your father hate Baman Marker so much?'

'My father did something wrong a long time ago,' Daniel said. 'He got caught. My mother could never forgive him for the shame. All that my parents wanted was for it to be forgotten. But Mr Marker and Aunty Almeida kept it alive. Every time they needed something from my father, they threatened to start things all over again.'

'What kind of stuff did they want from him?' I asked, startled. What could a discredited physics teacher possibly do for Baman Marker and Lina Almeida?

Daniel laughed, and I heard the first note of bitterness in his voice. 'How do you think Kysha managed to pass her

Standard 10 exams?' he asked. 'Everyone agreed that it was a miracle. Who do you think organized that miracle? Not the Lord, that's for sure. But Nandini, it's your turn to tell me something now.'

'What?'

'Do you believe me?'

I thought about it for a long moment before I said, very quietly, 'I'm not sure. But I think I believe you.'

'I'm so glad,' Daniel said as quietly.

To my great disgust, my eyes filled with tears. If I wasn't careful, I would turn into Drippy Nandini. Assuming my briskest voice, I said, 'In which case I guess I still have work to do and a killer to catch.'

Daniel laughed. 'That you will. For the first time in her fifty-eight years, Florence hasn't exaggerated. Thank you, Nandini Venkat from next door.'

25

At around 10 a.m., Ved, Shanaya and I had a quick moan about the horrors awaiting us. Then we settled down to deal with those horrors.

First, I stocked up for a day of soul-destroying screen time. The only snacks in our depleted kitchen were Marie biscuits and Cheeslings. I snatched the Cheeslings before Ved could get to them and slouched back to my bedroom.

I was in charge of the CCTV footage from 1 February, which was a Saturday.

The footage started at 12 a.m. and little happened during the sleepy hours of the night. Night Mishraji strolled past a few times. At around 2 a.m., Ruby Vaz and her husband bounced in with three friends. Although there was no soundtrack, you could tell that they were happy and laughing. At around 4 a.m. a car halted at the gate, a door opened and Kysha half fell out. She was so unsteady on her wedge-heeled feet that the boy who was driving the car hurried out, propped her up and virtually wheeled her into the compound. A few minutes later he returned to the car and drove away.

I'd started taking notes on a crisp yellow pad, but once morning rolled around, that became impossible. There were too many people walking in, driving out, hanging around near the gate and chatting. I spotted myself, dashing out in a tight T-shirt and that insanely expensive pleated skirt from Japan. I must have been on my way to Tanishka's birthday party. I looked skinny and the skirt looked great.

It struck me that I hadn't seen the skirt in ages. Could it have gotten lost? I hoped not.

Meanwhile, there was plenty of action on the screen. The problem was that none of it was worth a raised eyebrow. It astounded me that the Hon Chairperson had actually spent his free time watching this dire footage.

Ved and Shanaya complained that their day was going quite as badly.

'Nothing,' Ved barked when we did a group call at noon and again in the late afternoon.

'Nothing,' Shanaya snorted. 'Not a blood-dripping dagger in sight. This is a waste of time. I think we should just stop.'

'Nothing,' I sighed, 'and my head is reeling.'

By early evening, I was both puky and panicky. Could Kenneth Fernandes have gotten the dates wrong? Were we barking up the wrong tree entirely? Had we missed something major?

Then, just before dinner, Ved hurtled into my bedroom with his laptop and a huge grin. 'Got it,' he announced.

'What? Whatwhat? What?'

Instead of answering, Ved put his laptop on my desk and pressed play. Together we watched as, at 10.57 p.m. on 20 February, a lanky figure strolled out of the compound and onto the pavement. At first, all I could make out was that the person was male, smoking a cigarette and moving to an energetic rhythm.

'Neville Khambata,' Ved said.

'What's he doing? Why is he standing on the pavement?'

The question was unnecessary. Another figure had stepped onto the screen, also male, also young, but somehow dishevelled. We watched as Neville Khambata stepped back into the shadows, beyond the gaze of the CCTV camera. We could still see his acquaintance, however, as he removed a tiny packet from the pocket of his jeans. We saw the little white packet being handed over and what looked like a roll of notes being stuffed into the same tight pocket.

The new man walked away and Neville Khambata hurried back into the compound. Although I couldn't see his face, I decided that he looked pleased with his little shopping expedition.

We watched the sequence twice. Then we phoned Shanaya, who was even more excited than we were. 'Kysha was right after all,' she gloated. 'Shouldn't we tell the police?'

'I don't know,' I said. 'I still find it difficult to imagine Neville Khambata as a killer.'

'But it's the only thing we've got,' Shanaya protested. 'I just finished watching 16 February. There's nothing there at all. It was just another sleepy, boring Sunday.'

'Nothing on 1 February either,' I said. 'Which is strange, because Baman Marker was so specific with his dates.'

We disconnected the call and Ved and I hurried to the living room, where my mother was sketching something that was a cross between a mushroom and a side table. 'You have to see this,' Ved said, putting his laptop on top of her drawing.

My mother seemed eager to get away from the mushroom-table. We were huddled around the laptop screen in the living room when my father entered. 'What are you guys doing?' he asked, and came to look over our shoulders. 'What's all this?'

We were so chuffed by our ingenuity, that we gave him a full account of our sleuthing and snooping. Too late, we realized that his face was turning tighter and tighter and his voice was becoming colder and colder. 'Are the three of you completely insane?' he asked when we came to the part about the CCTV footage. 'You really don't see that you've done something stupid?'

'But I've already told you most of this,' my mother protested. 'Why are you going nuts?'

'Because I never imagined that you would go this far,' my father seethed. 'What is wrong with you? Watching CCTV feed like a bunch of voyeurs. Priti, I told you not to interfere.'

'But,' my mother started to protest. 'I don't understand what's so wrong. The point of CCTV—'

'I TOLD you not to interfere,' my father exploded. 'Amrita, Amrita, Amrita. All the time Amrita. Enough. It is not your job to save her. Leave it alone.'

He stormed off just as Alfonsa, who relished family fights almost as much as she adored murders, sidled into the room. She looked over our shoulders at the CCTV feed. Neville Khambata and his little white packet had exited the screen, to be replaced by Amrita Aunty and Shanaya who seemed to be returning home from a wedding.

Alfonsa smacked her lips and whispered, 'The police found some pictures in Chemmen Saab's room. There were two pictures of Amrita Madam.'

My mother was flushed, miserable and in no mood to listen to Alfonsa's innuendoes. 'Let's start heating the food for dinner,' she said brusquely.

Alfonsa ignored the instruction. Instead, she licked her lips and said, 'When they found Chemmen Saab in the bedroom, there were many things and papers lying on the floor. After they took Chemmen Saab to hospital, Maria did some cleaning. She picked up all the papers. Then the police came and took the papers away. They asked Maria lots of questions about the papers.'

'And?' I asked, suddenly attentive.

'Maria said that there were two photos of Amrita Madam. She was wearing a very tight black dress,' Alfonsa paused and added with a sly smile. 'She was with a MAN.'

I was perilously close to going at Alfonsa with one of the wooden Ganpatis, and I'm sure my mother would have joined in with the second. It was fortunate, then, that Ved asked his question. 'What were the other papers?'

'All the other papers had English writing on them,' Alfonsa said, oozing regret as she headed to the kitchen. 'We don't know what they said. Maria doesn't know how to read English. But there was one newspaper article—it was so old that it was tearing—in which there was a photograph of Mr Alimchandani. And there was one photograph of those ground floor Habibullahs standing in their kitchen.'

Photographs of Amrita Aunty. A newspaper article about Mr Alimchandani. A photograph of the Habibullahs' kitchen. Ved and I glanced at each other. 'I bet some of the documents had to do with the Burmans,' I said with sudden excitement.

'Why?' my mother asked.

'We've never understood why the police searched four houses—Amrita Aunty's, the Habibullah's, Mr Alimchandani's and the Burmans,' Ved explained. 'Maybe it was because of the photographs and documents they found in Baman Marker's bedroom…'

'Amrita told me about those papers lying near Baman Marker, but I'd forgotten about them,' my mother mused. 'And anyway, those papers just don't make sense. He must have been feeling really unwell by then, but instead of getting into bed, he pulled out a file full of random documents and photographs about his neighbours. What could he have been thinking? I just cannot imagine.'

I didn't reply. I guess I was too busy watching a scene in my head—a scene that might or might not have unfolded in the Marker apartment on that deadly Friday night:

It's past midnight. Baman Marker is woozy, unsteady and full of Ethylene Glycol. He hears a rap on the door and opens it to find a neighbour. The neighbour enters the flat and demands the documents that Baman Marker has been using as a tool of blackmail for seventeen painful years. During their argument, a porcelain shepherdess shatters and a chair topples. The Hon Chairperson is too unwell to hold out. He pulls out a plump file. There's a scuffle, the file falls—scattering dirty secrets on the floor of that blue-brown room. Glass objects tumble to the floor. A chair is knocked down.

The violent, enraged neighbour is, of course, Mr Carvalho. He finds the documents he wants, grabs them and leaves. The Hon Chairperson feels too unwell to do anything more. He tumbles into bed. The lights go out.

I didn't describe this scene to my mum or to Ved. What would I have said anyway? It was based on guesswork but it did provide explanations for the little mysteries surrounding the death of the Hon Chairperson. The shattered shepherdess and the scattered documents. The fact that Mr Carvalho had hidden on the terrace rather than left the building as soon as he possibly could. The fact that he had told Daniel that he was going up to look for his phone and had then vanished for almost an hour.

Dinner was a strained affair. My mother was not talking to my father. My father was not talking to anyone. The cabbage bhaaji and daal were limp, tasteless, and carefully curated for this dismal Saturday evening.

After dinner we fled to our own lairs. I brushed my teeth, slipped on a grey T-shirt and black pajamas and turned off the lights. I did one thing before I shut my sandpaper-dry eyes. I checked my phone. There were eighty-nine messages, but only one that mattered.

'How's it going, Nandini Venkat from next door?' Daniel had written. 'How many villains have you caught today?'

'Watch the headlines,' I typed back.

It was not very clever, but that was all that my fried brain could manage. Then I sank into bed with a goofy smile and tumbled into a midnight-dark well of sleep.

26

It was still dark when I surfaced from those dreamless depths. I drank two glasses of water, went to the toilet, returned to bed and shut my eyes. I was exhausted, but once again, a gang of anxieties had hijacked the night.

They jostled and pushed and demanded answers. Had my blue pleated skirt from Japan gotten lost? Should we be telling the police about Neville Khambata and his late-night activities? How long would my father remain cold and angry? Had I missed a vital clue in the CCTV footage? Did I need to watch it once more?

After ten wakeful minutes, I checked the time. 5.35 a.m. Already, a couple of birds were getting a head start on their day. Following their example, I got out of bed. Twenty minutes later, I was at my desk, emanating Dove soap, aloe vera shampoo and determination. I was going to crack this mystery today.

My plan had been to revisit the CCTV footage of 1 February. But, as I booted my computer, I decided to take a quick look at 16 February instead.

I admit it. I'm a control freak. One of the reasons I'm so lousy with group work is that I can never accept that things have been done right unless I do them myself. While I do trust Shanaya, I trust myself more. So even though the thought of watching more footage made me queasy, I clicked my way to 16 February and got to work.

16 February was a Sunday. Mini and Kysha were the first people to stroll into the compound, soon after midnight. They were holding gigantic tubs of popcorn and wearing tiny shorts and sneakers. The light of the two false moons that sat on our gatepost hit Kysha's shoes, which flashed a sharp silver.

Aashu's father arrived in a taxi a little later. Then nothing for ages till, at 3.17 a.m., a sleek car halted a little away from our gate. A few minutes later, a woman stepped out from the back seat. She was slim and elegant in a short, dark dress. It took me a minute to recognize Amrita Aunty.

Amrita Aunty must have been returning from one of her trips with her girlfriends. I watched as she went around to the boot of the car. She managed to yank out one suitcase, but the second one was too heavy. I wasn't surprised. Amrita Aunty was a compulsive shopper and habitual excess-luggage flier. She paused, looked towards the compound—probably for Night Mishraji—and then continued to struggle with the bag.

I smiled fondly, but my smile froze a moment later. The backseat door on the far side of the car opened and a man emerged. He went to the boot and, although the car blocked him from view, I could see the second suitcase being placed next to Amrita Aunty. I was wondering how Amrita Aunty had ended up sharing a taxi with a man when I got an answer. Of sorts.

Even as the CCTV camera watched, a pair of arms went around Amrita Aunty's waist and held her tight. The arms stayed there for more than a minute, white sleeves vivid against the dark dress, till Amrita Aunty stepped out of the embrace. The man got back into the car as Amrita Aunty slammed the boot shut. She waved and seconds later, the car had disappeared into the night.

As Amrita Aunty dragged the two heavy bags across the screen of the computer, I wondered where Night Mishraji had vanished. Then I wondered how Amrita Aunty would carry those two bags up the steps of Daisy Apartments to the elevator. I guess I was trying to avoid thinking about the real stuff.

Amrita Aunty had gone for a week-long trip in February. She had told us that she was going to Thailand with her school friends.

She had definitely gone to Thailand. Just, not with her school friends.

Sitting in the half light of a Mumbai dawn, I felt disgusted. Not with Amrita Aunty, who had every right to have a boyfriend and to go to Thailand with him. But with myself for spying on something so private. Maybe my father was justified in his anger, after all.

I wondered if my mother knew that Amrita Aunty had a boyfriend. And if Shanaya had known about his existence before yesterday. And I wondered how she had felt as she watched her mother being embraced by her lover.

I remembered that when Amrita Aunty came back from Thailand, she had given us a box of exquisitely carved soaps. Perfect waterlilies in pale blue, baby pink, milky white. I thought about those delicate soaps while the night of 16 February replayed itself on my screen. I saw Night Mishraji entering the compound with a weary gait. Maybe he was returning from a nocturnal version of a lunch break. After some time, two more figures hurried into the compound, bringing with them their suitcases and their jetlag.

I gazed at the computer screen without interest. There were hours of footage remaining, but there was little point. I had already stumbled upon the secret of 16 February.

Hitting pause, I thought again about Amrita Aunty and her gifts. The box in which the soaps had arrived sat now on my dressing table and housed my rubber bands and scrunchies. It was blue with tiny pink flowers and gold lettering that said 'Banyan Tree Resorts, Phuket'.

Banyan Tree Resorts. Banyan Tree Resorts.

The words resounded in my head like an accusation. I had seen this name before, but where? I bit my lip and tried to retrace the twists and bends of the last few days. But it was only when I opened up the Google Doc that I understood why the name had filled me with unease.

Banyan Tree Resorts had popped up on the Lily-Daisy Apartments chat on that eventful, deadly Friday. Soon after Binaifer Marker had fled Daisy Apartments in a big white car, Amrita Aunty had sent a barrage of sarcastic messages to Baman Marker. Which was when the Hon Chairperson had struck back with a seemingly irrelevant response, 'She is not in Banyan Tree Resorts in Phuket. She is not in an apartment in Worli. Thank you.'

Baman Marker must have figured that Amrita Aunty had travelled to Thailand with her lover. He must have decided to use the CCTV footage as a weapon against his increasingly outspoken and troublesome neighbour.

Somehow, Shanaya had suspected the secret hiding in the CCTV tape, which is why she had volunteered to view the footage of 16 February. My poor, poor friend. No wonder she'd been so unenthusiastic about the whole business. How frightened she must have been that the truth would spill out.

I wondered if Baman Marker had told Amrita Aunty what he'd seen. I wondered whether he'd planned to pass on the footage to Shanaya's father. There was little doubt that Shanaya's father would have used it to prove that Amrita Aunty was an unfit, immoral mother. To get control over Shanaya and her life.

There was no doubt that this was a good reason for Amrita Aunty to murder the Hon Chairperson.

Except.

Except that while a killer dressed in black pants had been creeping up the stairs of Daisy Apartments, Amrita Aunty had been standing in her balcony.

Shivering and rubbing feverish eyes, I stood up. Outside my window, the sky had turned the colour of old bones. Outside my bedroom door, someone was clattering about. Alfonsa or my mother. It was still too early for breakfast. Unable to sit still, I moved around my room looking for something to take my mind off murder and fear. Maybe I should hunt for my blue pleated skirt from Japan. Finding it would make me feel better.

I wandered over to my cupboard and groaned when I saw the higgle piggle of crumpled clothes. Underwear threaded through T-shirts. Leggings knotted with dresses. Right at the bottom, I spied something blue and checked. The skirt?

I gave the triangle of fabric a tug and then shrieked. The bulging mountain of clothes moved along with that fragment and, before I could do anything to stop it, I was in the middle of an avalanche. A landslide of panties, jackets, swimsuits, shrugs, bunny ears, cholis, lacy tops, strappy dresses, camisoles, tank tops, a pink feather boa shedding fluff. Somewhere in the mess, I spotted the Japanese skirt. It didn't cheer me up as much as I had hoped.

In fact, it didn't cheer me up at all.

Standing in front of my cupboard, I burst into tears. Not just because of the heap of crumpled clothes at my feet, but also because of the lockdown and Amrita Aunty and what could so easily happen to Shanaya. Then, because it seemed to be the only way that I could bring order to chaos, I started folding the clothes, sorting them and arranging them in neatish piles. Skirts. Shorts. Pajamas. Jackets. T-shirts with slogans. Tops. Dresses. Jeans. And on my bed, a separate pile of Shanaya's clothes.

I was halfway through the task when I picked up a pair of red pajamas. I folded them mechanically and was about to put them onto Shanaya's pile on the bed when—I realized.

The truth smashed into me like a roaring truck. So hard that I couldn't breathe. All I could do was stare at the pajamas in my hand. They were red, with fried eggs and a few rips and holes in unfortunate spots.

I was clutching them so tight that my hands tingled. But that wasn't enough to stop the unthinkable thoughts.

These were the pajamas that Shanaya had said that she was wearing while we had watched *Mean Girls* on that Friday. These were the pajamas that Shanaya had said she was wearing when somebody in black pants was climbing the staircase of Daisy Apartments with a metal bottle filled with a poisonous smoothie.

But now, one thing was clear. Shanaya had not been wearing the red pajamas with the fried eggs and the holes. Which meant that she had been wearing something else.

Something that could well have been a pair of black pants.

If Shanaya had lied about her pajamas, she could have lied about other things as well. While she was supposedly making tomato soup and exploding the mixer and swabbing the kitchen, she could have whipped up a flask of Green Glow Detox smoothie on the side.

Shanaya knew *Mean Girls* almost by heart. She could recite entire chunks of the dialogue. She could easily have made a quick trip to the fifth floor without missing a beat. She could have sent me a few quick messages as she climbed. Maybe that's why she had needed to put down the Waffle Wonderland bag on the steps. So that she could send me those messages—so that I would believe that she was sitting snug in her yellow bedroom with her laptop, wearing her red pajamas with the rips and the fried eggs.

Shanaya had the motive. Shanaya had the yellow notes from Lina Almeida. Shanaya had the spunk and the brains.

Finally, I had my answer to the puzzle of Daisy Apartments.

My utterly, totally, forever best friend was a killer.

27

Soon after breakfast on the fifty-fourth day of the lockdown, the doorbell rang. For the first time in ten days.

Alfonsa got to the door first. She peered through the peephole and smacked her lips. 'Police,' she announced in a voice throbbing with anticipation. Then she opened the door with a flourish.

The two police officers didn't match Alfonsa's excitement. They looked hot and harassed by their blue masks and thankless task. We were the tenth family that they were interviewing in Lily Apartments. From their hopeless expressions, it was clear that none of our neighbours had seen anything, heard anything, thought of anything.

The two policemen shuffled in and sat on the carved wooden bench in a manner that, in Mumbai-speak, was called half-bum. They didn't plan to be here more than three minutes and saw no reason to get comfortable. They looked a little startled when Ved and I sat down on the sofa next to my mother. 'Children not required,' the younger police officer said kindly. 'This is a routine inquiry only. We only need to ask if you saw anything last Friday night.'

My father, who had perched on a dining table chair, gave us a 'keep your mouths zipped' glare. Then he smiled ingratiatingly and said, 'I didn't see anything. My bedroom is at the back of the house. And work is so busy.'

The police officers seemed resigned. 'Everyone is saying the same thing,' the bald one said. 'Madam, did you see anything.'

My mother shook her head. 'No. But my daughter has something to tell you. Nandini, tell them what you saw.'

My father glowered and raised a warning eyebrow. I ignored both the glower and the eyebrow and launched into my story. It took me about ten minutes, by which point both policemen were sitting full bum, and the younger one was scribbling notes.

I made it easy for them. I gave them a clear, concise, bullet-point version of what I had seen and heard on Friday night. The black legs, the Waffle Wonderland bag, the doorbell, the white legs. While relating the story, I made two things clear.

That while various legs were running up and down and poison-packed smoothies were being left outside doors, Amrita Aunty had been on her balcony in a short grey dress with billowing sleeves.

And Shanaya had been in her bedroom, watching a movie in her pajamas.

While I spoke, Ved and my mum nodded encouragingly. There was only one point at which they appeared unsure. This was when I told the policemen that while Black Legs was creeping up the staircase of Daisy Apartments, I had noticed something shine and flash. I couldn't be sure, of course. But perhaps the person was wearing glittery shoes. Possibly silver sneakers.

The policemen made a careful note of this.

Finally, the police got up and headed out. They were at the door when I asked them, most casually, if they had found out anything more about Baman Marker's missing parcel. Then, even more casually, I told them about my Baman-Burman theory.

The policemen sat down again and made more notes. They said that they would be in touch for a formal statement. They had gotten up to leave for a second time when I posed the question that had been niggling me. 'Could you tell me one thing?' I asked, in my most wide-eyed voice. 'What did the note say? The yellow note with Lina Almeida's name on it? I'm dying to know.'

The younger policeman found this hugely amusing. 'When you grow up, are you going to become a police detective?' he asked, before addressing my question. 'The note had only two words written on it—"Take care." And then the madam's name printed underneath.'

I smiled and thanked the policemen, but my stomach heaved. Almost as if I'd drunk a hefty dose of coolant.

Over the last four hours I had imagined many unimaginable things. I had imagined Shanaya stirring poison into a smoothie. I had imagined her leaving the smoothie outside the Marker apartment. I had imagined her waiting for news while Baman Marker lay sick in hospital.

These had caused me only mild horror. But the thought of Shanaya pulling out a yellow note from her school bag—one that said something like 'Your maths marks are falling. You should take care'—then sitting down with a pair of scissors and trimming the note to fit her purpose, that upset me badly.

After the policemen left to interview the Kurvillas upstairs and my father stormed out of the room, my mother remarked, 'Nandini, you never mentioned the shiny shoes before.'

'I didn't?' I asked, pretending surprise. 'It's something I see in my head whenever I think of Black Legs. But maybe I didn't actually mention the detail. Don't know.'

My mother was satisfied. Ved was not. 'You really hate Kysha, don't you?' he asked as we headed for our bedrooms.

I stuck a baffled expression on my face and asked, 'What are you talking about?'

Ved shrugged and asked, 'Do you know who killed Baman Marker?'

I shrugged back. 'As long as the police don't arrest Amrita Aunty, I don't really care.'

'You know, right, that I can always tell when you're lying?' Ved asked as he stepped into his bedroom.

I ignored the jibe and headed to my bedroom. Thirty seconds later, Ved was on his drums and I was on my phone and sending a message. A message that may or may not have yielded results.

'Hi Thea,' I typed on my phone. 'Sorry I never replied to your message on the kids' chat. The police had come today. I told them I saw a person wearing black pants climbing up the stairs of Daisy Apartments at 10.26 p.m. on Friday night. There is a chance that the person was the murderer. I also told them that the person was wearing really shiny silver shoes. Just wanted to let you know, in case you noticed something similar. Bye.'

I waited twenty minutes for two blue ticks to appear and then deleted the message.

Next, I called Shanaya. 'Two policemen came this morning,' I told her. 'I told them everything I saw. I told them that Amrita Aunty was in the balcony the whole time. I also told them that you were in your bedroom in your pajamas, watching a movie and chatting with me…the whole time.'

'Thank you,' Shanaya said in a flat voice.

I had planned to leave it at that, but I couldn't. There were too many questions rattling around in my head. 'Why didn't you tell me,' I blurted out, trying not to shout or to let my hurt show through. 'Why didn't you trust me?'

A sigh. Then a long and deep silence. And finally, a rush of words. 'I never thought…he called my mom…told her what he knew…said he was telling my father…I was so scared and angry…I just did it…never imagined it would work…I never, never, never…when I heard he was sick I was so scared…'

'Why did you ask me to google Ethylene Glycol? If you mixed the coolant into the smoothie you must have known what it could do.'

Another jumble of words. 'I had to know if he had died because of me…didn't dare google myself…it would have shown up on my computer…I had to know if it was really the coolant or something else…going mad, completely mad…'

'Where did you find the coolant?' I asked. This was the part that really puzzled me. Shanaya was not a Topgear kind of girl.

'When we changed cars, Murlidhar emptied everything from the boot of the old car into a cardboard carton and shoved it in the storage cupboard near the kitchen,' Shanaya said, talking more coherently now. 'I had moved my old doll house to make space for it. So I kind of knew that it was there. Then I noticed it again on Friday morning when I was hunting for my old computer charger. Then soon afterwards, everything went crazy. Baman Marker called my mom. She began to freak. I felt everything was falling apart. And then I thought about that can of coolant.'

'You already knew that coolant is a poison? How?'

'Oh yes, I knew,' Shanaya paused, and then continued with a small laugh. 'I spend a lot of time planning ways in which I can get rid of my father. This came up during my research. So yes, I knew coolant was a sort of poison.'

Shanaya's voice, when she said this, was so matter of fact, that I quailed. But then the panic bubbled up in her again. 'It all seemed to work and I thought we were safe…but then they…the police came and they thought my mom had done it…kept asking my mom questions…nightmare…I can't think, can't sleep…what is going to happen…'

'Nothing,' I said, calm and firm. 'Nothing is going to happen.'

'But—'

'Nobody else knows. And the police have other suspects.'

'But—'

'I haven't said a word to anyone. And I never will. You can trust me.'

Shanaya started out sounding relieved, but by the time we said our goodbyes she was wary. Even resentful. I guess it will take some time for her to get used to the idea that her best friend knows her secret. I'm not sure she understands that I don't care about right and wrong, good and evil. That I'm actually pretty pleased with this turn of events.

Why?

That's easy.

All these years, I've been the friend who's worked to keep our friendship going; the one who's fallen in with plans and given in to capricious demands; the one without power, without boyfriends, without a cool aura. But suddenly, the power has shifted. Now I'm the one on top.

It's a good feeling.

And the bonus is that I don't think Shanaya will be hanging out with Kysha any longer.

28

The BMC came today and took away their white, black and red banner. Lily Apartments is no longer a sealed building. Tomorrow, Daisy Apartments will shed its banner.

I can't wait. Amrita Aunty has promised me a big pani puri and sev puri lunch. And Shanaya has agreed to watch *Knives Out* and help me to decide which shoes will work with my purple skirt.

Daniel has suggested a walk. It's a pity that the lockdown is still on and that Waffle Wonderland is still closed. But I guess we can always look for mermaids at Sassoon Dock or visit Salman at Citypoint Vegetables.

Mr Alimchandani is doing well and is back in Daisy Apartments. I never did find out his secret. But it's possible that before he became a benevolent, old man he was a corrupt builder who had done something not-so-honest.

Mr Sevnani didn't make it.

Meanwhile, the smudges under my eyes are getting darker and I still wake up in the middle of the night. It's not a guilty conscience. It's the unresolved questions. How did Baman Marker know about Amrita Aunty's trip to Thailand? What was that stuff about the apartment in Worli that Baman Marker had posted on the chat? What did Mr Carvalho do when he went up at midnight to retrieve his phone on that dark Friday night? Did he really pay the Hon Chairperson an unwelcome visit? Was he responsible for the chaos, the smashed shepherdess and the scattered papers? Had that been his plan all along?

For the time being, the police are focusing their attention on Kysha and Mr Burman.

They will soon realize that Kysha is too moronic to commit such a clever crime. I'm not sure what they will feel about Mr Burman. I'm not sure what they'll find if they look carefully enough. Maybe a pen drive with CCTV footage. Maybe not.

There's one last thing I need to tell you. About that toxic CCTV footage. Let me just get done with it. About twenty-five minutes after Amrita Aunty dragged her bulky bags into the compound of Lily and Daisy Apartments, a man hurried through the gate.

It was Mr Burman, toting an expensive, medium-sized bag with zippy wheels.

Then, five minutes later, another figure walked into the camera from the street, wheeling a largish suitcase. This figure was also male and even more familiar.

It was my father.

When I wake up in the middle of the night, I sometimes wonder who went to Thailand with Amrita Aunty in February. Was it someone we know, or someone who is a total stranger?

There are ways to find out. But some things are better left alone.

This is one of them.

Postscripts:

1) In case you're wondering, this story is true, but the names I've used are not. So please don't peer suspiciously at every 15-year-old Shanaya you encounter.

   If, however, you do find yourself next to a 15-year-old South Bombay schoolgirl with a rude laugh, a capable air, a cloud of curly hair and a mother who makes mind-blowing dhokla, you might want to be a little careful. Don't leave your drink unattended.
2) I watched a movie called *Rear Window* yesterday. I guess I'm not the only bedroom-window detective around.
3) Do you know the unkindest twist of all? A few weeks after the murder of the Hon Chairperson, the BMC decided to seal buildings only if a large number of residents tested positive for coronavirus. If there were just a couple of cases, they would seal only individual floors.

   If the BMC had decided this earlier, Baman Marker would have been alive today. Not that I'm grumbling. For me, at least, this has worked out okay.